To my family, without whom I would not have had the rich source of information to write this book. To my two sons who patiently came with me on my worldly adventures.

Pamela was born in a small town on the North East coast of England. She is the youngest of five sisters and a brother. There was this restlessness within her from a very early age and she spent seventeen years in Canada before returning briefly to her home town.

Still eager to embrace life, Pamela sought out more adventure in the USA and stayed there for fourteen years before retiring back in her beloved Lincolnshire.

Pamela Martin

DOLLY DON'T CRY

AUSTIN MACAULEY PUBLISHERS™

LONDON • CAMBRIDGE • NEW YORK • SHARJAH

A CIP catalogue record for this title is available from the British Library.

ISBN 9781786122353 (Paperback)
ISBN 9781786122360 (Hardback)
ISBN 9781786122377 (E-Book)
www.austinmacauley.com

First Published (2017)
Austin Macauley Publishers Ltd.
25 Canada Square
Canary Wharf
London
E14 5LQ

Acknowledgements

To all those whose stories are intertwined with fiction.
Also to all the people who believed in me and did not
say I had ideas above my station.

Chapter 1

Dolly was plain. She knew she was plain but, as she peered into the old sepia mirror, the optimist in her saw a 16 year old girl with her whole life ahead of her. She had no doubt that her life was to be a life full of excitement and purpose. What difference did it make that her complexion was too pale, or that her eyes were too large for her face, or that her nose was a tad too broad; she was a free spirit with the world at her feet.

It was 1917. England was at war, but for Dolly all that was important was that she was finally leaving school today. She was born Doris Eleanor Daisy Marcum but the nickname Dolly had been her name, given to her by her father, for as long as she could remember. She had been protected by her parents and surrounded by love. Up to that day Dolly had no fears, doubts or trauma in her young life. She was blessed and she knew it. Things were hard in England in WW1, but the Marcum family was comparatively unscathed and optimistic about their future.

All her life Dolly had been called a free spirit, and she was still not sure exactly what that meant. Whenever she thought about it, she mused that she would soon find out. She had functioned as the teacher's assistant for the last three years in the same schoolhouse she had attended since she was only four years old, and knee-high to a grasshopper. The ever curious Dolly had taken the opportunity to access the available books around a learning environment, indulging her need to know about the world far away from her cosy Cotter's Marsh. Dolly had deliberately become lost for hours in the folds of the musty stacks of knowledge, much of which was far beyond her comprehension.

Dolly had travelled to places with names she did not know how to pronounce and had gone on adventures through history with heroes and heroines, real and imaginary, and was the better for it. No other person in her family had the privilege of so much education, not even her twin brother Everett. Dolly's twin had never been a scholar; he much preferred drawing and painting. Dolly thought that he was quite good at it. One day when he was a mere boy of ten, he had presented a watercolour painting to his mother for her birthday. He had captured the old Abbey ruin in the early light, the soft hue of the sunrise dappled along the crumbling parapets of the towers. He had added his mother's silhouette, standing on the rise surrounded by a field of lavender, so real that you could almost smell it. This painting had pride of place in the small drawing room of their modest house.

Everett had joined the British army in January, only one month after his sixteenth birthday. With coaxing from his friend George he had lied about his age and was accepted right away, leaving almost immediately to join his regiment in France. He had been away from home for nigh on five months, and Dolly missed him. There was talk that the war had taken a turn for the worse and Dolly thought about her brother as she dressed. Even though it was May the weather was damp and cold, especially in the early mornings. Dolly became impatient and pulled out the lace tie her mother had lovingly sewed onto the front. Picking up the camphor bag and placing it around her neck, Dolly wished she was already a grown woman. "Don't wish your life away," she imagined her mother saying.

Finally pulling up her stockings she looked at the combination of her attire and, satisfied, moved around the room and pushing off Rats the dog she made up her bed. The warm colourful feather bedspread was embroidered with bluebirds and roses. Dolly had helped her mother with this task many years ago. She was not very skilled at it but the effort was allowed to remain. Every night Dolly would seek out the imperfections and remember the many winter nights she sat with her mother, sewing.

Trying to put aside her dark mood our heroine sighed heavily before donning her hat and picking up her gloves. In her mind's eye she saw her brother's pale blue eyes and shock of blond hair. She remembered how her mother had tried to tame his mop with little success, saying that it seemed to be as wild as he was. However, his cherubic face with its cheeky grin assured him all kinds of leniency from his doting mother. He was a ray of sunshine that brought joy to everyone who knew him. "Not like serious old me," Dolly thought.

As twins they were nothing alike in appearance or personality. Everett was tall for his age, charming and handsome, and Dolly saw herself as plain and rather dull. Her best feature, she thought, was her thick long black hair which was almost as difficult to tame as Everett's hair, but hers shone like the polish on her father's Sunday shoes. Almost as far back as Dolly remembered she towered over her twin and he would grin at her and affectionately called her 'giraffe'. The siblings enjoyed a love-hate relationship with squabbles and pouting, but Everett would likely kill to protect her and Dolly knew it. "That's what he is doing now," Dolly thought with sudden clarity, "he is fighting in France to protect us all." Dolly gulped with the enormity of this revelation and a warm feeling came over her, just as surely as if her brother held her tight.

Dolly turned to the mirror and examined her image. She sighed once again as she had to stoop down because of her height. She stood up straight as she heard her mother approaching her room. Before she did so however, impulsively she stuck out her tongue and said to her reflection, "I don't want to be a shrimp like you Rett, so there!" She turned away from the mirror and forced a smile, remembering that today her life was to change.

Eleanor knocked quietly on the door and walked into the tiny bedroom. As she manoeuvred her way around the large oak bed, she smiled indulgently at her wilful daughter.

"I was thinking about Rett," Dolly spoke softly.

"Yes I know," her mother replied, "we are all so worried about him. He is so young to take on a man's task. Daddy won't talk about the war but I know he is worried, everyone is, but we try to get on with our lives the best way we know how, Dolly. This is your day, luv, try to put it out of your mind for now."

"Does this suit, Mam?" Dolly swirled around.

Eleanor appraised her and reached up to kiss Dolly's cheek. Eleanor did not see her daughter as plain at all. She saw a spirited imp in front of her, whose zest for life would take her far. She saw her own mother in Dolly's eyes and her father's mannerisms and wilfulness in her daughter.

"It does child, now button up your boots and don't be late for your last day, special day it is, so get along with you, and give my regards to Miss Arden."

Dolly beamed as the troubling thoughts of Everett evaporated from her fickle childish mind.

"Today is a special day, but I am also a bit sad, mam, why do you suppose that is?"

"Eee lass, you are leaving behind the last of your childhood and that is a sad time. It is all you have known since you were little. Now you are almost grown. Being grown up has its compensations too, lass, you will discover each one when the time is right."

Eleanor squeezed Dolly and turned her towards the door as she tapped her bottom affectionately.

Downstairs Eleanor gave Dolly a piece of fresh baked bread, cheese and half an onion wrapped in brown paper. She touched her shoulder gently as she opened the front parlour door.

"Good luck, Dolly luv, make this day a day to remember."

"I will Mam, see you at dusk."

"Get along now lass...they are waiting."

Eleanor stifled a cough as Dolly brushed passed her towards the door.

"Bye mam."

"Bye child, and enjoy every moment."

Today was certainly a special day, her last day at the village school. Later she would have to assume the role of a woman with a woman's responsibilities. She had one last wonderful day before she had to put away childish things. She would miss her school, her students, and especially Miss Arden with whom she had built a wonderful friendship. Miss Arden, a spinster, was devoted to her students. It was rumoured that she had once had a serious love affair, but her lover had died tragically. Dolly surmised that she showed the pain in her eyes, especially when she thought no one was looking. Dolly was fond of her and used her fertile imagination to weave wonderfully exaggerated stories about what might have happened.

The truth was that Molly Arden was planning her nuptials, when her fiancé died of pneumonia, they were both seventeen. She devoted her life to her teaching and never married. Molly never regretted her decision although she was now approaching thirty and thought more and more about her future alone, not knowing if this is what she really wanted deep in her heart. She had had her share of interested suitors but the time never seemed right to open her still vulnerable heart to love again. She was still an attractive lady, slim and tall, but now suitors had stopped trying to win her hand.

Molly's parents were both dead now and she lived in the old farm on the east side of the village. The house was rambling and very lonely at times, and apart from the children and the ladies at church, Molly saw no one. There had been no incentive for her to keep it a working farm and she had sold the animals long ago. Molly had a special fondness for Dolly and treated her as a younger sister. Dolly was a great help with the teaching duties, often taking the younger students aside and reading stories she had written herself about forest animals and creatures of the sea. Molly often thought that Dolly would make a very accomplished writer someday.

Dolly walked briskly down the lane in the early morning chill. Although it was almost June, it seemed as if autumn had visited for the day. The early morning mist had not yet dissipated and a slight drizzle of rain had just begun. Dolly's boots crunched the pebbles under her feet. Although barely started, she wished for this day to never end. The school had just three rooms: a large classroom divided into two areas, one for the small children and one for the older ones. The second room was Dolly's favourite because it was filled to the rafters with books. She had set out to read every one but had realized early on that it would take her two lifetimes to accomplish this task. The third room was the teacher's room with facilities to prepare tea on a large black wood burning stove. Sometimes, if the winter was particularly harsh, all the students clamoured around the warmth in this room and lessons were temporarily suspended as Molly Arden sang old English ballads in her wonderfully melodic voice which mesmerized all within earshot.

Times were hard in this little village of Cotter's Marsh. The Lincolnshire Wolds were flat and often inhospitable. Fog rolling in from the North Sea enveloped the village in a blanket of choking cloud. The housewives were hard put to dry washing in the inclement English weather. Some children were still sewn into their winter underwear, although with the new easier to care for fashions and fabrics this tradition was dying out. It was now late May and the sun had some strength in it at long last. The outhouses, at the rear of the little school house, often frozen in the winter, was now free of ice. The children no longer had to struggle with buckets of hot water to break it up. All in all the spring was a time of renewal, a time of relief.

The people were poor but the village was a wonderful environment to raise children. It seemed that everyone cared; the children were treasured and loved. There were only three large houses in the village: the

Manor, the farm, and the rectory. The rest of the houses were modest and usually consisted of two rooms downstairs and two bedrooms on the upper level. Dolly's house was considered large by village standards with three down and three up. The outhouses and coalhouses were often quite some distance from the houses.

Most villagers grew their own vegetables; Dolly's father was one of them. He owned a small allotment just off the village green where he would retreat to work and think. This is where the village men would gather. Charley Taylor, the next door neighbour, Trevor Dagwood, the pub landlord, Raymond Cowl, the butcher, and Harry White, now retired from the railway. They all met two or three times a week in one of the greenhouses. They would put the world to rights. Heated arguments often erupted from this men's haven. As the men became hot under the collar about some subject or another, the smoke from their pipes clouded the air as they huffed and puffed on them. Presently they listened to the war news on the radio and were free to discuss their fears out of earshot of the womenfolk.

Dolly played there in the allotments when she was a young girl and spent precious quality time with her father. She was not interested in the vegetable garden so she was given a small corner in which to grow flowers. She remembers vividly the day she took a small bunch of Michaelmas daisies she had grown to her mother. Eleanor was overwhelmed and reminisced about the wild flower gardens she tended as a young girl. Dolly loved her mother with all her heart but she understood that Everett was her mother's favourite. She was content to know that she was her father's little 'Doll."

There had been some pressure earlier for Dolly to take up teaching but instinctively she felt that she had some living to do first. Dolly had accepted what she saw as a temporary position as a general shop girl until it became clearer to her what life had in store. Dolly had realized as soon as Everett had left that her mother was not strong, and her father's hacking cough caused by the coal dust was just not going to go away. She knew she had been indulged by her parents, far longer than her friends' parents had indulged them. Nan Platt had been obliged to leave school at age twelve. Nan had been working now for four years in service to the Reverend Stuart, cooking and cleaning for him. He had a housekeeper but she could not manage the heavy work and Nan was there to assist her.

Nan's brother, George, aged seventeen, was also in the army fighting in France alongside Dolly's brother Everett. As lifelong friends, the two had conspired together to go and fight for their country. Walking along the village streets, they had been acting like the young boys they were, pushing each other, teasing the girls and not a care in the world. They came across a poster of Lord Kitchener saying that their country needed them to fight the Germans. They both stopped, and centuries of male testosterone rose up in their psyche. They were fond of pretending to be knights, soldiers and conquering heroes, and here before them presented an opportunity to do the real thing. They impulsively made the decision to join the army. They were both young and impressionable, they wanted to shoot some Germans, and they were terribly naïve.

Then there was Joan Walker, aged fifteen and a half, who had never actually had any formal education and relied on Dolly and Nan to share their lessons with her. Joan's mother Nancy was a dear friend of Dolly's mother. Joan was also in service but she was working at the convent just three miles down towards North Thorsby. Joan's father had been killed in a tractor accident when she was just a young infant, and she did not remember him. Joan was a small, thin girl. She was so quiet spoken at times that she was often nicknamed "mouse". A mouse she may be but her voice was powerful and strong, totally out of keeping with her demeanour. Dolly affectingly thought about her as a small mouse with a giant heart, and the voice of an angel.

Another member of this clique was Victoria, the daughter of Lady Katherine and Brigadier Sir David Hastings. Victoria was being schooled at home by private tutors. She had become friends with the local girls when they were all playing in the estate woods. Far from being angry with the children for trespassing, Sir David had encouraged the friendship, and occasionally all the girls visited Victoria for tea in the summerhouse. Victoria had a crush on Everett and the girls giggled in mirth when his name was mentioned. Dolly also had a secret crush on George but did not share this with the group. It was her secret and she nurtured it as carefully as holding a newborn lamb, her secret, her love.

The last person included in the group of friends was Anthony. Anthony was the son of the local doctor; Dr. Steven Preston. Anthony was, like Joan, small in stature but large of heart. Everyone loved Anthony. Some would call him effeminate, but that did not bother the group of friends, Anthony was the glue that held them all together. His sense of humour was often a lifesaver when things got a little rough for them all, which it was apt to do in these sparse war years. His mother, Susan, was very actively involved in the church and had met Dr.

Preston when they had both been missionaries in South Africa.

Dr. Preston had been friends with Dolly's father ever since they were boys. Dr. Preston had helped to save Albert's life twice when they were both caught up in the Boer War in 1900. Dr. Preston's wife had left just after the start of the local hostilities because it was far too dangerous to remain. Struck down with a fever, Albert was sick for many worrying days. His comrades had managed to get him to the mission and Steven Preston nursed him back to health.

After Albert recovered, the two spent many hours talking together, smoking their pipes, contemplating their fate. After three weeks Albert was well enough to go back to active duty. After six more months in Hell, an exhausted Albert was hit by shrapnel and it had pierced his leg and chest. Steven Preston was again there for him. Although not a surgeon, he had removed life-threatening shrapnel and once again nursed him back to health. They both returned to England at the same time.

Anthony was seventeen years old and was working with his father as much as he could. His father allowed him to accompany him on his house visits. Anthony absorbed his father's teachings, knowing he wanted to be a doctor from a very early age. He was also an intern at the hospital in Grimoldsby three days a week. He was tempted to go with Everett and George and was briefly caught up in the excitement. However his mother's teachings about the sanctity of life rubbed off on him and made him a poor choice for an effective soldier. He never regretted his decision to remain at home. He desperately wanted to become a doctor like his father.

The county of Lincolnshire could only be described as flat and wooded. Occasionally the landscape broke into sweeping fields, fertile and green. There were castle ruins scattered around which served as play houses for the local village children. There was one particular old Abbey that Dolly and her friends played in, the one that Everett was moved to paint. The ruins were tentatively held together on three sides by large flaking stones, and the outline of the dividing walls was visible. The crumbling parapets were dangerous to climb but this never bothered the group of friends. They nudged each other on to take risks and daring walks along the wide walls. Dolly was always in the thick of the excitement and never shirked away from the next daredevil trick the boys devised. The boys were King Arthur, Knights of the Round Table, brandishing imaginary swords, and rescuing damsels in distress. The girls fought to be Gwendolyn, the heroine. They cheered on their Knights and swooned at the imaginary wounds of their hero.

The local market and nearby fishing town of Grimoldsby was thriving due to the fishing fleet utilizing the inlet from the North Sea called the River Hamber. Grimoldsby and Immingham docks existed solely because of this inlet. Often shrouded in sea fog and mist, the river was treacherous and foreboding most of the time. Sensible people gave the sea the respect it deserved by not straying too close to the constant rip tides that were often whipped up in a frenzy on stormy days. Save for the hardened fishermen who ventured out to earn their living, the sea shore was deserted most of the time.

These hardy men were weather-beaten and often had missing fingers from filleting ice cold fish. They were habitual alcohol drinkers, and certainly not ideal family men. They stayed away for weeks at a time, fishing the inhospitable north sea, often venturing into the dangerous Irish sea waters to bring home the catch of haddock, cod, skate, halibut, or whatever else their nets could find. Lobsters were a rare treat for the Marcum family and Dolly remembers how they squealed as they were put into boiling hot cauldrons on the fire. For years she had refused to eat them and eventually her mother ceased to cook them.

Any time that the seafaring fishermen had at home in port was solely for the purpose of landing their catch and refitting the trawler. Family visits were slotted in between the 'meetings' in the public houses. Beer flowed freely and so did their hard earned shillings. Many a union was 'blessed' with fights and infidelity, as the women tried to find security from whoever was in town at the time.

Those fisherman and sailors, born in Lincolnshire were often referred to as 'Lime'ies', due to a history eating limes to stave off the scurvy. Their ancestry could be traced back to feudal times and the roads and hamlets from Roman occupations still existed. Royal Navy ships also used the inlet port. The locals were used to seeing masses of sailors in uniform milling around the town. The numerous local pubs would be awash with uniforms, painted ladies and ribald singing. On the day that the ships sailed, whether the navy or the fishing fleet, the jetty would be alive with wailing women bidding farewell. Wives were saying goodbye to their husbands, mothers to their sons, and blushing fiancées to their lovers. The port was vibrant and lively.

Eleanor and Albert Marcum had wanted their children to stay out in the country, far away from the seedier side of life in the big town. Albert had been born and raised in Cotter's Marsh; however, Eleanor was born and raised further south towards London town. They had met when Albert was in the army. Eleanor was from 'good stock' and was the granddaughter of the Honourable George Wilmington. When she was just fourteen her family had fallen on hard times, due mainly to her father's gambling and his failed attempts at farming. Her more affluent Southern English family disowned them after many years of loaning them money. Eleanor was never quite sure of the details and often daydreamed about reuniting with her southern relatives. It was not to be.

After he left the army in 1902 Albert had wanted to work in the open air and eventually to own a small farm at Brady Downs but that had not been possible due to lack of financing and the lung problems and leg injury he had contracted while fighting in the Boer war. He had suffered greatly at this time, and was silent about the horrors he encountered. The only other person who was privy to his suffering was Dr. Steven Preston. However, through an unspoken understanding they never talked about their shared experience.

Albert remembered the date of his own departure from Immingham by ship, landing immediately into battle, August 21st 1900. Still fresh in his mind was the fear in his throat and the names and faces of his comrades; Harry Green from Gloucestershire, only a young boy, James Hammond from Yorkshire, proud of his moustache, Peter Snow from Lancashire, the writer who chronicled as much of their experiences as he could, until survival forced his creativity to wane, and his best friend Hugo Herriot from Lincolnshire, the ladies man, all of them perished within weeks of arrival. Of the group of friends, Albert alone survived with comparatively minor wounds, and weak lungs.

Albert, exhausted and ill, returned to old Blighty in May 1902. On the same ship came Steven Preston, back to his own wife who was anxiously waiting for him back in Cotter's Marsh. Albert brought back with him the writings of Peter but up to that day he had left the journals untouched. He never talked about those horrendous times, but they were again fresh memories due to Everett's impulsive decision to join the army. Albert was having flashbacks and nightmares once again and he fretted for Everett. The news of the war was sketchy and he and Eleanor gathered around the radio every evening for the war bulletin. The names of the dead were read out, quietly but clearly. Each listener dreaded to hear their loved one's name. The newspapers were heavily censored as the country needed more men to fight the 'Krauts'.

However, all thoughts of war were pushed far back in our heroine's mind as she made her way along a very familiar path. Dolly tried to savour every moment as she walked for the last time down the country lane to school. Some early morning mist graced the fields and the sun was just peeping around the clouds to banish it away. She breathed in the smells and tried to capture the sights, one last time. She jumped over a stone in the lane, as she had done many times before. She swung her bag from side to side while she hummed a tune, "Twas the merry merry month of May…"

She peeped over the hedgerow into the field to see if farmer Wilson had any new cows. She watched as Bella, the big brown milking cow, looked up at her briefly then continued to chew her cud. Her eyes were diverted up to the sky as a hawk swooped down to get his breakfast. Further down the lane she stopped while a hedgehog crossed in front of her, his snout smelling her presence but sensing no danger. Dolly held onto every moment.

However much she tried, once again her mind wandered to her sibling. Everett had been gone for five long months now, and they had only received one brief correspondence that was heavily censored. She had no concept of where he was, or the horrors he was experiencing, just a spider web of sibling bond that gave her an uneasy feeling. Dolly shuddered thinking of her brother and her friend George, but as she approached the school her thoughts dissipated as she was interrupted by little Samuel Green running towards her and shouting her name.

"Miss Dolly, Miss Dolly come and sees what Mary has brought to school. It is a baby stoat, it was 'bandend'," he said, mispronouncing abandoned. He was dressed in too large short pants, tied with string, and an oversized knitted pullover, obviously belonging to an older brother. As he ran he winced because his boots were pinching his growing feet.

"Whoa! Young man, give me time to get there," Dolly laughed, all her gloomy thoughts disappeared. Dolly's day had truly begun.

Samuel pulled her along as he ran to show her what all the excitement was about.

Eleanor closed the door after her daughter and wiped a tear from her eyes. She held on tightly to the back of the horsehair sofa as she manoeuvred around it to sit down. The strain of hiding the severity of her illness was showing and she closed her eyes for a moment's rest. Eleanor had been a beauty. She still had a youthful skin and bright shiny blue eyes. "I could get lost in those blue caverns and happily live out the rest of my life," Albert had said when they were courting. Albert was not a poetic person, and Eleanor always remembered this comment, and today it was particularly poignant. She was drifting away into sleep when his voice broke through her pain-induced fog.

"Eee, lass, you look darn worn out, has Dolly gone?" Albert's voice was soft and caring. "I was trying to get back to see her before she left, last day an' all."

Albert worked night shift at the coal house packing coal into the sacks ready for delivery. He had tried to get healthier work, but his hacking cough prevented that. Albert had come through the courtyard door shedding his boots and overalls in the outhouse. He had quickly washed in the cold tap water using the carbolic soap and rough towel, set there for his use by his loving wife. He moved over to his Eleanor and with his large, coal blemished hand, gently felt her brow.

"The fever is no better, luv, let's get you upstairs and you can rest for the day. You have to tell Dolly soon."

"Yes, I know Albert, but not today, it's her special day. She will have to face the cruel world soon enough."

"Tomorrow, tell her tomorrow," he pleaded.

"Yes tomorrow," she replied, not too convincingly.

Eleanor let Albert help her up the steep flight of stairs to the bedroom. He helped her remove her shoes and gently lifted her up onto the bed. He pulled up the hand knitted coverlet and kissed her on her cheek. Albert turned to her as he walked out of the bedroom, "Rest my dear. I love you, sleep and dream of better times. Rett will be back with us soon, safe and sound… mark my words."

He moved his lanky body to the door and turned. His wife smiled and to Albert she looked just as beautiful as the day he met her. He smiled back and the look between them spoke of many intimate moments and half a lifetime of love for each other.

Eleanor blew him a kiss as he closed the door quietly. She looked around the room as she lay there on the marital bed that had been their haven for eighteen short years. Her twins had been born in this bed; she had had two miscarriages prior to their birth which made them extra special gifts. She noted the worn wallpaper with its large multi coloured flowers that were now faded and torn in a few places. Her head turned towards the dresser where her wedding picture was propped up next to her bible. Crushed lovingly between the pages, her bible held three pressed flowers from her marriage posy.

"I have had a blessed life," she thought and a smile creased her strained face which was contorted with pain.

She thought about the day she had met Albert at her father's house. Her grandparents and her mother's sister Daisy were also visiting from the south. The visit from her family made the day extra special for her. This was before the major family rift which separated them forever. Her grandfather, the Honourable George Wilmington, was a stately military man who lowered his stuffy class barriers to welcome all military men. Eleanor was familiar with the sacrifices military wives made through the stories her grandmother told her. She was aware of the many months her grandmother waited patiently for her grandfather to return from his duties abroad. Eleanor imagined she could smell the lavender her grandmother wore.

When Eleanor's grandmother shared some of her experiences with her beloved granddaughter about when they were posted to India, she had made it all sound like a wonderful adventure to the impressionable girl. As part of the British Empire, India had a special bond with the British and many prominent men were posted there. A subculture of British soldiers, diplomats, and their wives was created. Grandmother often talked to Eleanor of the opulence, the heat, the monsoons and the many servants fulfilling their every whim. This was a culture so foreign to Eleanor as to be a fairy tale. Although Eleanor did not know it at the time, this was the last day she saw her grandparents. It was also the day she met her life's love, Albert Marcum.

Although fascinated by her grandparent's tales of adventures abroad, never once did Eleanor imagine living anywhere but where she was. Years later she surmised that her own daughter, Dolly, had the same wanderlust that she saw in her grandparents. Her own mother, Sandra, and father Charles, were far less travelled. She knew when she was about fourteen that her parents were terribly unhappy. She understood some of the financial worries that the family experienced, although she was not aware at the time of the extent of her father's gambling.

It was fortunate and down to a twist of fate that Eleanor's father, Charles Brant, had known Albert's father James for years. They were in the same regiment, although different ranks. They became friends when James took the blame and punishment for Charles. Charles had smashed up his room in a drunken rage and James, hearing the commotion, went to investigate. He managed to get Charles into the tub of cold water to sober him up. Amidst insults and threats, James did what he could, but the damage was extensive so he devised a fictional argument between them in which it was James, not Charles, who had damaged the room. It wasn't until the following day when Charles was completely sober that the damage was reported. Charles remembered very little about the incident except that it was he and not

James that had damaged the room. James never regretted this lie, although his promotion was affected. Charles was forever grateful to James and they became friends.

On this day, James' son Albert was a new recruit and accompanied his father to the Manor house at Charles Brant's invitation. Charles had moved his family to Cotters Marsh because he wanted to try his hand at farming after failing to make a career in the army. His wife Sandra was homesick for the South, but Eleanor loved the rural life and her only regret was that she did not see enough of her grandparents and her aunt Daisy. Eleanor loved the freedom of the country, the fresh air and the openness of the marshes. She had made some good friends in the village and they would remain true to her, and she to them, for the rest of her life. No, she could never think of leaving Cotter's Marsh.

On this momentous weekend Albert and his father were both waiting for their battle orders. They both expected to be shipped out to the Sudan. James was eager for the next adventure but Albert was hesitant. Oh, he would go there, no doubt about that, but he lacked the enthusiasm that his father had for war. Albert did not shirk his duty to his country, but when his father was killed in a terrible battle a year later, he determined that he was not to be an army career man. It turned out that eventually he was wounded in battle and was invalided out with honour.

"What honour was there in killing and being killed?" he thought bitterly at the time.

They gathered around for tea at the Manor house on a Sunday after church. Just as soon as the tea and finger food was served the men retired to a corner of the room to talk. Eleanor's grandfather was in his element talking army strategy with James. Charles was noticeably quiet during this conversation.

"We had better not scare the boy," laughed George Wilmington after he noticed Albert's expression.

"He is fully aware of the risks, aren't you, Albert?" asked James.

"Yes sir, but the call of duty is paramount, far outweighing any personal misgivings I may have," answered Albert.

"Well said, boy. I am sure you will make your father and regiment proud."

"Come along, gentlemen, there are ladies here and we are all being dismally neglectful," chastised Charles' wife Sandra, faking a pout.

"I do beg your pardon, daughter;" said George, "let us talk of more pleasant things, my granddaughter Eleanor, for instance."

George had a twinkle in his eyes as the company all turned to look at Eleanor, who blushed shamefully. Albert remembered how small and vulnerable she looked and he also remembered how she sat up straight and proud as she answered, "Thank you, grandfather, I do love to hear you reminisce about those days, I often wish that I was a man to enjoy the comradeship and adventures."

They all laughed and the afternoon passed very pleasantly.

Eleanor remembered how shy she was at thirteen and how handsome Albert was at eighteen. Their eyes met briefly and Albert tells that he fell instantly in love with her. Eleanor smiled and thought that she would not have changed anything. Albert was her love and would always be.

After leaving the army, Eleanor's father drank excessively and gambled away her mother's inheritance. Sandra refused to return to her family in Kent, and the rift ended in George Wilmington disinheriting his granddaughter in fear that Charles would gamble away Eleanor's money as he had Sandra's. Sandra took to her bed in shame and never recovered. Eleanor remembers how she had tried desperately to engage her mother in her life. How she would spend hours reading to her and chatted away about anything and everything, but to no avail. Each day, when her studies were done, Eleanor would take refreshments up to her mother's room and gently wake her. Sandra seemed to fade before Eleanor's eyes.

"Mama, please wake up. See what cook has made for you. Please mama, eat a little something," Eleanor pleaded.

"Thank you, dear, but I am not hungry, maybe later," Sandra replied weakly, trying to sit up and falling back onto her pillow.

Sandra's face was ashen gray and her eyes had no more life in them. Eleanor remembered how her mother's hair lay in clumps on her pillow. Sandra's hair had been beautiful and the envy of the country set. Now it was just wisps of cotton candy, dull and lifeless.

Eleanor tried to get her mother to eat until the nurse asked her to give up for the day.

"Mama, when you are well, let's go for a picnic to the old Abbey. You know, the one where you and daddy chased me around. Then daddy picked me up and put me on his shoulder, do you remember? The spring flowers will be blooming soon and we can take Tag the old Labrador with us. Do you remember how he loved it up there?" but her pleadings fell on deaf ears.

Eleanor walked out of the bedroom and stood just outside her mother's room and cried. Cook came for the tray that she knew would not be touched. She put her large comforting arms around the crying child.

"Nay lass, don't go on so. You mama has decided what she wants, but you have to live your life. Go now and take Tag for his walk. The fresh air will help you feel better, go along now and stop fretting," she playfully patted Eleanor's bottom and pushed her to go outside.

The tragedy did not end there for Eleanor. Her father, disgraced and desperate, shot himself in the autumn of her fifteenth year and her mother died not six months after, the doctors said of a broken heart. Only two months later Eleanor received a letter from her mother's sister Daisy, who was in Europe, telling her that both her grandparents were killed in a train accident. Eleanor had lost all four loved ones within a year. It seemed more than one person could endure.

It was Albert to whom Eleanor turned and they were married on the day she turned sixteen in a quiet ceremony at Cotter's Marsh village church. The small group at the church consisted only of Eleanor's aunt Daisy, who had recently returned from France, former housekeeper and cook, Mrs. White, and Albert's best friend Hugo Herriot. "Dear Hugo," Eleanor thought, "Such a handsome man, such a short life." She sighed as she remembered her wedding day, so wonderful and yet so brief.

Albert and Hugo were both on a week's shore leave and would be returning to set sail the very next day. Eleanor was staying temporarily with her friend Violet and regrettably Violet could not be released from her work to attend the wedding. The Manor House had been repossessed to pay for her father's debts; therefore

Albert had rented a small house in the village. Eleanor's aunt Daisy wanted her to return with her to Kent but Eleanor was looking forward to setting up home for Albert's return. "Thank God for the optimism of youth," mused Eleanor as she struggled to make herself comfortable in the bed, "everyone has tragedy in their lives, mine was no different."

She thought of her many miscarriages before the birth of her beloved twins and smiled through her pain. Tears came unexpectedly as her mind wondered to Everett.

"Oh! Rett, I love you so, be safe and return soon," she sobbed out loud.

Her mother's love dreamed of his safe return home. She knew that thousands had died in the war and news often took weeks or even months to filter back to England. Before Eleanor fell into a fitful sleep she thought she smelled her grandmother's lavender once more.

Albert had not gone straight downstairs but had lingered outside the bedroom and silently cried along with his wife as she cried out aloud for their son. In his heart of hearts he knew she would not live long enough to see her beloved son again, even if Everett was still alive. As a man he heard far more about the war than his wife. He knew the rats were eating the wounded that could not walk out of the trenches, he knew that the British were often outnumbered by the Germans and the fighting was brutal. Men were not taken prisoners and if they were they were horrifically tortured and starved in the camps. He also knew that the foot soldiers were often used for cannon fodder. His body shook as he stifled a cry and crept downstairs.

He made himself some tea and warmed thick slices of bread on the embers of the fire for toast. He absentmindedly stroked Petra, the silly old alley cat who had jumped up onto his lap. After he had given his bony body some nourishment he slumped back into his armchair and closed his weary eyes. Flashes of the horrors of war played themselves out behind his closed eyes and weary as he was, he forced them to open again. Something shook him fully awake. He thought he had heard a noise from upstairs so he pulled himself upright, much to the indignation of Petra. Stepping over Rats the mongrel dog, he climbed the stairs quietly in case his wife was sleeping.

He knew almost instantly that she was dead. Eleanor was only thirty six years old. She had reached for her bible that was now on the floor. Albert stood in the doorway of the bedroom transfixed at the sight of his love, lifeless but serene because she was out of pain at last. Eleanor was out of pain but Albert's pain descended upon him like a sledgehammer. He let out a guttural sound that startled him. Rats, sensing something was wrong, ran up the stairs to join his master. Albert did not see him. After what seemed to be an eternity, he moved to the side of the bed and picked up Eleanor's frail body and held her close. He rocked her as he would a baby and alternated between stroking her hair and showering her in gentle kisses. Rats whined and licked Albert's foot. Albert absentmindedly kicked him away and he retreated to a corner of the bedroom and lay down, watching, his head on his paws and his eyes alert in case he was needed.

It was late afternoon before Albert's senses returned and he covered her with a sheet and in just his socks walked slowly to the next door neighbour's house. Annie was a good friend of Eleanor's and as soon as she saw Albert's face she dashed to see Eleanor. Charlie, Annie's husband, was not able to find work and being too old to join the army, he spent his days in melancholic self-pity.

"Sit down, mate," Charlie was stunned.

"Aye I think I will, just for a minute," said Albert. He staggered to a chair at the large kitchen table. Charlie awkwardly hurried around preparing the inevitable mug of tea trying to find words of comfort and grateful for something to do. The best he could muster was a brief touch of Albert's shoulder as he handed him a mug of steaming hot tea.

Annie soon returned and put on her headscarf saying she was going to get Dr. Preston. She left without another word. The silence in the house was palpable until Albert said he would return home because Dolly would be home shortly. Charlie put on his boots and went with him. As if to mimic the sombre mood, the fog descended, thick and damp as it shrouded them like a blanket. Even though it was spring, the marshes often emitted a fog as soon as the sun lost its strength and night time began to fall. Albert never noticed he was without boots, or that the lamps were not yet lit in the house. He was walking rigidly and felt nothing.

The house was eerily silent when they entered and Albert sighed deeply. Charlie busied himself by lighting the gas lamps. The fire had gone out so he set about relighting the embers. He filled up the kettle and hung it over the fire. He found Albert's mug and added three tea spoons of sugar, took the jug of milk from the cooler coalhouse and sat to wait for the water to boil. He sat down beside his friend; it was some time before either of them spoke.

"Dolly will have a shock so she will, poor bairn has no idea her mother was so ill." Albert's voice cracked, "She should be home by now. Perhaps she was delayed, her last day today."

"Annie will break the news," offered Charlie, "a woman's touch an' all."

Dr. Preston arrived with the local undertaker's wife. He busied himself for a while and then came downstairs.

"She is at peace now, Albert, she suffered for a long time."

"That's as maybe, but she was a loved woman and will be missed," Albert struggled with his words.

Dr. Preston sat beside his friend and awkwardly rested his clean, smooth hand on Albert's dirty, calloused one. Neither of them noticed the coal dust under his finger nails, nor that he sorely needed a change of clothes. The situation was far beyond the mundane niceties of the genteel world. Albert had lost his wife, his friend, his soul mate, the mother of his children, and the men who were his friends could do nothing to ease his pain.

The undertaker's wife, Mavis Thomas, stayed attending to Eleanor's needs for some time. She was still there at five when Dolly arrived home. Sensing immediately that something was terribly wrong, and before anyone could stop her, Dolly bounded up the stairs two at a time to her mother's bedroom. Her mother was laid straight and stiff with a white sheet covering her, leaving just her beautiful face exposed. Dolly screamed out, and Albert, shaken out of his inertia, ran to her, turned her face away from his wife and held her tight while she absorbed the enormity of what had happened. There was no need for words.

In the nightmare of the following days, Dolly was trying so hard to be strong for her father but there were so many adults around treating her as a fragile child that she could not cease crying. She had helped her father choose the burial dress for her mother and ever since then she had fretted, wondering if her mother would have wanted the blue calico they chose, or her only Sunday dress with the delicate pattern of tiny roses. She focused on this and asked her father for the zillionth time if they had chosen correctly.

"Lass, your mother looks beautiful and she was always uncomfortable in her Sunday best, you know that. Besides the blue calico was the exact colour of her eyes," Albert spoke gently, stroking her arm to comfort her. But Dolly was not comforted and she dwelt on that small detail for days.

The day of the funeral arrived, although to Dolly and Albert, time was irrelevant and could not pierce the shroud of grief in which they were both cloaked. They moved automatically to the coaxing and encouragement of their friends. The Vicar chose the sermon and psalms with the help of Nan and Joan; the undertaker took them gently through the procedures and daily living tasks were performed by Nan's mother Violet, and Molly Arden. They coaxed the duo to eat, drink and sleep as though they were bairns.

The old village church was Norman in origin; the windows were ethereal with their magnificent coloured glass that had been added just recently. The inside had remained largely untouched save for some minor repairs to the roof to keep out the rain. The pews were well worn dark oak wood that had been polished daily by the 'church ladies'. The day of the funeral the sun shone in a watery hue through the multicoloured glass giving the interior of the church a pink and rosy glow. Flowers were put at strategic places and their delicate aroma permeated the usually stale air. The organ was softly played by old June Lane, who missed some notes due to her creeping arthritis. No one noticed.

Three choirboys sang in unison and Dolly barely recognized them as Jake, Samuel and Thomas from the schoolhouse because they looked so cherubic and serene. Dolly's friends, Nan and Joan, sang a beautiful psalm and Dolly hung onto every note. The church was full to the rafters with mourners; every one of them cared deeply for Eleanor, their neighbour and friend.

Dolly went through the service as best she could. Periodically her father reached for her hand. Neither of them found a voice to sing or even pray. They were bereft of reason and mortal action was lost in the twilight world of grief. Victoria and Anthony flanked Dolly as she walked out of the church. Dolly moved over and took her father's arm and they were all silent as they walked to the churchyard. Dolly looked at the mourners around her without seeing. She listened to the comforting words without hearing.

As they made their way to her mother's grave Dolly noticed how calm her father was and part of her wanted to resent him for this. She knew that her parents loved each other very much and she wondered what her father's life would be like now. He was now in his early forties and Dolly knew that his work was making him ill. An overwhelming feeling of pity moved her and she reached once again for his hand. Albert grasped her with such force that she took a deep breath. Some instinct told her that her father was just hanging on to her for support. She moved closer to him. Neither of them spoke or looked at each other, they stood there, at the side of her mother's grave, stoic and emotionally overwhelmed.

Her last day at school had been only three days before, yet Dolly felt it was a lifetime ago. "What a child I was then," she thought ruefully. Everything had changed and yet nothing had changed. The house looked the same, her friends looked the same, and she still woke up in the morning expecting to hear her mother singing in the kitchen. The final straw came on the day of her mother's funeral, the day of Dolly's first menarche. The day that she needed her mother the most, a day when she truly became a woman, was the bleakest day of her life so far. After a fitful sleep she had woken up to a warm sticky feeling between her legs. At first her consciousness did not register what it was. Instead of being elated that she had reached a joyous landmark of womanhood, Dolly screamed inside that she was not yet ready for another change in her life. She reluctantly tended to her needs while all her thoughts were on her mother. "Mam, where are you now, I need you, it's all changing too fast. I want it to be as it was."

The funeral tea was held at the village hall. It seemed as if the whole village was there. The women had all contributed by bringing food, and the men milled around in small groups, unsure of what to do. What could they say? Talk of the war was a whispered buzz, but could be forgiven under the circumstances. Funerals were a woman thing, men don't cry. That is unless you are the bereaved. Children were on their best behaviour lest some adult should clip them around the head in punishment. A few mourners sat down and enjoyed the food. Slowly Dolly mingled, not knowing what else to do. After a while, as she fought to clear away the terrible fuzziness in her head, Dolly caught snippets of conversation ranging from the weather, to how Eleanor was everyone's friend. Mr. Brown ventured to speculate how Albert was to manage such a headstrong girl as Dolly.

"She be a wilful girl alright. Stan, but she has the heart of her mother and an inborn sense of duty. Stand by her father she will, to be sure," replied Mrs. Donavan. Neither of them was aware that Dolly was listening. Dolly was a little perturbed at their insinuation that she would be a difficult child for Albert. She was indignant at the implication that she would not stand by her father, her father was her world. However, Dolly did not even have the strength to speak up, she was depleted of emotion.

"Am I strong-willed?" Dolly thought. "I know I have been accused of being spirited, but maybe they are right. I know I have been indulged by my parents. Oh! Am I selfish, I did not give it all a thought? I could have been working years ago and helped out." Dolly wept and thinking it was her grief, she was comforted Joan.

After a while Dolly controlled her tears and self-loathing to try and get through this day the best she could. She sighed as she cleared the pots from the tables, and started to wash them.

"Nay lass, leave that to us," said the rotund Mrs. Martin, taking the plates out of her hands. At that moment Dolly wished she could be one of the nine Martin children with a large motherly presence hugging and protecting them all. Mrs. Taylor walked up, held her gently and kissed her cheek.

"We are here for you, Dolly dear. Come around to see us at any time. I know you are hurting bad right now luv, but it will ease, just you see."

Dolly wearily sat down and Mr. Graham, the local merchant, sat beside her.

"It will get better dear, get back to normal routine, it will get better."

Mr. Graham was to be her new boss and was kind to come to the funeral tea. He took Dolly's slim hand into his own fat sweaty one and stroked it gently. Dolly gave an involuntary shudder and put it down to the emotions of the day. She pulled her hand away, excusing herself as she went to talk to Vicar Simon and Molly Arden who were deep in conversation. As soon as Dolly approached they both turned to include her.

"The flowers are so beautiful, Dolly, everyone had a posy of summer flowers and your mother was well loved," ventured Molly.

"Are you alright, child? You seem so pale. Do you want to sit here for a while with Molly and me?"

"Yes please. I don't want to appear ungrateful but everyone is watching me, like I should be performing or something. Mam would have been proud of it all, but I don't know how to act or what to say to people," tears ran down Dolly's cheeks as she spoke. "I didn't think I could cry anymore."

Molly put her arms around her and Dolly sobbed for a while. Vicar Simon left them alone and went to talk to his parishioners.

Much of the day passed in a haze. Albert said very little but thanked everyone as they took their leave. As soon as the last person left he closed the door of the village hall and leaned against it. It was quite some time before he moved to go home himself. Dolly did not speak but looked at her father for some sign that this was all just a nightmare. It was not. They walked slowly back to their cottage. Albert opened the door and the silence roared in his ears. They felt like robots, hardly aware of their next move. He looked at his young daughter, sitting on the couch with her shoulders slumped. He started to sob. Dolly was alarmed and instantly ran to comfort her father. They stood with their arms around each other for some time. Dolly moved first and led her father to sit down.

"It will be alright, poppa, we are still a family and we will make the home nice just like mam was here." Dolly's voice cracked as she tried to comfort her father.

"I know luv," Albert blew his nose loudly, trying to regain his composure, acutely aware of his daughter's need for him to be strong.

"I hope Everett will be home soon. I hope he got my letter, but there is no way of knowing," he finally said.

"Me too. He will be grieved because he was mam's favourite."

Albert changed the subject once again. "Do you start working in the morning, and is Mr. Graham expecting you?"

"Yes, I think so. I need to be busy. Will you be alright?"

"I will return to work too, so we will both go on. Mam would have wanted that."

They both fell into a calm silence, the beginning of acceptance of a very different life ahead.

That night for the first time Albert opened the journal that his comrade Peter Snow wrote in the midst of the Boer war.

"One cannot adequately describe the horrors we have all seen today. Man's inhumanity to man will have its dubious place in history. No person can take all this pain and death, and still have faith in human nature or even faith that there is a God, how can we live a normal life after this….."

Albert cried.

Chapter 2

It had been four months of hell. An order to advance, retreat, pick up the dead, go on, stop, bunker down, and the worst of all was the periodic silence, eerie unsettling silence. The routine of eat and sleep when and how you can was now ingrained in Everett's psyche. He was huddled at the far end of the bunker that was comparatively well equipped. There was some shelter and he had just had his first warm meal in a week. Everett was cold, so very, very cold. It had rained nonstop for days and his army issue was not meant for these conditions. There was a rudimentary shelter he shared with twenty other men, but no one spoke much, everyone was too exhausted and traumatized.

The 'trench war,' as it was called later, was the result of both sides digging in to defend their hard-won ground. Whenever the enemy got close enough to aim a hand grenade the ensuing mayhem resulted in more dead and maimed comrades.

"Better that than the poison gas," reasoned Stan, as he tried to reassure a frightened Everett, after such an attack. The barbed wire stood firm and impenetrable on the rise of the hill. It stood out against the sky, a fortress of death and doom, specifically at sunset, when the golden-orange hues lent a surreal veil to the whole horrific affair.

Everett removed his boots to try and dry out his wet socks. He looked at them, darned heels already fraying. His feet were wrinkled blue with cold and they badly needed a wash. He had given up trying to tend to his blisters and they were now hardened and callused. He put his socks on the butt of his rifle and removed his trench coat and pullover. His balaclava fell into the mud and he shook it and hung it with his socks. The bucket of cold water he was given was a luxury after weeks of not undressing and he relished the cold refreshing wash. Somehow he managed to shave his adolescent fuzz that one day would be a beard. Finally he soaked his feet and dried them on a small cloth he had been given with the bucket of water. He felt refreshed and slept fitfully for a blessed four hours.

His unit had dug themselves in and for the last two days they had been awaiting orders. No news had reached him about his mother's death, but he felt that something was terribly wrong at home. He sat in his bunker weeping silently, missing his family. He saw grown men occasionally doing the same and no one felt they were lesser men because of it. He thought of Dolly and knew that she was ending her schools days soon. "She is the scholar," he mused, "and I am the doer." He daydreamed about the antics they got up to as children. He thought about the Abbey ruins where they spent carefree days of pretending to be soldiers, now he was doing it for real. Real was nothing like the imagination, he thought ruefully. He smiled despite everything, and marvelled at the joyfulness and naïveté of youth. Dolly always covered for his misdemeanours and they loved each other unconditionally. He missed her terribly.

His comrade Graham Sharp inched his way nearer. "Got any cigs, Rett?"

"A bit wet mate, but you're welcome to 'em." Everett pulled a squashed packet out of his pocket.

"It's getting bad out there. They just captured a Kraut and he said his unit just received reinforcements. Apparently the foot soldiers don't have much heart for the war. The sergeant said the Kraut was rather relieved to have been captured. That's a turn up for the book eh! If they don't want this war, and God knows we don't want it, then what the bloody hell are we doing here?"

"Doing our duty mate, just doing our duty," Everett replied wearily.

Everett hadn't seen his friend George for some days, he was worried about him. He was in the same unit but in the last horrific battle they had split up to go around the target and he hadn't seen him since. However, although he was worried about George, he did not feel alone because each man in the bunker was closer to him than even a brother could have been. They would each have given their lives for him and he knew that, young as he was; he would have done the same for them. He donned his still damp socks and prepared his backpack in readiness for the unknown. It did not take long. At first light; all hell broke out once again.

"Hey lads, get a move on. The air force is mounting an air strike, pray that's our lads up there and not the krauts," the sergeant yelled. Everett could hear the drone of a plane above him. Unused to the sound, he cowered and froze. He looked up to see a solitary plane through the smoke and it was so close he could see the young English pilot inside. Made more of cloth than metal, and with its 'pusher' propeller facing backwards, the plane looked so flimsy. Months later, astounded by his vivid recall, Everett remembered thinking that it would blow away in the wind at any moment. The din of the engine drowned out any other sounds but as it moved past his bunker he heard gunfire from above and he covered his head with his arms. The fledgling fighter plane was clearing the way for the foot soldiers. He heard but could not see other planes pounding the enemy lines.

"Go for it lads," shouted the sergeant, waving enthusiastically, "let's get the fucking bastards."

There was movement around him and instinctively Everett followed his comrades from the comparative safety of the bunker over the rise of the hill. Chaos erupted and the sounds of battle were deafening and the scene around him confusing. The ground was hard and wet. The rain was coming down in a steady drizzle.

"Get ready, here they come," someone yelled.

"Get ready for what?" thought Everett who was in a dangerous daze. Stan pushed him hard in his back and he fell down.

"Get your bayonet fixed, lad. Stay here but protect yourself."

Everett seemed to wake up from his inertia and fixed his bayonet. He aimed his gun towards the horizon and waited. He did not wait long before the enemy appeared. Much of what happened next seemed to be played and replayed in Everett's mind in slow motion.

He fired and reloaded and heard his comrades yelling to advance. He stood up and ran with the others until they were on top of the ridge they had abandoned three days before. Smoke obscured his view, the sounds of battle deafening and frightening. He looked around; as he climbed higher he could see where the source of the smoke was coming from. He heard Johnny Caruthers through the chaos and as he turned towards his voice

Johnny ran right into the line of fire. Everett stood transfixed as his comrade was mortally wounded. He watched as the bright red blood oozed from Johnny's head. He reacted by firing in the direction of the noise and saw the shadow of a German soldier as he fell and rolled to a stop a hundred yards away from Everett.

"Oh my God, I did that," he thought, shaking uncontrollably. He had no more time to think before more bullets were coming his way. He fired again, this time blindly.

He threw himself on the ground and focused on avoiding the smoke which was stinging his eyes. He reloaded and waited to hear orders, none came. He heard muffled cries of terror, cries in both German and in English. He knew that whatever the language, or the age of the warrior, the severely and mortally wounded inevitably cried in vain for their mothers.

There was no time for tears, no time for feelings at all as Everett moved around the battlefield in a mixture of self preservation and horror. His head felt as though it would explode, straining to pick up any commands he could hear through the din. In his confusion he thought he heard Johnny shouting somewhere ahead and Everett moved towards his voice without registering the carnal scene he had just witnessed. He moved forward and, passed the distorted body of the German soldier he had just shot. The soldier's helmet was lying at his side and Everett saw that the enemy was a young blond boy around sixteen years old. He had no feelings; he couldn't afford them, it was time to survive.

As Everett continued to climb the steep hill he lost his footing and momentarily rolled backwards, being saved from falling further by a large tree. With both hands on his gun he could not stop his fall. "Thank God for the tree, I might have landed in a German's lap," he thought. He lay there slightly stunned, trying to gain back reality, when he felt what he thought was someone touching his shoulder. Instinctively he swung around and fired his weapon. He wiped his eyes from the stinging smoke and prepared to fire again.

What he saw then was to haunt his dreams for years to come. The touch on his shoulder was from a boot. The boot belonged to a British soldier who had hung himself in the tree. He was dangling by his neck with a horrific purple bloated face, his eyes almost out of their sockets, the boy's body swinging from above. Everett stared in disbelief. The bullet from Everett's gun had pierced the boy's uniform in the chest. He recognized the young boy as Mathew Green but had never spoken to him. He knew only that two evenings ago they had supped cold tea from the same can.

"He must have done this in the night," Everett reasoned. "Hanging himself was quieter than using his pistol."

A surge of adrenalin, compounded by his own instinctive reactions, gave him strength. Everett scaled the large branches and cut the boy down. He was now totally oblivious to the sounds of battle raging around him. The smoke was clearing but still gave him some protection from the snipers. This was the day that Everett became a man and left childhood behind. He had dropped his weapon as he scaled the tree to cut the boy free. Now he used both arms to cradle the boy in his arms, cooing as his mam had cooed when she held him. He was crying openly but silently, emotion too deep to escape his lips, too primal to be heard by mortal men. Time stood still.

In this timeless void, George appeared out of the smoke and slid down the ridge to join Everett. Everett was overwhelmed to see him because they had lost contact three days ago.

"What are you doing mate?" hissed George, "leave him and get going."

"Get going where?" stuttered Everett.

George grabbed him by the arm and made him stand. Everett was shaking uncontrollably as reality once again invaded his numbed psyche.

"Follow me."

Gently and unhurriedly Everett laid the boy's head down on the grass and, using the boy's jacket, he covered his head. Everett picked up his gun with the bayonet still attached and crouched as he hurried after George. George at seventeen was a year older than Everett and a stocky redhead. They had been friends their whole lives and it was with George's urging that Everett joined up. George led him back to the bunker where some of the men in the unit were recovering. The sound of gunfire was deafening but suddenly it all stopped and there was an eerie silence once again. No one moved for what seemed to be an eternity. They were sprawled in the bunker next to Craig Phillips and it seemed that Craig had joined at the same time they had.

"What yer' mate," Craig said good-heartedly, as they settled in for what they thought was the night.

"Craig, do you have any chow?" George asked.

"Here mate, take this." Paddy Jones offered some dried bread and a tin of spam.

Everett felt that if he ate anything, he would be sick. He declined the food but accepted the canister of water. He tried to keep his mind focused on the present, but knew as surely as he knew the insanity that was war, he would carry these memories with him for a lifetime.

The comrades settled in for the night, hoping to get a couple of hours rest, but that was not to be. Sergeant Westerman slid into the bunker and gave the order to retreat. Pandemonium reigned as the men pulled back. Advance, retreat, advance, retreat seemed to make no sense to Everett at all. The wounded and dead were all around and even lay in the same bunker where they had settled down momentarily. Everett was covered with the blood of his comrades and as they retreated they fell over dead bodies that had been there for days. Everett thought that this must be the definition of hell. Home and sanity must have been in another life.

As soon as the men moved again there was another round of explosions. They were given the order to retreat once again and they all reacted in unison. They all started to run back over the last hill, about one hundred yards to the west of where they were. Guns were firing and men were shouting. Everett joined in the exodus of the bunker and onto an open piece of no man's land. He crawled on his belly as he watched his comrades do. Snipers were hitting their marks and hand grenades were being thrown from both sides. Everett did not know what had hit him. Silence reigned. Slowly the haze cleared and he heard George talking to him.

"How yer' doing, mate?" the voice asked again.

Everett struggled to make sense of it. He saw the face of George swimming before his eyes that were not yet able in focus. He saw George grinning like a Cheshire cat.

"Thought you were a goner there, Rett, I'd say you were one lucky son of a gun," he continued to grin.

Everett tried to speak but a croak escaped, "What, where?"

"In the mobile field hospital, mate, we are both as lucky as Lucifer, me with a couple of missing fingers and you with a shattered knee."

"How long? Have..." Everett croaked.

"Couple of days, mate, and we have to move out tonight. Thank God you are awake, didn't want to leave you behind."

"How did we get here?" Everett struggled with his words.

"Craig Phillips was in the same explosion, it seems, he lost an arm though. He was shipped out yesterday because they couldn't fix him here. Hope the lad makes it. It was him who alerted the medics because you and I were unconscious, he must have been in agony but he saved us all."

Everett did not reply, he couldn't find any words.

Everett was slipping again into a pain-induced fog but not before he felt George take hold of his hand with his good one.

"Hold on, Rett, we will both get out of this alive."

Everett heard nothing as he slept on and off throughout the night. Even in his stupor he tried to get out of bed, he screamed as the pain in his leg broke through. George stayed by his side to comfort and calm him, even though he was also in excruciating pain.

The wounded were moved out as soon as dawn broke and thankfully most of the trip home over the choppy North Sea was a blur to Everett. He later learned that twenty three of his comrades did not make the journey, although seventy others did. Everett and George were both sent to a military hospital to recuperate and were honourably discharged as soon as they were fit to go home. Everett did not remember many details of those weeks, although he teased George often of flirting with the nurses.

"Just practicing," George laughed.

George stayed longer than need be, to be with Everett, and the chums talked often of their loved ones back home in Cotter's Marsh. They were both different people than they were a few months earlier, and they recognized that they could never pick up their lives again from the point that they had left them.

On one of their late night talks George shared his future dreams with Everett. He was sat on Everett's bed and Everett lit up a cigarette for them both.

"Against the rules, mate," someone called out. "Give us one, then."

George went over to the voice and put a lit cigarette in his mouth. He let him take a drag and took it out of his mouth. The voice had no right hand and his left arm was amputated.

"Thanks," the voice said. His eyes looked at George and there was a silent communication not to pity him.

"OK mate, anytime."

George gave him another drag and walked back to Everett.

"I am looking to get my own farm, Rett. I know it's a long shot. I was hoping to make a career out of the army until I lost my fingers, seems I can't shoot now and what good is that?" George laughed ruefully; there was a hint of disappointment about his statement. George though, was minimizing his injuries and, apart from losing fingers, he had also lost his hearing in one ear and was prone to debilitating migraines for the rest of his life.

"Looks like I may have to marry that sister of yours and raise dozens of kids," he laughed but this time with light-heartedness. Everett knew that a union between George and Dolly was in the cards but this was the first time the true relationship had ever been brought out into the open.

"Honestly George, you are welcome to her, she is obstinate, a pest and will not mind her own business." They both laughed.

"I need a strong willed gal to keep me in line," retorted George.

"Maybe mam has other ideas though," Everett surmised, "you know how mam is for her to be independent."

"Oh, not to worry, your mam is putty in my hands."

George was loved by the whole family and Everett conceded that if George wanted Dolly, then the only thing stopping him was Dolly herself.

The orderly arrived with the long-awaited mail. Everett had two letters and George had one. Everett opened the military one first. He had been honourably discharged due to his injuries. George also had the same letter and they grinned to each other as Everett opened his second correspondence. His father was informing him of his mother's death.

July 1st 1917

Dear son Rett, I hope and pray that this letter finds you safe. I have to inform you that your mam passed away yesterday. She died peacefully in her sleep and is to be buried next to her mother and father at St. Mark's cemetery. Dolly is obviously distraught and we are both worried about you. I hope this letter gets to you. Keep safe and come home soon. There is talk of the war being over soon, we are all praying that this may be so.

With the greatest affection,

Your father.

Everett's face turned white and his hands shook. George snatched the letter to read.

"Oh my God, Rett, I am so sorry."

They both sat for some time stunned.

"I knew she was not well, but I had no idea," Everett said.

"We will be going home at the end of the month so you can comfort Dolly and your father."

"I had no idea," repeated Everett.

Both friends sat there holding on to memories of better times. That night Everett did not sleep. He thought of how his mother had loved and cared for him and his twin. Tears would not come, he was all cried out by the loss of souls. He had witnessed mayhem. It was not supposed to spill into his home life; that was sacred and safe, or it was supposed to be.

Three weeks after her mother's funeral, Dolly was walking arm in arm with Joan and Victoria after church. They were all wondering what had happened to Nan. Nan sang in the choir and had the voice of an angel, so when she was not there she was sorely missed.

"I hope she ain't sick," Joan said.

"Isn't sick," corrected Dolly.

"I mean she was looking peaky on Wednesday at the market. Maybe she got the gripe," continued Joan without missing a beat.

The friends walked on when they heard a whistle from Anthony.

"Hey, wait up. Where are you going?"

"Just down the lane a ways, getting some air after sitting next to Mrs. Jones and her brood. I need to breathe," Dolly laughed.

Mrs. Jones was fat, to put it bluntly, and her eight children were less than clean, with running noses and nits in their hair. The group were sympathizing with Dolly and for the first time in three weeks Dolly forgot her mam's death, albeit briefly. The realization that she was laughing descended on her like a cloud and her eyes lost their sparkle once again.

The friends walked along in companionable silence until they reached the turnstile at the edge of the village. The watery sun was not enough to cast shadows but was a welcome relief from the last rainy days. In the meadow they saw the children playing and laughing as they climbed a rope attached to a big old oak tree.

"See this is how to do it," shouted young Samuel, no longer looking cherubic, as he swung to and fro.

"Let me have a turn," pleaded Shirley, trying to grab Samuel as he avoided her arms. Shirley's hair was unruly and blowing in the breeze, she had long since abandoned her ribbon and wanted to challenge the boys to tree climbing.

Dolly laughed, remembering that it seemed only last year they were all doing exactly the same thing. George and Everett were the ringleaders in any mischief, followed closely by Dolly, the tomboy.

Nan appeared from across the field and they called her to join them. Nan was out of breath. She smiled to be among her friends. She was a plump attractive girl with a ready smile and long curly black hair. Dolly often envied her her curls.

"Where were you? I suppose you were daydreaming again and forgot your appointment with God," Anthony said sarcastically, without waiting for Nan to say a word.

Nan ignored him but put out her tongue cheekily.

"You little minx," laughed Anthony, pretending to be annoyed.

They all sat down around the wooden stile and listened to the birds singing and the children laughing. Anthony broke off a dead branch and Joan picked off some blackberries, offering them around the group. They languished for a moment in the aroma of the fresh cut grass. Nan cleared her throat.

"I have something to tell you all but you must swear to keep the secret. I am mortified to have to tell you my terrible news," Nan blurted out. She looked so serious they paid her mind.

Such urgency in her request took them all back momentarily to when they were eight. Nan had captured a live baby rabbit and they all kept it a secret and had tried to rear it in vain. However, they were all well past eight years old now and the fear in Nan's eyes and voice gave Dolly shudders down her spine.

"Nan, you're frightening me," said Victoria, who had also felt the chill in Nan's voice.

"There is no way to say this, except just to say it. I… I think I am with child."

They all gasped. No one spoke as they tried to absorb this devastating news. Anthony went over to Nan and held her gently on her shoulder.

"How long?" he asked.

"Nigh on nine weeks," Nan whispered.

Victoria thumped loudly as she fell off the wooded style. She was as white as a sheet and could not contain herself, "Why, Nan, what have you done?"

Nan started to cry. Anthony put his arms around her while glaring at Victoria. Dolly and Joan came closer.

"Shush… the others will hear us," said Joan, looking back towards the church. The children had gone to the church hall to get some refreshments. She could see a few remaining parishioners still talking to the Reverend.

Dolly knelt down besides Nan. "Tell me what happened, I am sure you are not to blame," she said comfortingly, taking Nan's hand and kissing it gently.

"It was when I was returning to the Reverends house a few Sundays ago. Dolly, do you remember that I was worried about being late because he had some guests arriving from town, and wanted me to serve supper? It was very unusual but it was because the housekeeper was nursing her own father who died that night." Nan's words were fast and she barely took a breath.

"Yes I remember, go on."

"Well I was late, so I took a shortcut over the marshes towards the sand dunes, and when I was almost past the churchyard and into the copse, I knew I was being followed."

Nan paused and her voice faltered. Anthony, looking grave, sat at her feet and took her other hand in his.

"Well, I hurried as best I could, I knew I was being followed but every time I turned there was no one there. Then out of the darkness a man appeared with a hood on his head. I would have screamed but he punched me in my face and I fell down. Before I recovered he put a grain sack on my head. When I struggled to get away another blow to the side of my head dazed me."

Joan gasped and held on tight to Victoria, who was openly crying in fear for her friend.

"Go on," encouraged Anthony.

"Well, I think I was assaulted," Nan's voice became naught but a whisper, "as no nice Christian girl can comprehend."

Nan paused for some time, no one spoke. The air was electric with fear. Nan's face was ashen.

"Did he... do it?" Victoria asked.

Anthony again glared at her. "Vicky, what a puerile question to ask her, how else could a baby be conceived?"

"Please don't squabble you two, this is far too serious," pleaded Dolly. "Nan, please go on."

Nan's mind was racing. She did not want to tell them all the details of how her assailant had ripped her underclothes and forced her to open her legs so brutally that she could not walk properly for days, or that he pushed his manhood into her so roughly that she thought she had been split in two. She could not share with her dear friends how the beast had crushed her beneath him with such force that she could feel a branch searing into her back, or that her head had crashed onto a rock so hard that she was only semi conscious throughout. Even through this ordeal, she remembered his panting breath vividly, and the way he uttered disgusting obscene words in her ear. She could do nothing but lay there. He slapped her again as he forced her into submission and finally finished his business, releasing his vice-like grip on her.

Nan had lain there motionless for some time after the man had jumped up and disappeared into the copse, with as much stealth as he had arrived. She wanted to die, wanting to be divorced from her body that had been so forcibly invaded. Slowly she regained her reality; she moved carefully, trying to kneel on all fours. She tried with great effort to stand, forcing her legs to support her weight, fighting through her pain. She tried in vain to brush away the blood on her skirt. No tears would come; she was temporarily devoid of feeling. Her head hurt and throbbed so much she was dizzy. It took some more time for her to stand up fully. She then made her way unsteadily towards the vicar's house. Nan does not know when she decided that she would not tell anyone of the rape. It just evolved that she just did not say what had happened. It was not a conscious decision, she was in shock at first and then it seemed to be too late.

"Yes it was so... horrible... he hurt me so bad," cried Nan.

"Why didn't you tell us? Or at least the constable?" asked Joan.

"I don't know... I was ashamed I think."

"You must have suffered greatly, Nan," Dolly comforted her.

"Do you know who it was?" asked Anthony, himself a white as a ghost.

"I can't be sure but I could smell horses, and when I struggled and pulled off his hood I felt hair that was curly and a clean-shaven face... but I can't be sure," Nan cried.

"Did he speak?" asked Joan in a small shaky voice.

"He said, 'You asked for it, I watched you and you asked for it. You are a strumpet'... I think something like that."

"So it is someone who has seen you before? He said, 'I have watched you'," offered Victoria.

Nan started to cry louder. "I never thought that it could be someone I know. I just thought it was a town boy, someone who was just passing through. Do you really think it could be someone I know?" Nan broke out into a fresh bout of tears.

"I'll kill him," announced Anthony, springing to his feet and pacing around like an angry bull.

"But she is not sure who it was," reasoned Joan, "it could be anyone from the town or the village."

"What did you do then?" asked Dolly, trying to keep Anthony focused and calm.

"I was so ashamed I just sat there stunned and relieved to be still alive, although a few moments before that I had wanted to die, but I suppose my survival instinct kicked in. I think he threatened to kill me if I told. I was just a mess emotionally and could not think."

"The bastard," spat Anthony, completely out of character for him, forgetting he was in the company of ladies.

"Please don't say anything until I have told Mam," Nan pleaded.

"Why didn't you tell the vicar?" asked Joan.

"When I recovered enough to go there I wanted to clean myself and he already had guests arriving. I just wanted to be invisible; I just wanted it not to have happened."

"Did he not notice anything?" asked Joan.

"Well he said I looked feverish and I made the excuse of running through the marshes because I was late. I told him I had tripped and fell onto a branch that had scraped my face. I don't know why I didn't tell him everything there and then. I think he did not believe me and he gave me the night off and sent me to the room I was to use that night, he seemed angry that I was late."

They all sat silently with their own thoughts, and it was Anthony who spoke up first.

"Maybe you are just in shock. I think my dad needs to see you. You may not be pregnant at all so don't let's panic until we are sure... then we can panic," he smiled to break the tension.

"Maybe Anthony is right," spoke up Victoria, relieved to have a plan.

The little troupe all walked with purpose to Dr. Preston's house. Anthony led them into the parlour, thankful that his father had lingered at the church. He furnished them all with a glass of lemonade.

"Ma is visiting so she will not be home until tonight and Pa will keep your secret Nan, so try not to worry," Anthony kissed her forehead and she smiled.

Dolly looked around the beautifully furnished room. Although she had visited Dr. Preston many times this was the first time she had sat in his parlour. Anthony was a gracious host, making sure they were all comfortable.

"Maybe it ain't a good idea for us all to be here," said Joan.

Dolly did not correct her this time. They all agreed that only Dolly and Anthony should be there when the doctor arrived. Joan and Victoria bade a tearful but relieved goodbye and left, promising to keep Nan's secret.

Dr. Preston was surprised to see Nan and Dolly in his parlour when he arrived home. Anthony soon explained that this was more than a social call, Nan needed his medical skills.

"Alright young lady, come with me to the study."

There was a large brown leather couch in there that the doctor used to examine Nan.

"Now don't be afraid of me, child," he said gently as he carried out his duties.

Nan was overwhelmed with shame.

"Well, young lady, it appears that you are going to be a mama," said Dr. Preston kindly.

Nan stared at him bereft of tears. He went to his desk to write something down while Nan dressed herself and sat there with her head down and her hands clasped so tight in her lap that they were white. Eventually Dr. Preston spoke.

"Does your mother know?"

"No sir, I thought it best to be sure before I told her," Nan whispered, not lifting her head.

"Get dressed and we will talk some more."

They moved back into the parlour where Anthony and Dolly anxiously waited for news. They only had to see Nan's stricken expression to realize that all hopes of a false alarm were dashed.

"Both of you go into the kitchen," Dr Preston ordered.

"No please let them stay," pleaded Nan.

"Well alright, young lady, if that is what you want. Now tell me who the father of the child is?"

"I...I don't know sir," she spluttered.

"Now child, come along. You have to know who he is; I refuse to believe you are a child of ill repute. Was it a beau who has deserted you? Does he know?"

Nan quietly repeated her story and Dr. Preston looked grave.

"We must inform the constabulary; this man must be found and punished."

"I am so afraid sir; he said he would kill me if I told."

"But you cannot take responsibility for this alone."

"My mam will know what to do. I will tell her tonight."

"Very well then, you must do what you think fit, however I can arrange for the birth and adoption. Tell Violet, your mother, to come and see me and I will arrange something for you."

At this Nan burst into fresh tears and Dolly went to comfort her.

"Sir, what do you think will happen?" asked Anthony.

"Well, to have a child without wedlock is a very serious thing, whether a crime has been committed or not. First things first, Anthony and Dolly please take Nan home to her mother, and with Nan's permission I will talk to the vicar, I am sure she can continue to work for a few months yet, Simon is a kind and understanding man. Even if you choose to have the child adopted, your employer must know what is happening, don't you think?"

Nan nodded.

Anthony and Dolly went with Nan to her mother's house. Dolly could not imagine what was running through Nan's mind at that moment. Violet had been a good friend of Eleanor, Dolly's mother, and Dolly knew that she would help Nan to get through this trauma. It was getting dark and a fog had moved up from the marsh and was starting to swirl around them. They walked hand in hand without talking. A dog barked as they passed farmer Prichard's farm. They saw a couple of bats hovering over the church belfry. It took only a few minutes to reach Nan's home but for all of them it felt a very long time. Anthony left them at the front gate and kissed Nan, trying to reassure her things would work out fine. Dolly hugged her before they entered the house, and Nan smiled bravely.

Violet's house was modest but warm and welcoming. It was sparse of furniture but Dolly recognized a few pieces her mother had given to Violet. The library chair and the large wooden kitchen table had been salvaged from the manor. Dolly had heard stories from her mother about the grandeur of the manor. She never got a clear explanation about what had happened to her grandparents, except that they both died within months of each other. Every time she went to Nan's house she saw the evidence of what her mother's life had once been. In her own home, her mother had refused any connection with her past and her father had provided everything the family needed.

The fire was alight in the black iron grate and Dolly was glad of this because Nan was shivering with fear. Violet was only forty but her hair was grey and her posture was already bending to arthritis. She was sat close to the fire, polishing the horse brasses that lined the mantelpiece.

"Well, what a surprise. Dolly, you are looking better. You have some colour back in your cheeks," said Violet, who had not yet noticed her daughter's swollen eyes and puffy cheeks.

"Thank you. I came home with Nan because... a terrible thing has happened."

With Dolly's encouragement, Nan shakily told her mother the news. Violet just sat there, stoic and motionless.

After a few moments, which to Dolly and Nan, seemed like a lifetime, Violet went to her daughter and gathered her into her arms. Nan rested there on her shoulder, and closed her eyes. Violet said not a word but caressed her daughter's hair, as only a mother can. Nan was shaking.

In answer to Nan's fears, Violet just rocked her gently and quietly sang a lullaby she had sung to her as a small child.

Golden slumbers kiss your eyes,
Smiles awake you when you rise,
Sleep,
Pretty baby,
Do not cry,
And I will sing a lullaby.

Care you know not,
Therefore sleep,
While I o'er you watch do keep,
Sleep,
Pretty darling,
Do not cry,
And I will sing a lullaby.

Dolly rose from her chair and hugged them both as she took her leave.

"I will check in tomorrow, although it will be after six if that is alright?" Dolly asked.

"See you then child," Violet agreed in a whisper, not pausing as she rocked Nan like a babe, her face now ashen white.

Dolly knew then that Nan would be alright. Violet loved her daughter and would help her through this terrible ordeal.

Even though it was a summer night, Dolly shivered as she hurried home to the comfort of her father's love. Things were happening too fast in her world. She was not ready to face all the hardships that adulthood seemed to bring. She was now aware of her surroundings, as she had never been aware before. Every flutter of bat wings, every hoot of the owl, every bark of the dogs, every shadow from the swaying branches, seemed to be an omen, a threat. If this was adulthood, she did not like it at all.

Chapter 3

Everett and George were on their way home, the telegram said. Dolly was elated and all the bad things that had happened in the last month were pushed out of her thoughts. She was to accompany her father to the train station and they had hired Harry Brent to take them in his horse and cart. The morning of her twin's arrival seemed to move excruciatingly slow. However, the time arrived at last. Dolly could not contain her excitement and rushed around the house preparing for her sibling's arrival. She knew he had been through hell, and that he would need to grieve their mother's death, but he was coming home and that was all that mattered.

In due course Dolly and her father waited impatiently at the train station. Dolly was too excited about her twin's return to give George much thought, but George's grandfather was also waiting at the station. Violet had remained at home with Nan because they did not want George to find out about her condition at the impersonal train station. Albert went to stand at the side of George's grandfather.

"Richard," acknowledged Albert.

"Albert."

"Rain's stopped."

"Aye... late again," remarked George's grandfather Richard, referring to the train. No one mentioned the war or the horror their children were returning from. There was only today. Today was a good day.

Half an hour later they heard a whistle sound in the distance. They all heard the chug chug of the train as it inched its way into the station. The arrival of the train sent steam billowing out, covering the waiting people with a thick mist. Dolly couldn't care less and was anxious to see Everett. The train ground to a screeching stop. Waiting friends and family surged forward for the first glimpse of their loved ones, many of whom were hanging out the windows, waving.

Passengers alighted from the carriage. Some were soldiers returning from war and some were local people returning from work in the countryside. The station was awash with tears of joy at the reunions of families. Dolly strained to catch sight of her brother through the thick steam. She spotted George as he was the first one down and he turned to assist Everett, who was still on crutches. Dolly gasped. Her brother was so much older, and as he made his way towards her she ran to meet him. In her enthusiasm she almost knocked him down and George steadied them both. Dolly did not notice the bandages on George's hand.

"Dolly, you look beautiful," said George, hoping to get some attention from her.

"George, Everett, Rett oh, Rett," was all she could manage. Albert walked up to his son and shook his hand in both of his. He then embraced him and tears fell down all of their faces. George was greeting his grandfather, who would never have owned up to the tears in his eyes. George turned to Albert, and, as the surrogate son he was, grabbed him and hugged him with as much fervour as he had his grandfather. George kissed Dolly on the cheek and she smiled, but did not let go of her sibling's arm. They all made arrangements to meet the next day.

When Dolly, Everett and Albert were settled in the carriage, Mr. Brent spurred his horse on towards home. Harry Brent also had a son in the army, and was looking forward to the day when it was his own son he was bringing home from war. Harry had heard no news from him or the army for over six months.

When they were underway Everett turned to his father, "Mam?"

"Aye lad, she went quickly in her sleep," answered Albert.

"If I knew she was so sick I would have stayed at home."

"Nay lad, you have to live your life, mam understood that, and she was proud of you for fighting for your country."

"Dad..." started Everett, "I..."

He could not continue to explain that it was not patriotism that spurred him on but adventure and youthful selfishness.

"No need son, I understand. Nothing matters except you are home safe," answered Albert to the unspoken statement.

Everett collected his thoughts, sighed and turned to Dolly. He reached out and held her hand.

"Are you doing well, sis?" he asked.

"I want to hear all about your adventures, we have had enough sadness around here," smiled Dolly in her innocent way.

"Nothing to tell really, it was hell and I am more than happy to be home."

"Well said lad, I am here if you ever want to talk," said Albert, touching his son's shoulder affectionately.

Their eyes met and they both knew that neither of them would talk about their experience with the horrors of war. It was a bond they shared and a special mutual respect had blossomed that would last for the rest of their lives. The last time Albert had seen his son he was a child. He had returned to him a man and their relationship was based on ultimate respect.

Everett sighed as he tried to focus on his family; it all seemed to be surreal to him as they chatted idly about unimportant things, until they reached home. Dolly did not share Nan's troubles with her brother; there was time enough for that. Today was a wonderful day, Rett was home. He needed assistance to get out of the cart and both men helped him down. He slowly limped into the house as his father settled with Harry.

"Not on your life, mate," Harry said, refusing payment, "these lads are fighting for us, bringing Rett home is the least I could do," Harry doffed his cap and climbed back up in the cart.

"I hope you have some good news of your own soon Harry," Albert said, as the horse started to turn the cart around towards his home. Harry's son was already dead, although they did not yet know it.

After the joyous meal Everett and Dolly went into the garden, Everett using one crutch and Dolly's arm for balance. Dolly sat on the swing and Everett leaned on the big oak tree and pushed her gently. It was dark but the earlier rain had given way to a full moon and there was not a cloud in the sky. The stars were brilliant against the blackness.

"Hardly the same stars that shone over the carnage of war," Everett thought ruefully, but silently. He looked at his sister.

"What are you not telling me, sis?"

"How do you know there is anything to tell?"

"I know you and there is something…"

Dolly reluctantly told her brother about Nan's predicament. Everett was quiet for some time before he asked if the constable had been informed. Dolly said that he had, but because time had passed the culprit may never be caught. Everett sighed.

"So how is Nan now?"

"She is still working for the vicar but in a few weeks she will be sent to the convent to have the baby. They will find a home for the child."

"So our childhoods are officially over."

Dolly did not reply, there was no need. The siblings then sat on the garden bench in silence holding hands and wishing away the horrible months that had changed their lives forever. Dolly moved the leaves about with her feet and waited for her brother to process the information.

"Victoria, how is she? And Joan and Anthony, are they well?" Everett asked, to quickly cover his first question about Victoria.

"Yes, they are sad about Nan but they are well, Victoria will be happy to see you," Dolly managed a small grin.

"No hope in that area," surmised Everett.

"Love conquers all," laughed Dolly.

Everett started back towards the house. He was overcome with a deep sadness and an overwhelming weariness.

"We will talk tomorrow sis, I need to rest my leg now."

Dolly helped him up the steps and he went to his room. Dolly joined her father in the kitchen.

"He looks as well as can be expected given the circumstances, lass," Albert offered at the sight of Dolly's grave face.

"Nothing stays the same, does it?"

"Nay lass and it is as well, being a grown up can be good too, you have to make the best of it."

Dolly went to her father and kissed him.

"I love you... so please live for a long time. I miss mam so much."

"I don't plan on going anywhere yet awhile," Albert smiled at his daughter's spontaneous show of affection.

Nan could not postpone telling George the news of her rape and, as expected, he took it very badly.

"I'll kill him if I get my hands on him, I'll split open his belly and spill his guts and feed them to the vultures, I'll...," George broke down and cried, for his sister, for himself and for lost innocence.

Nan went to him and quietly put her arms around him and let him cry. Violet absorbed this scene. The depiction of the raw pain of her children was almost as devastating as the untimely death of her husband, their father, in a tractor accident. He had been working from dawn to dusk in the bitter cold of winter to earn a sparse living for his family. She thought then that nothing could be worse. She walked out of the house and sat on the stoop lost in her past and present pain. "Where are you Eleanor, I need my best friend to help me through this?"

Violet sat in the quiet night, looking at the same moon and stars that Everett and Dolly were looking at. She thought about her life at Nan's age. How hard it had been even then. Many a day she went without eating, as her own father struggled to make ends meet, tilling a cruel land. Some winters were harder than others and the villagers struggled to survive. She remembered the good harvests, when there was plenty, when neighbours were kind to neighbours and lifelong friendships were formed. She saw this same companionship in her daughter's choice of friends. Dolly, who was the serious scholar, Vicky, the spoiled one with a good heart, Anthony, dear lovable Tony who wanted to take care of the whole world, and Rett. Rett was destined for great things and knowing her Georgie, he would follow wherever Rett led him. Violet smiled through her pain. In a while she heard laughter coming from inside, "Thank God for the resilience of youth," she said out loud.

Nan came out to her mother and sat beside her. She took her hand gently and laid her head on her shoulder.

"Do you want a cup of tea, Mam?" she asked.

"I will be there soon, lass, I will join you both in a little while." Violet knew it would be alright; everything would work out, George her beloved son was home.

"So what for the future?" asked George when his mother returned to the kitchen.

"Well, for Nan's sake the baby will be adopted."

"Why don't we help her to keep it?"

"Well for Nan it would be too hard; it would ruin her life forever."

"So you have already decided?"

"Stop it, stop talking about me like I am not here," Nan cried, suddenly losing her calm façade.

"Sorry sis."

"Well I have not yet decided, so both of you must give me time," Nan ran to her room. George went to go after her but his mother stopped him.

"Let her be, lad, she is going through a lot of changes, we will have to give her time. She will see the sense in adoption, just wait and see."

"But I don't see it, no matter the circumstances this child is your grandchild, Mam, it is my niece or nephew."

"Aye lad, I know, but the news is new to you and I have had a few weeks to think it out. We will talk another time. Right now you are home, you are safe and we have to rejoice in that."

Violet took George's injured hand gently in hers.

"This is of no importance; you are alive and back with us."

George laid his head in his mother's lap and cried.

A few days later the friends met up after church. They strolled around the village green and settled in the bandstand.

"Well, I think the news is splendid," said Anthony. "We will all help Nan bring up the child."

"I agree," said Everett; "I for one will give her a sum each week from my earnings. Nan is family."

"So will I. I don't earn a lot right now but I will be a doctor soon and then I can really help," said Anthony.

"And me," joined in George. "So it's agreed this child will belong to all of us, what do you think of that, Nan?"

"I am overwhelmed, you are all my true friends and I promise to be the very best mother ever."

The group was then joined by Victoria.

"Sorry I'm late. My uncle John just arrived from town and I had to wait to greet him."

They told her of the decision that the child would be protected and adopted by the group of friends.

"This is the best news ever, Nan. I will start a fund with my stipend for her, it has to be a girl," Victoria laughed.

"Well I think we have enough feminine influences around, the baby will only add more fuel to the growing Women's movement," teased George.

"What shall we call the baby, whatever it is?" asked Dolly.

The group spent a pleasant hour discussing the name of the unborn child and the final decisions were Grace if it was a girl and Andrew if it was a boy. Nan was beaming with happiness and was smiling for the first time in months.

"You will all be the baby's godparents, every one of you."

"Absolutely," Anthony agreed. They all chatted happily as they made their way to Victoria's summer house for tea. It was just like old times. Everett and George were back home safe. The others had no clue about the happenings of the war and it was a relief for the chums not to have to talk about it.

"Papa," said Victoria as she entered the summerhouse, "Nan is going to keep her baby."

Victoria's father, Sir David Hastings, was a distinguished-looking man in his early forties with greying hair and a military stance that showed in a ramrod-straight back. He was reading the newspaper when they all invaded his peace and quiet.

He was taken aback by Victoria's news, but seeing the determined look on the group's faces he remarked, "Well, it sounds as though you lot have reached the decision for her."

"Oh no sir, I did it all by myself before I told them," spluttered an embarrassed Nan.

"Do you know the difficulties raising a child, Nan?"

"Yes sir, I most certainly do, but I can work and Mam will take care of the child in the day. The vicar said I did not need to live in, as long as I start at six in the mornings. I can do it sir, I really can."

Sir David laughed at her youth and enthusiasm. The group told him about their pledge to assist Nan with the child.

"This is one lucky baby," Sir David chuckled. "I suppose Victoria can set up a trust fund with my help, a small amount mind, but if it is left untouched the child could have a tidy sum at age twenty-one."

"Sir, I am overwhelmed, thank you, thank you."

Victoria stared at her father with her mouth open.

Just then the tea arrived and true to form Katharine Hastings had provided light refreshments, which were very welcome to the group.

"I will leave you all now as my brother and I have business," Victoria's father said, as soon as the group was settled.

Sir David left the room and was met in the garden by his brother John. Nan stood by the open window and just caught a glimpse of John from the back. He was tall but well built, with blond hair that was unfashionably long and curled over his collar. His voice, there was something about the voice, but he was speaking low and moving away from earshot. Nan shuddered; there was something about the voice. She struggled to join in the good humoured chatter of her friends.

"So George, what will you be doing after the army?" asked Anthony.

"I am apprenticing with Mr. Wright as an accountant as soon as my discharge comes through. He knows I am still recovering with my hand, but dammit I won't let the loss of a few fingers ruin my life. How is your work going Tony, are you still at the hospital?"

"I am studying now to be a physician, my father has managed to get me some tuition from the professors at the hospital as an intern."

"Wow, and I thought Rett and I were leading the exciting lives. Are you pleased?"

"Yes, it is what I always wanted to do, I think I will be good at it."

"Any ladies in the cards yet?" teased Everett, and he could have bitten off his tongue at the faux pas. He quickly recovered because Anthony did not know he and George had talked about their friend's failure to form intimate friendships with the opposite sex. Everett thought Anthony was ashamed of his small stature and baby features.

Anthony went bright red. He had never had a girlfriend and the group was all he wanted as far as relationships go. What they did not know was that Anthony had grave doubts about his sexuality and was struggling with this. He took great pains to keep these feelings secret. What could he confide in them anyway, he had nothing to say.

"I am too busy for that," Anthony replied.

"I don't doubt it, being a doctor is a hard-won profession, is your father happy?"

"You bet, he feels proud as punch, especially because I have free tuition."

Everyone laughed because Dr. Preston's parsimonious nature was legendary in the village.

"Still, big heart empty pockets, eh!" George quipped, and they all laughed once again.

Victoria, Nan, Dolly and Joan were all discussing the fair that was coming soon to Cotter's Marsh and they were making plans to go together.

"Hey, what about the men in your lives?" teased Everett.

"Of course we meant all of us, but maybe it would be too tiring for Nan."

"No it won't. I am not missing out on all the fun, time enough for that later," Nan protested, pouting like a young child. They all laughed. George and Everett stayed for about an hour then left together to take a leisurely walk.

"Say George! I have been offered a job with Mr. Symes on the estate as a gamekeeper. He knows about my gimpy leg but does not think that will be a problem. He says that in a year or two he will be too old for the job and wants to leave Four Winds estate in good hands."

"That is wonderful, if that is what you really want Rett, but what about your painting, are you giving up that dream?"

"Well as far as I can tell I won't earn money as an artist and perhaps I can still paint in my own time."

"Then if it's what you want it means we are all lawfully employed in and around Cotter's Marsh," George laughed, "I will take care of everyone's finances, Anthony will take care of our medical needs and you will take care of our land and food."

For a while there was a companionable silence as the chums walked.

"George, do you have nightmares?" asked Everett.

"About the war?" George asked.

"Yes. I cannot get a night's sleep without waking up sweating like a pig and shaking."

"Yes, that happens to me too. I also have splitting headaches but that will pass I am sure."

George looked briefly at his hand missing two fingers but Everett saw him.

"Any regrets?" Everett asked.

"No, do you?"

"Some. I think we were young and had no idea what was in store, did we?"

"Not on your life, if we did we would not have gone. We have grown up, Rett."

"And survived."

"Yes, and survived."

They walked on and stood looking at the flock of birds flying in the distance, seeing but not really seeing.

"Do you think we made any difference? It seems as though we accomplished naught but death and sorrow," Rett broke through the silence.

"We have to believe we did some good, Rett. We will thank God when the war is over for good and we will make sure it will not be repeated in our lifetimes, we won't allow it. Too many young men suffered and died. They are still suffering and dying."

"I think we can name twenty of our own friends who perished, so there is little wonder we still have nightmares. I wonder what happened to Robert; someday I would like to thank him for saving our lives."

The chums walked on until Everett had to rest his leg. They sat under a poplar tree and Everett absentmindedly picked at the bark. He shuddered, remembering the young soldier he had cut down.

"The ladies must never know the real horrors we went through," said George quietly, sensing what his friend was thinking. "No one who has not experienced the carnage of war knows what it is like. Words are inadequate to explain it all. I remain perplexed at the continuation of man's brutality to man. History keeps repeating itself. Most of the soldiers on both sides were mere boys like us."

"I know George, and I am thankful to be standing here once again on English soil, safe and sound."

"That is the point, Rett; we must keep our homeland safe and sound."

"You are right there, mate, we both know deep in our hearts that we would do it again to protect our own."

"Idealism is easier when there is no threat."

The Monday morning after Everett's return Dolly was waiting for Mr. Graham to collect her in his horse and cart. It was a clear early summer morning and although it was still dark it held the promise of a beautiful day. It had been unusually warm of late and Dolly had put on her light calico dress without the collar and shoulder trim, which she had removed. Dolly wanted to become more fashionable as befitted a young lady of the Edwardian era. With her breasts and hips developing she was becoming a very attractive girl. She still thought of herself as plain but with the glow of youth and blossoming figure she was very passable and pleasing to the eye. As she climbed up the cart to sit alongside Mr. Graham he admired her longer than was politely acceptable. Dolly felt a slight discomfort.

"My girl, you are quite a treat for an old man's eyes," stated Mr. Graham.

Dolly blushed and pulled her shawl close. She kept her eyes fixed on the back of the old gray mare, and concentrated on the rhythm of her trot.

"Don't take offence, Dolly. You must expect compliments, being so pretty an' all."

"Please Mr. Graham, I don't like that talk."

"Nothing meant by it, I'm sure," he huffed, amused.

Mr. Graham tapped her leg a little too intimately and Dolly pulled away. He smiled, "I got patience, Dolly. I can do good things for you, but I got patience."

Dolly cringed at this statement and her mind was in turmoil. No one had ever been so suggestive to her before and she did not know how to handle it. However for the rest of the day it was all as normal, nothing untoward was said. Dolly put it down to her misunderstanding Mr. Graham's intentions. Nothing else happened for the next week and Dolly put the incident out of her mind.

Sunday came around and the friends planned to meet after church as usual and visit the fair. They were all excited at the event. For the last two days they had heard the music and the vendors shouting to the punters to gather around and win prizes at their stalls. Dolly had saved up nine pence and Joan eight pence. They were comparing their bounty as they walked arm in arm towards the fairground. The boys were not yet with them because they had stayed behind to help with the church repairs, but would be joining them later. Victoria and Nan were also walking arm in arm, and this was the first time that Nan had had time to ask any questions about Victoria's uncle John.

"I have never met your uncle John, Victoria, why has he never visited Cotter's Marsh before?"

"Oh, he has been in India for years, and only returned a few months ago."

"So last week was his first visit to four Winds?"

"No, he came a few months ago and he visited in the past but I don't think you ever met him before, he had to leave again on business."

Nan did not want to go any further; she needed time to think, but she could not help herself.

"Is he married?"

"Oh no, he has never been married but he does have a shady reputation with the ladies, I think," Victoria laughed.

"Is he going to stay around here?"

"Yes, papa would like to find him work locally. He used to be quite the horse breeder. Papa said that as a young man he bred champion steeplechasers, but that was a long time ago."

The reference to horses made Nan feel sick and she had to stop a while to stop herself from retching.

"Nan, are you alright?" asked Victoria, alarmed.

Dolly and Joan ran to catch up. They all surrounded Nan who was trying to regain her composure posture.

"I'm fine, thank you all; I just needed to stop a minute."

"You sure scared me," puffed Joan taking hold of Nan's hand.

"We can rest a while longer if you want, Nan," offered Dolly.

"No, let's go on; I want to be first at the toffee apples," Nan laughed, which greatly relieved her friends.

The fair was being held in the field just at the verge of the marshes. The friends all gasped with delight at the colourful displays around them. There were booths that tested skill at throwing, water ducks with prize numbers at the bottom, food stalls of all description, five different carousels, and the 'Greatest show on earth'.

"Let's go there first," said Joan, and they all agreed.

The little troop walked into the darkened tent but not before a group of young men had spotted them. The men went into the tent and started to tease the girls.

"My, what have we here Todd, me thinks we have stumbled across a bevy of beautiful women."

"They can't be the local crop, Gerry, because they are so pretty."

"Do you imagine that they are all so rude as to ignore us? The cream of the crop of this year's eligible men?" laughed Todd.

The banter between the youths went on for some time and the girls started to giggle. They hardly noticed the bearded lady or the Siamese twins in a bottle, nor were they impressed by the headless dwarf. They huddled together delighted at the advantages of blossoming into women and the attention of lustful males.

"Let's go," giggled Joan who was the youngest of the girls. She was feeling very uncomfortable even though the others were obviously enjoying the encounter.

They all left the tent and laughed out aloud as they got into the fresh air. The young men followed.

"Shy ones here, mate. Now do you suppose they need a little coaxing?" remarked Todd.

"But such beautiful ladies," answered Gerry, leaning on a bale of hay and exaggerated his hand on his heart, followed by a low bow. As he did so he fell over the bale and ended up side down behind it. His friend laughed and as much as they tried not to the girls laughed too.

"Anything to oblige ladies," Gerry joined in the laughter as he struggled to regain his composure.

"You're a clumsy oaf, Gerry, now these beauties will never take us seriously."

The girls looked around to see if the boys were coming and were relieved when they spotted George's red head above the crowd. Dolly waved and George waved back. Admitting defeat the two town youths walked away.

"See you later," called Todd as they moved back into the throng of fair goers.

Gerry just carried on brushing hay from his hair.

Nan walked home that evening the happiest she had been for months. She was just beginning to show and found herself holding her growing child as she hummed a tune and walked through the field next to her house. The ground fog was swirling a little but the weather was warm and she was happy. Some instinct stopped her in her tracks. A dark shadow was near the hedgerow and was walking in pace with her. The shadow stopped too.

"Who is it, stop frightening me," shouted Nan bravely.

"So you're carrying my spawn, keep looking forward, don't turn around or I will hurt you," whispered a man's voice.

"Who are you?" Nan's voice was tense and she was ready to scream.

"Now little lady, keep your voice low or I will silence you forever."

"Who are you?"

The shadowy figure moved closer but Nan could not see clearly in the fast approaching night. The man had a hat pulled over his head and a muffler over his face.

"I said, don't turn around."

Nan gasped and her heart was pounding with fear. She thought she knew who it was, and she was terrified at the knowledge. She knew no one would believe her.

"I've got something for you, some hush money. Say anything my pretty maid, and I will put an end to both your lives. Now don't turn around, and tell no one or the money will stop. How stupid of you girl, for keeping the sprigget. Now everyone's watching you, including me. Keep quiet or it will all end for you and the bastard," threatened the shadow. There was some rustling of leaves as the shadow drew closer. He stopped.

Nan stood holding her breath, transfixed to the spot. The shadow threw something at her feet and she was startled. She heard footsteps walking swiftly away, leaving her alone. Nan picked up the small packet and inside the piece of sackcloth she found five guineas, a small fortune for her. She gasped and clutching the money she ran the last couple of hundred yards to her house. George had stayed behind at the fair and Nan had left because she was tired. She was no longer tired but was fired with adrenalin, fear, anger and confusion. Why would a man who had raped her give her money? 'Hush money,' he had said.

"He must think I know him," thought Nan in a moment of clarity. "I think I may know him but I can't be sure," she mumbled.

"What dear?" her mother asked.

"We had a wonderful time," answered Nan, making the decision not to explain what had just transpired.

"Oh, I am pleased. I hope you did not tire yourself, and that all the girls have gone home safely. There is still a rapist out there. Where is George? Why did he not escort you home?"

"Mam I am alright, I really am, and I am now home safe with you. Poor George deserves some time with his friends without his sister tagging along."

"Nevertheless I will have a word with George. What is he thinking?"

"Mam, he has been through so much, let's let him have some fun for a change."

"You are a wonderful sister."

"I love him so much, I am happy he is home."

Nan clutched the sackcloth and guineas to her chest and went up to her room to think.

She knew that to bring up this child would require money. As she stared at the 'hush money' she determined to save it for the child's future regardless of its source. She found a long-forgotten music box she had been given as a young child by her father. She opened it without winding up the mechanism so as not to alert her mother. She placed the money between the layers of red velvet, and put it back into her wardrobe where it was to represent the future for her baby. Then Nan returned to keep company with her mother.

When she returned to the comforting presence of her mother Nan felt calm. Her mind was spinning with the knowledge of who her baby's father was but she was no longer afraid. She sat next to her mother and started to assist in the hemming of a baby blanket that someone had left at their door. Money was tight for the family but George's army pay had been a blessing. He had sent home every penny and Violet saved half for when he returned. Nan knew she would need a little time off work when the baby was due, but for now the little family was managing just fine.

George, Everett and Anthony did not leave with the girls; they were looking for some male entertainment. They found it in a tent where girls were scantily dressed and suggestive in their dancing. They drank ale and were merry. The chums made bawdy remarks and revelled in their youthful testosterone. George and Everett didn't notice that Anthony did not contribute to the revelry but he laughed alongside his buddies. They thought it was hysterical when a young lady sat on Anthony's lap. She kissed his, as yet, hairless cheek and left a bright red lip mark. Anthony tried hard to go along with the fun. The chums lingered in the tent discussing the possibility of going to town to visit a brothel that they had been told about.

Anthony walked part way with them, excusing himself from further involvement in the evening's entertainment. He said he needed to be up early the next day to assist in an operation at the hospital. He then parted company with George and Everett and started on his way alone. The two chums were slightly drunk and laughed as they manoeuvred their way along the country road towards town. They stumbled along holding on to each other. Anthony walked swiftly and straight because his alcohol consumption had been only a fraction of the amount the others had imbibed. Everett shouted, slurring his words, "Tony, we'll thinsh of yer…"

When they were out of sight, Anthony stopped at the village green and sat on a bench trying to collect his thoughts. He looked up at the almost full moon dappled between the leaves of the big old poplar tree, swaying gently in the breeze. He wanted more than anything to accompany his friends and not have the feelings of repulsion that he felt at the thought of making love to a woman.

"I'm not a real man," he chastised, "I cannot lead a normal life."

A tear fell down his cheek and he felt a shiver in the cool summer night air.

A chill again went through his body as he heard an owl hooting above. "Bad omen or is it just nature sympathizing with me?" he mused.

Lost deep in his thoughts, he slowly made his way home, where he was surprised to see the lamps were still lit. As he entered the parlour he noticed that his father was still up reading, his mother had retired to bed.

"Son," his father acknowledged, "did you have a good time?"

"Yes dad, it was splendid, loud, colourful and a little like being in a lunatic asylum at times," Anthony laughed.

"Oh yes, I remember my own forays to the fairs and the mischief I got into. Watch the girls though we don't want another incident like Nan, no pregnancies without marriage."

"No chance of that sir," Anthony replied, shocking himself with the bitterness in his voice.

His father heard it too and was about to ask what his son meant when the words died on his lips. He hoped he misunderstood the interchange.

Anthony smiled to buffer the remark and left his father to ponder something he had suspected for some time but had no tangible evidence to back up his fears. Even now one remark was not evidence, but it was enough to push his thoughts further down a road he did not want to go. This was his son and he wanted a happy life for him, not a life of secrets and intrigue that could lead to being hanged if made public.

"I'm just a silly man, suspicious for no reason and letting my fears rule me," but he shuddered just the same.

Everett and George had brought a jug of beer with them and were more than a bit drunk as they made their way to the Market Street brothel. As they approached the house two sailors came out talking quietly to each other. They did not say anything to the chums. George was not a virgin because he had fumbled around with local lasses before he left for war, but he was as nervous as if this was his first time. For Everett it was his first time and he felt physically sick with nervousness.

"Maybe not one of our better ideas," he said to George.

"Come on Rett, you have to do it sometime."

They knocked on the door and an old woman answered. Her hair was the colour of dry straw after the harvest, and she wore a bright multi-coloured robe that gapped slightly open, exposing her obvious nudity underneath. Her ample breasts moved freely and she made no attempt to cover up.

"Got the money lovey?" she cut right to the chase, no pleasantries from her.

Everett, even through his drunken haze, blushed bright red. George pushed him into the room. Everett was about to protest when he was caught up in the absurdity of it all. He stifled a giggle to hide his naiveté.

"Dam you, George," he spit out through clenched teeth. George laughed nervously but continued to pull them into the house. The old woman opened a door to a room just off the hallway.

"First time my lovelies, my girls will take very good care of you."

They entered a parlour all decked out in red satin brocade fabrics and large pillows. In this room were about eight women of various ages and attractiveness, although in retrospect Everett realized that none of them were the least bit attractive. The chums stood there transfixed at the sights, sounds and smells of the whorehouse. One woman, about thirty years old, came up to George. She was reed thin with rouged red cheeks. She wore, or rather didn't wear, an undergarment that barely covered her body. She whispered something to him and Everett caught his eye as he left the room.

"Take care of my friend, it's his first time," he laughed nervously, speaking to no one in particular.

Everett wanted to hide, or even leave, but a young girl with long auburn hair slipped her arm in his. "Are you ready sweetie?" His mouth was open like a young schoolboy with his first pornographic picture. He was not aware of time or space; he was in some slow moving picture show.

She pulled his arm slightly and he unsteadily followed her upstairs. The room they entered was dark, with just one dim lamp on the windowsill. There was a large bed draped in the same red satin brocade as downstairs. Everett felt as though he had entered a world of dreams, of unbelievable fantasy, that even in his private world of paintings, he could not have imagined. Sweet scents added to the illusion of being cocooned from the outside world. The young girl was no more that fifteen but was very confident in her trade. She had large doe-like eyes. Her lips were painted an unbelievable shade of red which added nothing to her youthful beauty. She smiled sweetly at Everett and sat on the edge of the bed, pulling him next to her. He felt her hair swish past his arm as she shook it provocatively.

She began to undress, slowly and tantalizingly. Everett sat there with his mouth open, not able to take a deep breath for fear that the fantasy would fade away. The girl knew how desirable she looked as she removed her stockings slowly; rolling them down. As she looked over at Everett, with her tiny pink tongue, she wet her lips. Before he knew what was happening, Everett's manhood responded to the sight of exposed female flesh. He shifted uncomfortably on the bed. It was not long before his instinct kicked in and his penis strained to be released. Everett stood up as the girl assisted him to

89

remove his breeches and shirt. She understood his urgency, even if the befuddled Everett did not.

"Hold that thought luv, don't be in a hurry, yer gets what yer pay for remember."

The young girl skilfully laid him on the bed and took some time pleasuring him by running her hands over his chest and thighs, she used her lips and tongue to tease and arouse him until he could stand it no longer. Everett abruptly turned her under him and with a little of her expert guidance, entered her waiting body. He was driven by an instinct as old as man. She assisted him rather than taught and they moved with a rhythm that was designed to quickly accomplish the act. When he had finished he rolled off her and enjoyed the moment of ecstasy.

"Regrettably you only have five more minutes sir, and then you have to leave," the girl was enjoying the company of a handsome young man for a change.

"Are you alright, did I hurt you?"

"God luv yer sir, no one ever asks me that. Thank yer kindly, you were a gentle man."

The girl kissed his cheek as she started to put on her clothes once again. Everett watched her in wonderment. Because of her age her breasts and thighs were firm and her skin soft and taut. He had never seen a young lady naked before. His sister he once saw by accident when she was just little but this was so different. He was erect again and the girl noticed.

"Can't oblige sir, we have a time limit and your time is over."

"I have money to pay."

The girl turned and smiled, "In that case I got dressed too soon. Let's try something else sir, I am sure you will enjoy."

She pleasured him once again, only this time she put his throbbing manhood into her hot moist mouth. Gently she moved her tongue around and brought him to the brink of ecstasy. He groaned as she stopped and sat astride him. Everett gasped.

"Steady sir, just enjoy a while."

When they returned to the parlour George was waiting for him, drinking a glass of gin. George winked and they said nothing until they were well clear of the house.

"Gentlemen don't discuss their adventures," George said.

"I don't have the words anyway," Everett replied.

The chums walked in contented silence until they were nearly back in Cotter's Marsh.

"Of course this little adventure has nothing to do with the love I feel for Dolly," George felt the need to clarify this with his friend. "I know that women marry expecting their husbands to know how to treat them in bed. Dolly is special and will be a virgin on our wedding night."

The double standard made Everett laugh.

"Men are so selfish you must admit, George."

George joined in the laughter and then, embarrassed, abruptly changed the subject.

"Do you stand a chance with Victoria, is she interested?"

Everett did not reply for a while, while he pondered the question.

"I think even if she were interested, her family would not approve. We have years yet and there are many adventures to be had before marriage."

"You are right there Rett, let's just enjoy our lives. After what we have been through there is no hurry is there?"

"Not on your life mate. I do wish we had persuaded Anthony though. Do you think he has a secret girlfriend?"

"He has a secret, but it is not a girlfriend," George answered.

"What do you mean?"

"I have some suspicions that girls are not his thing."

Everett stopped in his tracks and stared at his friend.

"No it can't be, we have all grown up together, we would have known, he would have told us."

"Grow up Rett, would you share a secret as devastating as that with your friends, even if you were not ashamed of it?"

"I suppose not."

Somehow the elation that Everett had felt fizzled into a dark cloud that spoiled his evening.

"I may be wrong, let's wait and see and if he wants to tell us he will," George continued lightly. "I may be totally wrong."

"Yes I hope you are. They hang men for less than that."

Chapter 4

Dolly was tired. She had worked for four twelve-hour days at the grocery shop, and the work was physically tiring. She sat in the stock room on a crate for a moment to rest. Her hair had tumbled down her shoulders as she had lugged the sacks of potatoes through to the shop. Dolly took this opportunity to try to pin back her hair.

"My! What a beautiful girl we have here," Mr. Graham remarked as he entered through the back door. He sat beside her. Dolly tried to jump up but he held her arm so she had no choice but to sit down again.

"I am so sorry, sir. I was just resting, only for a moment."

"Don't worry about that Dolly, you work hard and deserve a rest. Here, rest on my shoulder."

He pulled her head across him and instead of stopping at his shoulder he pushed her down to his lap. Losing balance, Dolly slipped down.

"No sir, please don't," protested Dolly, instinct telling her that this was terribly inappropriate. Mr. Graham was strong and forced her head down on his lap and she could feel the hardness of him as he breathed erratically.

"Oh, you little tease," he said, pushing her head down.

Dolly struggled and cried out. He let her go but not before he had roughly squashed her face into his hardened manhood.

"Sir, don't," Dolly cried.

"Now don't you go making a fuss over nothing?"

Dolly struggled free and escaped. She stood up and quickly ran towards the door into the shop. She was so shocked she did not know how to react.

"If you get it all out of proportion and say anything they won't believe you, and besides you brought it on yourself with your wicked ways."

Dolly glared at him in defiance, even though she was shaking.

"Don't get into a mood girl. I have your wages here, and if you are good I will give you an increase."

Mr. Graham smiled and took advantage of Dolly's confusion to get between her and the door once again. As Dolly pushed him aside and ran through the door he caught her and put his hand on her breast. She pulled free and ran outside.

Dolly was seething with anger but totally confused as to what to do about the situation. Mr. Graham called after her.

"I have to go out of town for a few days girl, so behave yerself until I get back. Take care of business, won't you. You don't start until seven am while I'm away, what a treat eh!" he smirked, knowing Dolly's confusion.

Dolly did not answer; she just kept going, her skin crawling with the insult of the older man's touch.

By the time she had reached home she had made up her mind to tell her father what had transpired. She was surprised to see a horse and carriage outside her house. The driver was napping under a large leather hat and the horse was standing patiently, decked out in red ribbons and a beautifully engraved yoke around his neck. When she entered the house there was a stranger sitting talking to her father. It was a lady clad in a fur coat and a hat covered in peacock feathers. She was mature but very beautiful. Her father saw Dolly and stood up.

"Dolly, I am pleased you are home, we have a visitor, this is mam's aunt Miss Daisy Wilmington."

Dolly politely took her gloved hand and sat down in shock.

"It took some time," Albert continued, "for mam's relatives to hear of her death, I wrote to them and Daisy came as quickly as she could. She had been travelling in Egypt and had just returned home."

"My dear, I am so sorry. If I had known sooner…"

"It was not your fault, Daisy," Albert said.

"There is more I must explain to you both," she spoke directly to Dolly.

"I am so sorry that the family never forgave your grandfather for gambling away my sister's inheritance. Your own mother, Eleanor, had to endure her parents' death at a very early age. I was so worried about her when she would not return to Kent but insisted on marrying your father. I can see that your father loved Eleanor very much. Then they had you, a beautiful child, and of course your twin Everett. Am I to meet him too?"

Before they could answer, Daisy continued. She turned to Albert, "I am so sorry mother and father never saw Dolly, she is the image of Eleanor."

"Thank you for saying so, I think so too. Rett should be back fairly soon."

Dolly found her tongue at last.

"Mam talked about you sometimes and she always cried when she did. She wanted to see you very much."

"While my parents were alive it was not possible, they were against your grandfather's choices in life. His gambling caused a great rift in the family. My sister, your grandmother, Susan, stuck by him of course. You know how that ended. Later I moved out of Kent and spent a great deal of time in France. Then with the outbreak of the war, I moved around and stayed in Egypt for some time. I returned as soon as your father's letter reached me. Time has moved on but I see Eleanor had love, which is more than a lot of the so called upper class can boast. I think the problem was that my father disinherited Eleanor fearing her father's gambling debts. Charles made some bad choices in life. Before they had time to reconsider Eleanor's inheritance after her parents died, they themselves were killed in India in a train derailment. There was an uprising… but that is not important. You, my child, were forgotten and your mother's inheritance was never rectified."

"I do not care about the money, but I know that mam suffered because of the family rift. How could you all have forgotten her, she suffered greatly?"

"I am sorry, child. We did occasionally exchange letters and she said nothing of the hardship you were going through. Last year I offered to install you a telephone but Eleanor refused it. She was just as proud as you, Albert."

"That's because we were happy. We were a family and we cared for each other very much. No amount of money could replace that. If I had been physically stronger we could have managed better. As it was, I was invalided out of the army and had to take what work I could do," Albert explained.

Dolly ran to her father's side and hugged him.

"Poppa you were, are, a wonderful father and old great-grandfather Wilmington can keep his money, you were the best parents ever, I love you both and would not change a thing about our lives together, except for mam to still be here with us."

"Hush girl, your great aunt Daisy was not insinuating anything, she was just explaining that everything was out of her hands."

"My, my child I had no intention of upsetting you, or criticizing your parents. Your mother made it very clear to me that she had no regrets at all."

"And you Daisy, what of your life?" asked Albert.

"My life was happy and also sad, Albert. I married a colonel in the army and had a daughter Nancy. Nancy and her husband Ronald died fifteen years ago of the fever, but not before she had just given birth to a son, Samuel. Tragically, two months later this child also died. My husband has been dead these last twenty or more years. I have some wonderful friends although, sadly, they are all dying off now. The side effect of living a long time," Daisy spoke without rancour, just relating a fact.

After absorbing all the sadness Daisy had suffered alone, Dolly was moved to go to her and hold her hand. Daisy smiled and her eyes reminded Dolly of her mother.

"How long can you stay?" inquired Albert, with hope in his voice. "You can have my room and I will sleep down here?"

He desperately wanted this contact which brought his dead wife a little closer.

"Thank you, Albert, but I have booked into a hotel in the town. I would like you and Dolly and Everett to join me for a meal tomorrow night; I can send the carriage for you."

"Dolly?" asked Albert.

"Yes of course we would love to. Thank you."

Dolly was stunned at the turn of events and could not take her eyes from Daisy. She thought that her great-aunt, apart from having her mother's eyes, also had the same facial features as her mother, but Daisy was obviously a lot older and her hair was grey. Daisy got up slowly to take her leave. She was smiling and seemed very satisfied with her meeting. She had a slight stoop when she stood up, and Albert lent her his arm as she went out of the door. Albert helped her into the carriage and the driver covered her with a blanket. They waved goodbye with promises of meeting up the next day at the hotel. Dolly and her father were speechless and could not wait for Everett to return home to tell him the news.

Anthony was tired. He had just finished sixteen hours at the hospital and was getting ready for the long walk home. He sat in the orderlies' room and rested on the bench, closing his eyes for a second.

"That was a difficult day, three deaths and four broken bones," remarked Mathew Scott, another intern.

"I am so tired I could sleep right here on the bench," replied Anthony.

"Crash in my digs, it is only twenty minutes away," offered Mathew.

"I would, Mathew, but my father is expecting me to help in the clinic tomorrow, thank you anyway."

"Maybe next week? Perhaps we can go to the picture palace, I hear they have a Charlie Chaplin film playing?"

Anthony sensed something but could not describe it. He looked momentarily into Mathew's eyes and blushed at the unspoken desire he saw there.

"I must be wrong. It can't be true because Mathew was once engaged," he thought rapidly because his own emotions were heightened.

On the way home Anthony thought about Mathew's friendship and offer. They had a bond of sorts and Anthony put it down to them both being in the same boat as interns. He knew that Mathew's grandmother had sold her house for him to attend medical school. She was not rich and Mathew said that she had taken care of him when his parents died of influenza when he was three years old. Mathew was twenty-two and had struggled to get all the funds he needed for his education. He was not good looking but had a kind face and disposition and Anthony liked him. He was once engaged to the daughter of a local farmer but this engagement was broken when she was unfaithful to him. He spoke about this unemotionally and matter of factly. There was no animosity in his voice and he seemed quite relieved and over the whole affair.

Anthony was tired, bone tired. He put all thoughts about Mathew out of his mind on his long walk home. He did not usually mind the four mile hike to and from the town but today he could hardly put one foot in front of another. He cursed as he remembered he was supposed to buy a bicycle on his last trip home and he slept the whole time and forgot about it. He thought about his upcoming exams for his first year as an intern and ran over the skeletal bone names in his mind as he trudged homeward.

"Hey there, fella," a voice called. "What yer doing out by yerself?"

In his half sleep Anthony did not focus.

"I said, hey there!" the voice repeated, this time louder.

Anthony turned to see three youths following him.

"What is it?" Anthony asked, totally oblivious to any threat.

"Oh I see, the Toff is too hoity-toity to give us the time of day," another voice spoke.

"Please just go on your way. I wish just to be left alone."

"I wish to be left alone," taunted one of the youths.

They rushed up to Anthony and one youth pushed him roughly.

"I am in the mood for some fun," said the boy with an oversized army coat.

"Give him one to remember," egged on the smallest of the three.

Anthony was alarmed. It was not that he had never had a fight before, but it was usually one on one. He was bone tired and there was no reason to engage them in battle. He tried to hurry away but the youths blocked his way. He was held by one of them and he struggled to free himself.

A blow was struck at the side of his head and for a moment he did not understand what it was. He wiped his head and saw a trickle of blood on his hand. He shook his head and tried in vain to protect himself from six fists all hammering him at once. He endured this for a moment and then rage took over and he started to kick out and hit back. He was overpowered and was pushed onto the ground where they started to kick him brutally.

"Not an even fight," a familiar voice came out of the chaos.

Mathew waded in and was by far the tallest and strongest of the three youths. He pulled the tallest boy off Anthony and landed a hefty left hook on his chin. The boy stumbled backwards.

"You bastard, take this," Mathew turned and kicked a second in his groin. This gave Anthony time to recover and he pulled one of the youths to his feet and sent a lip-splitting punch to his mouth. After a few minutes the youths realized the fight was not going their way. They all ran off, leaving Mathew to pursue, and Anthony struggling to remain standing. The adrenaline was flowing and he was incensed at the unexpected brutality towards him.

"Are you all right, Totey?" Mathew returned and assisted Anthony to remain standing up. He was sporting a red and bleeding eye and a few sore ribs.

"Thanks, I thought I was a goner," Anthony was amused about the nickname.

"No way, Totey, although I am happy I decided to leave right after you."

Anthony could not help it; the tears slipped down his cheek and no amount of self-control could stop him shaking.

"Let's get you home," Mathew took control. He held him with strong and willing arms.

He hailed a passing carriage and they rode the last three and a half miles back to Cotter's Marsh. As they approached Anthony's house Mathew leaped from the carriage and assisted Anthony down. By now Anthony's ribs were so sore as to restrict his breathing. Mathew sent away the carriage and helped him into the house. Anthony stumbled as he tried to walk and breathe. He wanted to cough but it hurt too much. A particularly hard blow to the head had made him dizzy.

Dr. Preston had heard the carriage pull up and met the men at the door.

"What... what?"

"There was a fight, Totey was attacked," blurted out Mathew, not remembering to give Anthony his full name.

Dr. Preston ignored the nickname and helped Mathew to get Anthony to his room. Mathew left the room while Anthony's father examined him. After a sleeping draught was given, Anthony sleepily asked his father not to let Mathew go out alone again and to stay the night.

In the library Dr Preston saw that his wife had brought in a tray of hot tea and scones.

"Thank you, ma'am, this is most welcome," Mathew smiled gratefully.

"Well, young man, it seems as if my son has invited you to stay the night as our guest. He told me how you rescued him and we are eternally grateful."

"I wanted him to stay in town with me and not take the walk home but he insisted. I am pleased I left the hospital right after him and saw what was happening."

"You are also an intern?"

"Yes sir, and I will be a general doctor in one more year."

"Well done, young man, on all accounts, you are very welcome to stay here for the night. Anthony will not be able to work with the clinic in the morning so he will rest. Do you have to be back at the hospital tomorrow?"

"No sir, I have two glorious days off and when I get home I plan to sleep them away."

They all laughed and Dr Preston reminisced about his own intern days.

"Now come along, we don't want this boy up any longer. My son will be in pain when he wakes up so feel free to spend the day with him. Dr. Preston and I will be out until four o'clock so you have the house to yourselves," Mrs. Preston was concerned.

She showed Mathew to the guest room and after supplying him with towels and a sleeping robe they both thanked him once again and left him to sleep. Mathew had sweet dreams that night and they all involved Anthony.

Mathew was sitting in the study reading the newspaper when Anthony eventually came downstairs. It was ten in the morning and Mathew had been up for two hours already.

"Mat, you stayed, I am so glad."

"Totey, how are you feeling?"

"Well, I've had much better days." His voice was low and shaky, due to his broken ribs.

"Let me take a look at your ribs, they really pounded you and I can hear your laboured breathing."

"I think a couple of ribs broke," Anthony replied as he removed his robe.

Mathew examined him and then looked at his swollen eye.

"Show me where to get water and supplies and I will clean it up," he asked.

Anthony showed him where the supplies were and Mathew administered some aid to his injuries.

"You know what, Mat?"

"What, Totey?"

"Well, I was just thinking I would have been a lot more injured, if not dead, if you hadn't been behind me."

"Damn right you would have. But Totey, I was actually following you. I needed to talk to you some more. I wanted to tell you something."

"Tell me something?"

"Yes... but it will wait. Totey, you should rest now. I will get us both something to eat."

A short while later Anthony was dozing in the study while Mathew removed the pots to the kitchen sink.

"What did you want to talk to me about yesterday, Mat?"

"Well, it seemed so important last night, Totey, but today not so. It can wait and you will understand better later."

"Now you have piqued my interest. It is not fair to just leave me hanging," laughed Anthony, but Mathew would not explain further.

The chums spent a pleasant day together, debating politics, talking about their medical interests, and enjoying each other's company. Before dark Mathew made his way back to his own apartment. On the way home he berated himself for not speaking to Anthony about his homosexuality, although he instinctively knew that Anthony was not yet ready to hear it. He was troubled as he walked. He knew that if he spoke up too soon he would lose his friend. He felt trapped in this dilemma.

Joan was on her knees cleaning the kitchen floor at the convent. She stopped for a while just to listen to the nuns singing a beautiful psalm. Every sinew of her being was touched at the melodic vibrations which permeated the whole convent three times a day. In the mornings she was usually in the nuns' bedchambers, cleaning and tidying, but she often sat on the bed closest to the door to listen to the chants of Morning Prayer and she had memorized every one of them. Often she would join in the singing, alone and at peace. In the afternoon Joan was usually near the cloisters to hear them practice there and the echo was magnificent. Evensong was just as she left for home but rarely did she leave until the services were over and then, embarrassed, she sneaked off through the gardens and took a short cut over the marshes. This was not a route recommended by the wise, due to the uneven terrain she had to travel at dusk.

One day Mother Superior sent a message that she wanted to see Joan after her chores, before she went home. Joan was worried all day that she had done something wrong. She worked diligently and every time she found herself stopping to listen to the music she chastised her loss of focus and worked harder. The day seemed much longer than usual and she was comforted when Sister Josephine smiled at her and winked. It was nearly five pm and time for Evensong when Sister Ruth came to take her to see the Reverend Mother.

"Sit down, child, you look worn out, are we working you too hard?"

"No, Reverend Mother, I love working here."

"Good, now to business."

"Am I in trouble?"

"Bless your heart, girl, on the contrary; we are very pleased with you. Tell me Joan, are you a believer?"

"Oh yes, with all my heart, Mother. Have I offended anyone?"

Mother Superior smiled and sat down at the side of Joan and took her hand gently in hers.

"My Sisters have reported that you are interested in the services, especially the singing. They also have said what a sweet voice you possess when you sing the psalms. They all tell me that you are pure of heart and spirit. Do you believe this to be so?"

Joan's breath left her and she felt the colour rising in her cheeks.

"Now don't be embarrassed girl. The Sisters think you are enchanting, and they enjoy it when you sing."

"Thank you, Mother. I don't wish to cause any trouble."

"May I suggest something to you child?"

"Whatever you think, I will obey."

"I want to… we want you to join us in Morning Prayer and Evensong, if you would like to. Mind now, that would add three more hours to your day and we suggest that you use the small bedchamber off the kitchen in the week so you will not spend so much time travelling. Now this is just a suggestion so don't feel you should say yes to please us."

"If I say yes, would that please God?"

Reverend Mother knew then that the nuns had read the situation correctly. Here before her stood a pure, chaste child whose heart was already given to God.

"Yes child, I think it would please Him very much."

"May I speak to my mother first, Reverend Mother?"

"Of course child, take all the time you wish. If you do join us for worship you must sit only in the atrium, you understand. As soon as you are ready, if you want to that is, we will prepare for you to enter the one true church.

"Yes, thank you, I think I would like that very much."

Joan left that evening and did not notice one step on the walk home. She had so much to think about. She was a smart girl and knew that this invitation was a serious step towards a religious calling. Was she ready, was she up to it, was she ready to change her life's course, her religion, she did not know for sure. She thought that perhaps her mother would not wish to see her cloistered. She knew also that her mother was a religious woman, but not of the Catholic Church and she was not sure how she would feel. The only thing she was sure of was that her heart was singing and she was so happy she thought she would burst.

Victoria was in the parlour talking to her father. She was petulant and moody. As she stood talking she stamped her foot in temper. Her father, as usual, tolerated her inappropriate behaviour.

"I will not go one more time to Latin, father. I am seventeen tomorrow and far too old now for a tutor. I want to pursue other things in my life." Victoria's voice was far louder and angrier than she had intended.

"I think you may be right, Victoria, I suppose I want you to remain a child. I don't want you to grow up, you are our baby," Sir David replied, walking over and gathering her in his arms.

Victoria's frustration dissipated just a little, and she hugged him back.

"Papa, I think it is time. Some women are arranging their marriage trousseau at my age, please allow me to grow up."

"She is right, David," her mother said as she came into the room.

"Mama you see, don't you?"

"We do want you here as long as possible but you are a young lady now, so I will reluctantly agree tutors will stop," her father acquiesced.

Victoria kissed him quickly, pulled away from him and went over to kiss her mother's cheek. Now she had achieved her goal, Victoria had no reason to continue her tirade.

"Can I have gentlemen callers now?" Victoria teased, looking at her father and running from the room laughing.

"I know she was teasing us, David, but she is right, marriage has to be considered sometime soon, a year or two at the most."

"Maybe you are right. No suitors around here though. Maybe you should start taking her for the waters at Bath, or to the Proms at Brighton. Cousin Mavis will be pleased to arrange her coming out, whenever we wish, she hinted as much last Christmas."

"Oh David, it will be hard for us to let her go. Now is the time I wish we could have had more children. Vicky is so precious."

Sir David Hastings went over to his wife and put his arms around her. He nuzzled in her neck and she giggled like a young bride as his beard tickled her.

"Maybe we can start again."

"David," she gasped, feigning shock.

Sir David took his wife's hand and pulled her gently into his arms and kissed her passionately. He led her to their bedchamber to discuss the matter further.

Later that day the family was all in the parlour. Sir David was reading a book on world travel and Victoria was asking him questions about his own extensive forays into the world. Katharine Hasting was finishing her embroidery, thinking about starting on items for Victoria's Hope Chest, when the maid knocked lightly on the door.

"'Scuse me, sir, there is a gentleman outside wishing to talk to Miss Victoria. It's her friend Mr. Everett Marcum," she curtsied and stood waiting for a reply.

"Rett's here?" Victoria was surprised because Everett only ever came to the Manor when invited.

"Miss Victoria will meet him in the summerhouse and my wife will bring them tea."

"Very good, sir."

"Victoria, before you go, I must speak to you," her father sounded solemn.

"Well, young lady, if you want to grow up there are a few things that will have to change."

"Sir?"

"For one your male friends can no longer see you alone..."

"But Papa, we have grown up together."

"Precisely the words, 'grown up' and we must not act as children. There is a certain decorum we must follow."

"Do you mean Rett and George... and Anthony, oh no father, this is too much."

"Vicky you cannot be a child forever, as you have so eloquently pointed out. The 'boys' you grew up with are now men and as such restrictions must be put on your relationships. I will talk to Everett myself so that he understands fully your position."

"No papa, let me, he will be crushed, let me tell him."

"Very well, but make him understand, and to tell the others. I like them all but they are hardly suitors for you, and they may compromise you unwittingly."

"I understand, sir," Victoria whispered, fighting hard the tears that threatened to spill. She walked slowly to the summer house trying to formulate the correct words to let Everett down gently.

Everett was happy to see Victoria. He stood by the window and as Victoria approached he strained not to rush up to her and take her into his arms. He knew he was smitten but was cautious about how to let this be known to her.

"Victoria, I apologize for the intrusion. I wanted to wish you a happy birthday for tomorrow. I know I won't see you until after church on Sunday and I have a small gift for you."

Everett was smiling broadly. He was only using a cane now and she knew the walk up the drive was difficult for him but he showed no signs of discomfiture, on the contrary he was beaming. His eyes were a sparkling pool of excitement, twinkling in merriment and hope. Victoria was taken aback, she sat beside him. Her mother entered the room with a polite cough.

"Good afternoon, Lady Hastings, I trust you are well. I hope I am not too presumptuous but I have come to wish Victoria a very happy birthday because we will not see her again until Sunday after church," Everett knew he was babbling but could not help it, he felt the tension.

"How thoughtful of you, Everett. I have brought you both some tea and Victoria would like to talk to you, it is very important."

The tone of her voice made Everett stop in his tracks. She smiled and gently touched his shoulder as she left them alone for the last time.

"Victoria?"

"Please take some tea, Rett, mama has made it especially for us."

"What is it, Vicky, you look so white, are you ill?"

"No nothing like that, I suppose I had better just start. Rett, as you know it is my seventeenth birthday tomorrow and my parents have conceded that I have finished my schooling."

"Yes, I know that you wanted that, and I am pleased for you."

"Rett... I... I have to stop seeing you... George and Anthony without a chaperone, as my parents feel it is unseemly for a young lady to..."

"Vicky, we are friends from childhood, I know that you are a beautiful young lady, and all grown up, but it never once occurred to me that we would ever be separated."

Everett's voice shook with emotion as he realized what Victoria was saying.

"Rett, I know it is so unfair, but please see it from my point of view. I need to be seen as beyond reproach and it is unladylike to go on our jaunts now."

"Yes I see," Everett took a few minutes to process this.

"I am still your friend, Rett, just now there are restrictions on us being alone. Please forgive me."

"The son of a labourer is hardly a suitor for a lady, how stupid I am," Everett abruptly turned and left the room.

Victoria stood up and was about to run after him, but stopped, not knowing what else to say. She moved to the window and watched as her childhood friend limped his way back down the long driveway. She was crying and wanted to go backwards in time for a while, back to their carefree days in the woods, playing together and laughing. She was torn between childhood and adulthood, and it was painful. After a while her mother returned and put her arms around her.

"Child, this is just another stage of growing up, and you will always have friends. Your father and I have decided to take you to Bath for the rest of the summer. You need another perspective and to see the advantages afforded your station."

Victoria did not answer. Her hands were shaking as she opened the small gift that Everett had left on the table for her.

"Mama, look at this, it is so beautiful and I will treasure it all my life."

The gift was a silver and jade cameo brooch. Everett had hoped that this gift would signify his deep feelings for her and represent a pre-engagement gift, but she was not to know that now. Everett made his way slowly home with a heart so heavy as to be a burden in his chest. He had never once thought the relationship with Victoria through to its conclusion. He had preferred to hope, to dream. Everett knew now, as clear as the sky after a storm, that it was not to be. Victoria was always there in his mind, a special place reserved only for her. It seems she did not return the favour. The only reality that he knew was that while he spent those months in the trenches he spent part of every day with her, in his mind. She was there when he opened his eyes, and was there when he closed them, and she was there through his pitiful sleepless nights. Now she was not there for him, their relationship was being ripped apart. He doubted whether her parents would let him be part of her life in any capacity. He wanted to talk it over with Dolly. He quickened his step as best he could.

Nan was cleaning Reverend Simon's fireplace when he arrived with a guest. She was brushing the soot into a small receptacle. The work had begun to take longer and she tired more easily. The Reverend was tolerant and never chided her for her slowness.

"Leave that be now, Nan, I will need the library for the next hour. Please bring us some tea, if you are up to it, Nan dear. Please sit down Marcus."

Marcus was a fresh-faced young man, who was looking to become a man of the cloth. He was sent to Cotter's Marsh to assist Reverend Simon and learn about being a parish vicar. He smiled kindly at Nan as she struggled to her feet. She was showing her pregnancy now and wore her mother's pinafore to hide her growing girth. She left, quietly, taking her brushes and pan with her.

"Your maid is with child, Simon? I did not see a ring."

"Yes. Poor child was assaulted on the marshes when she was coming here one evening. The culprit has never been found. It caused quite a stir in this small village."

"Did you believe her, was she chaste prior to this?"

"I would stake my life on it, Marcus, she is a good child. She wants to keep the baby and is prepared for the backlash of bringing up a bastard."

"What a brave soul, and she has forgiven the baby for the circumstances of its conception, a rare girl indeed."

"Rare indeed, but one could make an argument for also being naive and possibly stubborn."

The men got on with discussing Marcus's duties over a glass of port. Nan had gone into the kitchen to prepare some refreshments for them both. As she entered the room with a tray laden with food, Marcus jumped up from his chair to assist her. Nan's cheeks went bright red.

"Thank you sir, most kind," she stammered.

Simon smiled and Marcus looked her in the eyes and said, "No heavy lifting from now on, young lady, call me if you need assistance."

"Sounds like you have made a friend, Nan," Simon laughed.

"Sir...," Nan almost raced out of the room with embarrassment.

"I fear I have embarrassed the girl, Simon. I do apologize, no harm meant."

"Think nothing of it. Nan could do with a little moral support right now. Now for Sunday's sermon what about 'suffer little children to come unto me'?"

Marcus smiled at the irony.

Nan finished her chores early and decided that she would go and see Dolly. She could use the exercise, she reasoned, but when she arrived the house was empty. Dolly and Albert were out for a walk with Everett. They were all engrossed in the newest turn of events. Everett asked a multitude of questions, most of which his father could not answer. They were all anxious for the meeting at the hotel with Daisy. It was well past eight and getting quite dark before they turned for home.

Nan wandered where Dolly could be and she had no idea that for Dolly life was about to change dramatically. As she hurried home she saw Joan walking towards the rectory. She called over to her and Joan looked startled.

"My goodness, Joan, you were a million miles away. Are you alright?"

"I am more than alright and a little stunned." Joan related the conversation with Mother Superior and Nan looked surprised.

"Does this mean that you have leanings towards the order, Joan?"

"I honestly don't know. I only know that while I am within the confines of the convent I feel so much peace I am reluctant to leave."

"It is a monumental decision, Joan."

"So was yours, Nan, to keep your baby, but just as that was the right decision for you, I am thinking that this may be the right one for me."

The friends walked arm in arm through the village until they reached Nan's house.

"Come inside Joan, I am sure George will be home from work soon and we can discuss it all together, just like old times... before they went to war."

"I must discuss it with mam first, Nan. Please don't say anything yet, I will see you all on Sunday, after church."

Nan walked slowly and she sighed. The baby was growing inside of her and she felt protective of it. Her friend had shared a very important event with her and she had mixed feelings. She knew that Joan's life was going to be vastly different to her own if she became a nun. She also knew that she would see much less of her and that they would never celebrate Joan as a wife and mother. Nan went into her house and was greeted warmly by her mother. She knew that without her mother's support, having the baby would have been impossible. She knew she was fortunate to have such loyal family and dear friends.

"Mam, I just met the new curate. His name is Marcus and he is so kind and nice."

"A new curate eh! Is the Reverend moving somewhere?"

"I don't think so. Marcus is just learning, I think."

That night Nan could not stop thinking about the nice young man she would undoubtedly see every day from now on, and somehow it pleased her. He was not exceedingly handsome, just good looking. Nan smiled and said his name just before falling into a peaceful sleep.

The Marcum family, dressed in their Sunday clothes, walked into the hotel and were struck by the opulence of it all. Everett stifled a giggle because he remembered the last time he was surrounded by red velvet and satin.

"Rett, what is amusing?" asked Dolly.

"Nothing sis, I was just thinking about how different this is to Cotter's Marsh town Hall."

They went to the reception desk and Lady Daisy Wilmington was summoned to the dining room where the bewildered group was shepherded. Tea and scones were promptly placed in front of them and Dolly felt intimidated by the grandeur of it all. The chandeliers sparkled and the white cotton table cloths gleamed. Dolly had never seen such opulence. As the group waited Dolly noticed that the diners all talked in subdued tones, adding to the mystique of fine dining. Daisy joined them as they enjoyed their second cup of tea.

"I do apologize for keeping you waiting. You must be Everett?" she held out her hand, and Everett was not sure if he should shake it or kiss it, he ended up just holding it and bowing slightly.

"Sit down gentlemen, Dolly, we have important family matters to discuss but first we must all enjoy a wonderful meal together."

Daisy ordered from the menu for them, including the wine. She did not hesitate to pour Everett and Dolly a glass each.

"If you are old enough to fight for your country then you are old enough to enjoy a good wine. As for Dolly, she is a working girl now and will thrive on a glass of full bodied Bordeaux."

Dolly sipped it and pulled a face. They all laughed and the mood was set for a very pleasant evening. Dolly had not seen her father this happy since before her mother died, and she revelled in the family gathering. Daisy talked affectionately of Eleanor as a child, and of Kent and her life there.

After the meal they retired to the privacy of Lady Wilmington's suite of rooms. She dismissed her maid with orders to return in one hour prompt. The maid curtsied and left. After they were all seated Daisy started to explain.

"I have some important family business to discuss with you all. Please don't interrupt me until I have said my piece and then I will hear your thoughts. As you are aware, my parents died in a train derailment in India. What you probably do not know is that the train was blown up in some domestic unrest in the province next to the one to which they were going. Father owned a tea plantation in Assam, and he was on his way to see his manager when the 'accident' happened. For some months the manager did not get word of what had happened but continued to run the plantation until finally Papa's lawyer contacted him. The manager agreed to maintain the plantation until the family decided what to do with it. This was many years ago, you realize, but he has apparently done a sterling job until last year...," Daisy paused and Everett was about to say something but felt his father's hand restraining him.

"As it turns out the manager died a few months ago and his son has no interest in the plantation now, so the lawyer was contacted as to what the family wished to do."

Daisy turned to Albert. "Albert, my family are all dead now, and I have no living children of my own. With your permission I would like to bequeath the plantation to Dolly and Everett."

Dolly and Everett looked at each other and both gasped with shock.

"I don't know if this is a gift or a curse, mind you," Daisy continued. "I have no idea how profitable it is now. I know there is a little money for immediate expenses, but I have never had a head for business you see and I left it all to the lawyers."

Everett and Dolly sat silent, too shocked to process the implications of the news.

"This is wonderful, Daisy. I am sure you have thought this out," Albert's mind was racing. "This means that Everett must go to India doesn't it?" Albert asked.

"Yes, there needs to be someone there immediately. We can't leave it any longer without an overseer. I believe that there is labour unrest there and the plantation is being neglected."

"Pa I don't want to go alone. Can I ask George to come with me, or perhaps you would come too?"

Dolly's world shattered. Everett and George would be leaving again? How could she cope, she had just got them both back from the war?

"This is work for young men, Everett, so you should approach George. This will be dangerous work, but it is your inheritance so you must go as soon as a passage can be arranged."

"There are arrangements to make. I will talk to the lawyers to release funds for your immediate expenses," Daisy offered.

It was all too much for Dolly and she burst into tears. A million things were racing through her mind. She thought mostly about Everett and George leaving once again, she thought about her mother and what her reaction would have been. She tried to mop her tears with her glove but Daisy came to sit beside her and gave her a delicate embroidered handkerchief. Dolly blew her nose so noisily that they all laughed.

"Dolly, I know some of what you are thinking, but we are young and there are many adventures ahead.

Please don't cry because it will be harder for me to go," pleaded Everett.

"Dolly will be fine, she just needs a while to adjust to all this news," Albert soothed.

"There will be a stipend for each of you starting immediately," Daisy continued. "It is sufficient to allow you all a comfortable life."

They all left the hotel in a daze, the news they had received meant a whole different direction for them. It had been so sad for them all since Eleanor's death that they needed to enjoy the moment.

That week Dolly did not see much of Mr. Graham, who had business out of Cotter's marsh. She went through her daily routine in a daze and welcomed being alone with just the customers to contend with. She was looking forward to Sunday and being with her friends; she had so much to share with them and wanted their comforting presence. George had agreed to go with Everett and it seemed as though there was a hole in her heart. Her father was very busy helping Everett to make the arrangements and going with him to Kent the next week to see the lawyers. So many changes and Dolly was somewhat lost in her thoughts. She knew a little about India from her studies and it fascinated her. She briefly thought about going with Everett but she needed to care for her father, and she dismissed these thoughts willingly.

Sunday after church arrived and they all met in the grandstand of the village green because it was raining. Dolly, Joan and Nan were huddled together for comfort as, even though it was early September, there was a chill in the air. When the North East wind blew it held no prisoners, it cut through the thickest of clothing.

"Nan, you are looking so well, are you getting tired now from working?" asked Joan.

"I am a bit," said Nan and she blushed as she thought about work.

"What do I see?" asked Dolly. "Come on Nan, what is going on, you are as red a beetroot."

Nan looked shyly at them both. "It is something really silly I'm afraid. You see there is a new curate helping Vicar Simon and he is living at the vicarage."

"A new very handsome man, by the look of it," Dolly and Joan laughed.

"Well yes, but he was... is so kind to me and this is the first time I have ever felt this way. I have no right to these feelings though... my compromised state is a barrier to any romance now or in the future."

"Don't say that Nan, if he is as nice as you say he will wait until the time is right. Your life is not over because you are having a child," Dolly hugged her and Nan smiled.

"And he is handsome and his name is Marcus."

They were joined by George and Everett.

"Have you said anything yet?" Everett asked Dolly.

"No, I was waiting until we were all here."

"What is going on?" Joan asked.

Just then an automobile arrived and Victoria emerged looking wonderful in a new dress and bonnet. She had adopted the more modern style of dress that was less formal and the hem of her skirt was above her ankles. She had cut her hair into a short bob but this was mostly hidden under her bonnet. Victoria was very beautiful. The group waved to her mother who smiled and waved back but did not alight from the automobile which they had just purchased for their visit to Bath.

The friends were aghast and curious about the new means of transport but before they could comment Everett spoke.

"Hello Vicky," said Everett, his voice showing his coolness towards her. The others looked his way, surprised at his tone.

"Rett, we will talk later but I have some news that I need to share with you all," answered Victoria.

"It seems that everyone has news. Who is going first, Vicky, what about you?" Dolly suggested.

"Well, mama said to come and tell you all that we are leaving for Bath tomorrow for a couple of months so I want to say goodbye to you all," she looked searchingly at Everett who did not meet her gaze.

"This is a surprise Vicky, when this was decided?" asked Joan.

"Well, it was supposed to happen next year but mama thought it best for me to go now. I do want to go though; I think it will be an adventure."

"You will not want to talk to us when you return. You will be a 'proper' young lady and we will have to curtsy to you an' all," teased Nan.

"No more scraped knees, no more torn skirts climbing up trees and no more scrumping apples from the orchard. What a dull girl you will be," George laughed and they all laughed except Everett. Dolly noticed and made a mental note to talk to him later about it.

"What other news?" asked Victoria, relieved they took her news so well.

"May I tell you my news?" asked Joan shyly.

They all turned to her and her courage failed.

"I... I eh... I spoke to Nan already and I... I"

"Oh Joan, tell them your news, you are happy aren't you?" interrupted Nan.

"I am considering entering the order. Mother Superior asked for me to stay there while I decide, although I will be coming back home at weekends at least for another year."

"Is this what you want?" Dolly was surprised because Joan had never mentioned this before.

"I really don't know yet, but I think I might have a calling for it, I want to try anyway," Joan's voice faltered. Dolly stooped down beside her and looked her in the eyes.

"Joan, we all want you to be happy and if this is what you want then we all support your decision, although our objections may have a very selfish side, we do love you."

Just then Victoria's mother called for her to leave and without waiting for the others' news she said her goodbyes and left. Everett was aloof as she tried to kiss his cheek.

"Well, so much for solidarity," George was sarcastic. "What else is there to say except explain our good fortune to Joan and Nan?"

Everett and George told their news and the look of shock was palpable. Nan had stood up to say goodbye to Victoria but now she had to hold on to the balustrade to stop from falling from shock. Joan's tears fell as she tried to make sense of the news.

"You are both leaving us again and we have just got you back safely from the war," Joan said.

"My words precisely," Dolly replied, in obvious pain.

"What about my baby?" Nan struggled to speak.

"Nan dearest, Dolly is staying and you will have Joan and Anthony... by the way, where is Anthony?" Everett asked.

"I'm here," shouted Anthony, running towards them. He tripped up and that broke the tension as they all laughed at his antics. He arrived soaked by the rain and more than a little dishevelled. When he got to the bandstand they saw his black eye and cut face and he told them briefly what had happened to him. In turn they all related their news.

"Hold on, you cannot be serious. Here I leave you all alone for a full week and look what happens. Are we growing up and apart?"

"No chance," answered George.

"Seriously George, are you up to a trip to India. How are your headaches now?" Anthony was concerned.

"Well I think they will always be a problem and I have to learn to live with them. The emphasis is on 'live' Tony, I want to live before I die."

"I would have thought the war would have been enough excitement for one lifetime but no... my friends desert me once again." Anthony put his hand on his heart and gestured his grief.

"Trust you to lighten the mood," said Everett. The friends continued to enjoy each other's company until dusk and they all parted with affectionate kisses and promises.

Dolly decided that she would no longer work for Mr. Graham. When she went to work the next day she informed him of the same.

"Thank you for all you have taught me, Mr. Graham, but I will be leaving to care for my father." She felt she did not need to explain any more to this man she detested.

They were both in the stockroom and Dolly went to leave but the exit was blocked by him. He put his arms out to prevent her leaving. She turned to go out of the back door but found to her dismay that it was locked.

"Now little miss, what ungratefulness is this. I take a chance on you, train you in a good profession and this is the thanks I get. You need to get off your high horse and live in the real world. You need to compensate me for the time I took with you, you ungrateful wench."

With that he lunged at her and after a struggle he succeeded in pulling up her frock. Dolly smelled the pungent sweat of the overweight man. He held her shoulder so tightly as he tried to kiss her that she knew he had bruised her. She tried to hit him but he held her hands so tightly together that they hurt.

"Stop, oh! Please stop," she cried as his free hand yanked at her underskirt. He let go of her hands and pulled her head back by her hair. Dolly squirmed and fought but he was strong and succeeded in touching her most secret womanhood. His rough stocky fingers tried to gain entry. She kicked and he slapped her face. He roughly kissed her neck as she twisted and turned. Some primal instinct gave her strength and she kicked and pulled away as he fell on the floor. He was still blocking her way and he stood up grabbing her arm, she screamed out loud.

Just then Reverend Simon arrived in the shop with his curate, Marcus. They heard her cry and ran into the storeroom. He understood the situation instantly as he saw Dolly struggling to free herself. The surprise made Mr. Graham loosen his grip on her enough that she became free. Dolly ran into Vicar Simon's arms sobbing while Mr. Graham tried to make some excuse that he was restraining her because she was out of control.

Marcus took Dolly outside while the two men argued. Vicar Simon was very angry and said he would return later. They both walked with Dolly and she could not stop her tears. She felt defiled and dirty and kept pulling at her skirt. Reading the situation well Marcus removed his jacket and draped it around Dolly. The church was nearer than Dolly's house and she asked to rest there a while.

"Please don't let my father know, it would break his heart," she sobbed.

"Has he…" asked Simon.

"No but he tried once before. I thought it was just a mistake and he would not do it again," Dolly could not talk anymore as she shivered uncontrollably. Marcus took her hands and rubbed them as you would to a young child.

"Dolly, we have to talk to the constable. Don't forget what happened to Nan, this man is still on the loose… do you…?"

"No it can't be. Mr. Graham was not even in Cotter's Marsh that week. He is just a…a… you know."

"Yes, we know only too well, Dolly. You must decide if you want to take further action or not."

"I just told him I would be leaving his employ today and that is why he tried to…" Dolly whispered, unable to put the horror into words.

"Alright, my dear, we will keep an eye on him."

After a while Dolly regained her composure and they escorted her home. Dolly was sure that her father was still preparing to go to Kent with George and Everett. If he knew what had happened he would not go. She explained about the plantation and the family's inheritance to the men while they walked because she wanted to think of something more positive than what had just occurred. She also told them that now she did not have to work unless she wanted to because she had a stipend from her great-grandfather. Dolly said that she intended to care for her father until she figured out what to do. She knew she was rambling and the two men knew it too, but she was in shock and whatever she needed to do to regain her composure was fine with them.

"My father should also stop working because he is sick, but he said that the money is mine and Everett's, so he will continue to provide as a father should. We both tried to get him to change his mind but to no avail."

"He is a good and proud man," Vicar Simon said.

"I want mam to be here, I miss her," Dolly started to cry again.

"I know, child, but you are loved by many and they want the best for you. This is good fortune and you will be happier for it."

Marcus said very little as they made their way towards the house, but he was very kind and she leaned heavily on his arm as they walked.

They saw Dolly safely home and the two discussed events together. They wanted to go to the law but thought about how Dolly would be dragged into a terrible scandal.

"He should have at least a stern talking to, Marcus, would you accompany me back to the shop?"

"It would be my pleasure. Do you want me to challenge him to a duel at dawn?"

"I don't think that will be necessary, Marcus," Simon laughed.

The following Sunday meeting of the friends was very sombre, quite different to the one before. Everett and George were leaving on Wednesday to go to Kent and they were booked on a ship leaving at the end of the month. It was already September and they wanted to sail before the weather broke. Nan was looking tired and she said that Vicar Simon now allowed her to work eight hours with a two hour break in the middle of the day.

"He is a saint," commented Anthony.

"I second that," said Dolly, remembering how kind he was to her. She was debating whether or not to tell them all about her assault but she looked over at Nan and decided that it would bring back her terrible ordeal so she kept it to herself.

"Joan, what happened, did you discuss the situation with your mam, what did she say?" asked Dolly.

"It was a strange reaction. She just sat there not speaking or moving for... I swear... at least five minutes. I just stood there thinking she did not hear me or understand what I was saying. Then she burst into tears and I ran over to comfort her. I was shaken at her reaction."

"Was she angry?" asked George.

"No, I don't think so, she just asked that I wait until today after church to discuss it further. I think she wants to talk to Vicar Simon."

"I can see that it is a life-changing decision, for her too," Nan said.

"Am I being selfish?" asked Joan.

"Of course not. Your mother would want what is best for you I am sure, she loves you very much," Dolly reassured Joan as she put her arm around her. "There is no hurry, you are young and you must be sure it is the best thing for you."

Anthony told them once again all about his friend Mathew and how he had been saved from the thugs that night. He sang Mathew's praises, both personally and professionally.

"One day he will be a brilliant paediatrician. He is liked by everyone. I will bring him and introduce him to you if you agree," Anthony gushed.

George and Everett exchanged a cursory glance with each other, too brief for others to notice.

"Any friend of yours is a friend of ours, Tony," Dolly smiled and went to hug him. "Are you still hurt?"

"My ribs are still sore but apart from that I was lucky it wasn't worse. A fair fight is one thing... do you remember George when we got into it because you stole my fish and said you had caught it. What were we, about six, seven?"

"It was my fish, I remember it well," laughed George.

"No it wasn't," retorted Anthony, holding his ribs as he laughed.

The friends chatted amiably for the next hour and then they said their goodbyes.

"We will make sure we see you again before we go," said Everett.

"I will not see you again before you leave, mates, because I have to work long hours in the next week. I have exams to take." Anthony choked as he realized that they were leaving very soon.

"But we are here, Anthony, and you will have to be our knight and protector once again," Dolly knelt down and gestured her submission to Anthony and they all laughed.

Anthony did not feel like anyone's protector. He was confused and whenever he was alone he slipped into a deep depression. He thought of why he felt different, why it was so easy for Everett and George. He knew that the day he spent with his friend Mathew was the happiest he had felt for quite some time. Although Mathew did nothing improper or in the least suggestive, they just enjoyed being together as friends. Anthony had experienced an acceptance of who he truly was and he wanted more of that feeling of belongingness, of fitting in at last. He liked not having to pretend to be someone other than Totey, now he was Totey; he knew for the first time that he was Totey. Totey alone could love only men in the deepest sense possible, but that was a sin. Anthony cried and wished it were different.

Chapter 5

Victoria revelled in the adoration. She was the belle of the Bath set. She became the most fashionable, the most accomplished and the most spoiled young lady ever to come out. Her skirts were the first to go to mid-calf, trimmed with fur, and she attended many of the tea dances that were becoming popular. The invention of the gramophone made it easier for the young people to have their more intimate dances in the home. The advent of jazz meant a whole new era of music that made Victoria's life more exciting.

She had many young men and not so young men vying for her attention. Her breasts were forming and her womanly curves acted as a magnet for all the eligible bachelors. She was a little tall but compensated for this by wearing slippers that were low but exquisitely embroidered. She loved the dances of the day and excelled in them. Although she was reticent at the start of her adventure she soon became eager to meet everyone who could be of use to her. It was a fine line between being socially astute and being discriminating but no one noticed that she gave her time only to those of class and was impatient with all but the bourgeois. Her mother was proud of her popular daughter.

"My, my, I feel absolutely exhausted, Victoria. This may not have been such a good idea," Lady Hastings remarked to her daughter, who was busy writing letters.

She took great delight in writing about her exploits to Dolly, believing that she alone was enjoying the privileges of money and class, and that Dolly would never amount to much more than a bookworm with an ordinary life. She knew nothing of Dolly's ancestry or good fortune, or that now Everett would have been an acceptable suitor in her parents' eyes. She bragged to Nan and Joan too, feeling that they would be envious of her. She was wrong. Nan would never give up her life, even though the future was uncertain and bound to be hard. Joan was above the mundane worldly pursuits, although she wished her friend well. Nan was happily anticipating being a mother. She had no time for Victoria's silliness. Victoria's letters to Anthony were different, introducing him to the art and architecture of Bath. She wrote about the wonderful hospital there and some of the prominent doctors she had met.

"Mama, this is a wonderful time and I am sorry it has tired you so. We must cancel our dinner engagement tonight with Lady Myers. We can go another time when you have recovered."

"That would be so rude, no we will go. Which gown will you wear?"

They took some time discussing the appropriate attire and Victoria became impatient with her dresser.

"Stop fussing around me, just wait until I need you," she said crossly.

"Sorry ma'am," the flustered dresser replied as she left the room.

"Victoria... dear, you must watch your tongue around the staff. You will get a reputation and no one will work for you."

"Yes mama, I am sorry."

The dinner party was to be at the Pavilion and Victoria and her mother arrived late. The room was decked out in various flags depicting the British military accomplishments and battalions. The room was already filled with uniformed officers and ladies in fashionable gowns. Victoria thought that she had never seen anything so colourful because the wartime trends had been leaning towards more sedate and drab attire. There was no evidence of this patriotic parsimony today. The conversations were buzzing around the room and for a moment they both stood transfixed at the splendid sight.

"Lady and Victoria Hastings," announced the Master of Ceremonies Matre'd.

"How wonderful of you to come," Lady Myers met them at the door. "Come with me and I will introduce you. You know Major Brown, I believe?"

"Yes, how are you Major," answered Lady Hastings, Victoria bobbed in a curtsey.

They moved around the room with introductions to new and old friends.

The party went as planned, with Victoria being a popular dance partner for many beaux. She relaxed after a while and was enjoying herself. She joined a group of young ladies while her mother talked with the older dowagers. They drank champagne instead of fruit punch and giggled at their daring.

"Watch you do not get caught," Sissy Moore laughed as the tray was passed around once again.

"The bubbles make me sneeze so I won't have any more," Victoria replied, screwing up her nose.

"Ladies, may I join you?" a handsome officer bowed in jest.

They giggled and Victoria thought he was the handsomest man she had ever seen.

"Why, Lieutenant Gordon, what mischief have you been up to tonight?" teased Sissy.

"Who me?" he laughed. He looked at Victoria and stated his name as Mark Gordon. Victoria held out her hand and he gently kissed it. They all giggled once again.

"The next dance is mine, I believe?"

"It would be my pleasure," answered Victoria.

The evening ended far sooner than Victoria wanted and she went home dreaming of a handsome Lieutenant.

Joan was to move into the convent and just return home at weekends. The nuns often employed the village girls in acts of charity but to everyone's knowledge this was the first time any girl had been made an offer to stay within the confines of the convent overnight. Joan did not know what to expect but was looking forward to being more involved in the religious life. She knew her clothes were fine for now because she would still be working there. She took her Sunday best in case she needed them when she was asked to sing for the nuns. Apart from having a superb voice Joan did not know what else she could offer them. She was aware that some were translating various religious texts into English but she was far from a scholar so was therefore quite perplexed.

On the way there early on the Monday morning she felt sick with excitement. Her mother had been visibly upset, but after she had spoken to Vicar Simon she seemed more at peace with Joan's decision. They had had a quiet meal together that night and her mother had reassured her that she could change her mind at any time. This was only the first step. They had talked about the differences in religions and that Joan would have to convert from the Church of England to Catholicism. Joan had remarked that God was the same and the only difference was how they worshipped. For the first time that Joan could remember, her mother spoke to her as an adult and they reached an understanding.

Joan had spent a restless night and at two am she went into the kitchen and put the old black kettle on the dying embers of the fire and pulled her night robe tighter. She added a shovel full of coal and prepared a teapot. The old calico cat jumped on her knee and demanded attention. Joan chuckled and scratched him behind his ears.

"Well Patch, I will be going to a new life soon, I won't be around so much to spoil you. You will take care of mam, won't you?"

Patch snuggled deeper into her lap and purred contentedly.

"What is it child, are you sick?" Joan's mother joined her and put her hand on her brow.

"I'm fine mam, I just couldn't sleep. I am sorry if I disturbed you."

"No, I couldn't sleep either. Are you brewing tea?"

They both enjoyed each other in silence for a while.

"Mam, where do you think I get this inner need to learn more about God? Was I always like this? I remember that I would be just as unruly as Dolly and Everett, scrumping apples, teasing the others and being a general pest."

Her mother laughed. "Yes, you were a right tearaway."

"They all took it well. I will miss them all so much when I become cloistered… I mean if that is the way I choose. Will they forget me when they don't see me for long periods?"

"That is impossible, child. They are all your friends and we never forget our friends. I remember my own youth and how attached I was to Violet. Later as a young woman we both made other lifelong friends. Eleanor, Dolly's mother, was a great friend to us both. We talked about our lives together and supported each other and you will get that from the sisters, so it will be different in many ways from the path that the others will take but the same in the companionship you will receive. Women will always have a special bond together and care for each other deeply. Today's politics prove that, with the movement by women for women's vote and the way they have banded together against the male-dominated government," she paused and smiled. "No, child, you will not want for love and caring, that is what will give me comfort later when you stay there as a novice and later to become a nun."

"I am opting out of all of the political turmoil. The war still rages and the civil unrest is still part of life and I am choosing not to engage in it all. Look at Nan's life path. It will be so hard for her to raise a child without a husband and yet in a way I envy her. I know that my own path will mean I will have no children. For that I feel sad for you mam."

"Don't fret child. They say the war will be soon over. I want only your happiness and maybe Nan will allow me to be a second grandmother to her baby." Her mother laughed, "Don't forget Dolly will also be a mother one day, but I dare say she has some living to do yet. She is a restless child and won't just settle for marriage and children, what do you think Joan?"

"I did not think you knew her so well," they both laughed good-naturedly.

Eventually Joan fell asleep and had dreams about goodbyes and drifting away on water. The next day she did not remember them and started for work at the convent with a valise perched precariously on her bicycle. As she entered the gates of the convent she had to pass through the gardens which were beautifully adorned in late summer foliage. She rested at the iron bench and was met by Sister Josephine.

"My, my child, you have quite a burden to carry there."

"Yes," answered Joan and then she looked Sister Josephine straight in her beautiful green eyes. "Maybe I am leaving my burden the other side of the gate."

Sister gave her a hug, "Well said, my child. We have a lot to teach you but we are thinking that with your purity of heart, you have things to teach us too."

"But I don't see the problem," Mathew said through clenched teeth. "What difference does it make to your friends if I just tag along to meet them."

"I did not imply that you would be unwelcome," answered Anthony. "It's just that there have been a lot of changes recently with George and Rett leaving for India, Victoria away until the autumn and then Nan being very sensitive about her condition. I don't think it is a good time right now, Mat."

"So it is not that you are ashamed of us?"

"God no! What have we to be ashamed of? We are good friends and men can have friendships just as women can."

"Oh, Totey, when you speak like that I know you are running away from who you really are. I will be patient because I see something special in you. When you are ready we will be more than good friends."

Mathew put his arm on Anthony's shoulder and Anthony put his hand on top of his.

"You may well be right, Mat, but right now I am not sure, please remain my friend."

"You have it, Totey, what do you want to do now?"

"Do you want to walk to town, I have to look for some new surgical instruments as a gift for my father?"

The friends walked together talking amiably and enjoying a rare sunny day. Eventually they entered an old book shop. After browsing for a while Anthony heard someone call his name.

"Anthony, is that you?" Professor Taylor's voice rang out.

"Professor Taylor, what a pleasant surprise, I thought you had moved south to London?" Anthony exclaimed.

"Yes my boy, so I did, but my sister is still here so I visit twice a year."

Introductions were made and the three retired to a café for tea and crumpets.

"Mathew, now tell me how you came to be interning here, what of your family?"

"Well sir, there is only my grandmother now and she is in her seventies. She is the one I have to thank for putting me through medical school."

"I see boy, so it is not easy for you I can see that."

"He will be a great doctor, Professor, especially with children. Why the other day Sister Lamb almost threw him off the ward because he was making the children laugh so much," Anthony spluttered out through laughter.

"Alright Totey, let me tell the Professor what you did with the bedpans..." Mathew began.

"Don't you dare!"

The group spent a very pleasant hour exchanging stories and reminiscing. Professor Taylor was in no doubt about the nature of the boys' relationship and it made no difference to the old man, who was a homosexual himself.

"Well, gentlemen, I am afraid I will have to take my leave of you both. Here is my card, so please drop me a line every once in a while and if you get to London then look me up."

"Goodbye sir, and thank you," answered Anthony, tucking the professor's card in his pocket.

After they had walked a while Mathew said, "See Totey, there are people out there just like us and who accept us for who we are."

Anthony did not reply for a while.

"But it is not a life I would choose."

"Maybe we don't have much of a choice. God knows I tried the other way but willing it to be different does not make it so. Take everything slow, Totey, you have your life ahead, no rush, just 'be' for now. I will be your friend in any capacity you want. I leave it up to you."

They had arrived back at Anthony's house and they spent a pleasant evening with Dr. Preston and his wife.

"When are we to meet your grandmother, Mathew?" asked Dr. Preston.

"Sir, she would be honoured to meet you, too."

"What about if we send a carriage for her next Sunday after church, are you working?"

"I am and I think Totey pulls a late shift, Totey?"

This time the nickname was too obvious to ignore and Dr. Preston made a mental note to talk to Anthony about it in private.

"Yes I do, but not the following week."

"Sounds good for me then in two weeks, I will bring grandmother for Sunday tea."

Mathew walked the long miles back to the hospital without a care in the world; however Anthony was not so carefree. His father was closely questioning his relationship with Mathew. Anthony's mother was not part of the conversation, although she was aware that Mathew had stepped out of line by his familiarity with Anthony.

"We are friends, father, that is all," Anthony answered honestly.

After some time Dr. Preston believed his son but cautioned him about Mathew's intentions. Anthony told him once again that Mathew was once engaged to be married and he elaborated by stating some of the nurses in the hospital were attracted to him.

"Well, he just seemed to be over-familiar with you."

"I know father, and he is with others too. He means no harm but if you wish I will sever my acquaintance with him."

By now Dr. Preston's suspicions were laid to rest so he said that Anthony may remain friends but to be more careful with Mathew's familiarity.

"I will sir, and I apologize for him," Anthony was relieved but slept fitfully that night.

Dolly was just finishing clearing the pots after the meal. She prided herself now in being a very good cook and with the extra money from Everett she could get more fresh fruit and vegetables. She had inherited her housekeeping skills from her mother and took pride in everything she did.

"Dolly, we have a letter from Everett," Albert was excited and ripped it open before Dolly could join him. She dried her hands on her apron as Albert read it out aloud.

November 27th 1917

My dear father and sister, I have a lot to tell you both. George and I went to see great-grandfather's lawyer with great-aunt Daisy. The lawyer reported that the investments were far more lucrative than even aunt Daisy knew. He advised me to withdraw the stocks and bonds so that the funds would be more readily available to me in India. He surmised that the plantation would require quite a lot of labour and attention (and I know naught about tea). The sum of money available is astounding and I am sending you both enough to live on for the next two years, although I do not intend to be gone that long.

George and I have hired an advisor whose name is Montgomery Baxter. It seems that Baxter has had a lot of experience in India and can speak some of the local dialect. We hope to set sail next week and the next time I will write will be on the ship sailing towards our future endeavour. Now father, you must cease work and Dolly will now stay home and care for you.

P.S. There is a gentleman at my side who is anxious that I give his best wishes to you both (George of course).

Love always, Everett.

"Two years!" wailed Dolly, completely ignoring the rest of the letter.

"Nay, child, he will be home before that. What about the funds though, they belong rightfully to you and your brother?"

"Daddy, you are our life and we will take good care of you," Dolly was fearful that her father would continue to work in the coal dust, as ill as he was.

"I will maybe take a rest for a while child, but I won't totally give up work. I will return when I feel a bit stronger."

Dolly kissed him soundly on the cheek.

"Tomorrow we will go into town to the tea rooms to celebrate our family's good fortune. We will shop for new shoes and maybe even a new bonnet."

"Not me, lass," her father laughed. "Go get Nan, she needs some time away from chores and she needs some clothes for that bairn she carries."

Dolly smiled and ran to Violet's house to see if Nan was home from the vicarage yet.

Three Sundays later the friends decided to meet in Dolly's house because her father was staying behind with the other church elders for a while to talk about the progress of the war. As they went into the kitchen the fire glowed warmly and Anthony put another shovel of coke on the embers. The fire protested and spluttered by shooting out sparks. Nan was big with child now and pulled a chair close to the fire. She sighed heavily as she positioned herself comfortably. Dolly busied herself making hot tea for them all.

Victoria had made a rare visit with them and brought along some delicacies her mother had made for them all. She was very talkative about her exploits in Bath. She described the fashions of the young ladies and the antics of the pompous young men. She was entertaining and the group laughed and enjoyed her stories. She purposely left out any reference to the fact that she was corresponding with Lieutenant Gordon, or the fact that she was somewhat smitten by his good looks and his position in society. Victoria explained that her mother allowed her to visit for one hour today while she visited a distant cousin who was sick. Lady Hastings would be coming back for her in the automobile. Dolly had written to Victoria to explain her good fortune, but the self-centred Victoria dismissed the news and did not rejoice in her friend's good fortune.

"I know, we can have a tea dance just like the ones in Bath. I will get mama to approve it," Victoria suggested.

"Not until spring, please. Give me time to get my dancing shoes on," laughed Nan, pointing to her swollen feet.

"That is a wonderful idea," agreed Dolly. "But who do we invite?"

"Everyone, especially those who are not betrothed or married," answered Victoria with a wicked smile.

"Wonderful idea," said Anthony, winking at Mathew, who was now adopted by the group. His presence eased the void left by Everett and George.

Anthony had settled into the big leather horsehair chair that Dolly's father liked, and Mathew was perched on the arm. The men had just finished a gruelling thirty-six hour stint at the hospital. The group had accepted Mathew without question and they enjoyed his banter about hospital life. They instinctively knew that the boys were a couple but no one commented, they just accepted.

"Nan, are you well?" asked Joan, going over to her and kissing her cheek.

"Very well thank you, Joan, and Dr. Preston says my baby is big and healthy."

"I don't know if the 'big' part is a good thing," teased Anthony, and they all laughed.

"Well, I must say I will be happy when the baby is born, I have no clothes to wear, and even my boots pinch terribly," Nan complained light-heartedly.

Joan took off Nan's boots, which were almost threadbare, and warmed her feet by rubbing them gently. Nan smiled and visibly relaxed as she basked in the love of her friends.

Dolly shared Everett's last letter with them. Everett and George were now at the plantation and they were shocked at how vast it was.

"Are the labourers still there?" asked Anthony, always the practical one.

"Yes, many left when the foreman died because they were unsure of the future, but George is getting the men organized while Everett is learning how the plantation works."

"In a way I envy them," stated Mathew, "the adventure of it all, the unknown, the freedom."

"I don't know about freedom, think of all the work to do," retorted Anthony.

"But so romantic," Joan added, and they all laughed because it was a comment coming from Joan of all people.

All too soon Lady Hastings arrived, and Victoria left. They all were silent for a while. Joan began to sing, softly at first and then with gusto. She sang an old English ballad.

All in the merry month of May, When green buds they were swelling,

Young Jemmy Grove on his death-bed lay, For love o' Barbara Allen.

He sent his man unto her then, To the town where she was dwelling:

"O haste and come to my master dear, If your name be Barbara Allen."

Slowly, slowly rase she up, And she cam' where he was lying;

And when she drew the curtain by, Says, "Young man, I think you're dying."

"O it's I am sick, and very, very sick, And it's a' for Barbara Allen."

"O the better for me ye'se never be, Tho' your heart's blude were a-spilling!

"O dinna ye min', young man," she says, "When the red wine ye were filling,

That ye made the healths gae round and round, And ye slighted Barbara Allen?"

He turn'd his face unto the wa', And death was wi' him dealing:

"Adieu, adieu, my dear friends a'; Be kind to Barbara Allen."

As she was walking o'er the fields, She heard the dead-bell knelling;

And every jow the dead-bell gave, It cried, "Woe to Barbara Allen!"

"O mother, mother, mak' my bed, To lay me down in sorrow.

My love has died for me to-day, I'll die for him to-morrow."

The group sat transfixed and when the final notes died down they all had tears in their eyes, including the cynic Mathew.

"Joan, you are so gifted," Dolly whispered.

"A gift from God, the nuns say," Joan replied humbly.

Mathew put his hand on Anthony's shoulder and no one noticed.

Just then Albert returned home and the spell was broken. He shook a light cover of snow from his coat.

"You children had better start off for home, there is a snow storm coming," he remarked.

They all bundled up and Anthony and Mathew promised to see Joan and Nan safely home. Dolly draped another shawl around Nan's head as the group made their way outside.

Dolly went back inside the kitchen where her father was removing his boots. She made a fresh pot of tea and took out her knitting, settling in for a stormy night. Her father was not working now, and they were able to afford a few luxuries. They had a gramophone and a crystal radio. Albert, afraid of the new technology, had resisted putting in a telephone. He put on the radio to hear a scratchy commentary about the battles of war. Dolly sighed and was thankful the men she loved were home safe and sound. Everett and George were far away once again, but as far as she knew they were not in danger. A different world had beckoned, one she could not even begin to imagine, and was shaping her twin into a man she would hardly recognize next time she saw him.

The market day in early December was already showing signs of Christmas fare. Turkeys were hung aloft in the stalls and holly and mistletoe were hung around in a cheery attempt to deny the cold weather. Children were singing Christmas carols, hoping for a penny from those around them. Dolly was bundled up against the bitter North Easterly wind. The snow had ceased for some hours, but the roads were icy and traitorous underfoot. She had just completed her grocery and turned to go home when she bumped into a tall gentleman. For a moment he was stunned.

"Miss Dolly Marcum, is that you?"

"You have me at a disadvantage I'm afraid," replied Dolly, not altogether sure she wanted to converse with a stranger.

"Are you Rett's sister Dolly?"

"Yes, and you are?"

"Sorry, I am Phillip Chase, Pip to my friends," the young man smiled.

Dolly saw a tall man with a shock of unruly black hair. His smile lit up his eyes and he was dressed according to the fashion of the day, although Dolly briefly thought he was inadequately dressed for the cold. He bowed slightly with the introduction and Dolly nodded.

"I served with George and Everett; we were in the same unit. I know you are wondering how I knew you by sight. Well, Rett showed me your photograph. A photograph of you with a large bow on an even larger hat, and Rett in his father's extra large waistcoat pretending to smoke his pipe," he explained.

"Yes I remember he took that one with him because it was his favourite. The others he thought were too stiff and formal. We had them taken just before my mother died, before he left for the war," Dolly remembered how proud her mother was of these pictures.

"I hope you are not offended but I did not expect to just run into you, literally," Pip laughed.

"Not at all, Mr. Chase."

"Please, call me Pip."

"Alright... Pip."

"I was actually on my way to see Everett. He said to come by. I was on my way to Grimoldsby. I live in Kingston upon Hull you see, and I have business there."

They started walking towards Dolly's house, trying not to slip on the ice, when they were interrupted by Mrs. Clark as they passed the vegetable stall.

"Take these to your father, child," Mrs. Clark gave Dolly a packet of fresh greens.

"Thank you very much Mrs. Clark, he will enjoy these," and to Pip she whispered, "I think she believes I don't feed him well."

Dolly and Pip continued to chat once they were out of earshot.

"Everett told me that your mother died while he was away, I am so sorry, it must have been a great loss."

"Yes, we miss her terribly. Pip, are you staying long in Cotter's Marsh?"

"Only tonight. I have a room at the guest house because I hoped to spend some time with my friends."

"Dolly, wait for me," Albert called, as he came around the corner and saw her. He hurried to catch up and introductions were made.

"Come home for a while, young man. We welcome any friend of Everett's into our home."

"Oh my!" exclaimed Dolly, "I haven't had a chance to explain to Mr. ... Pip, that they are in India," Dolly exclaimed.

"India?" Pip was surprised.

"Come in and we will explain," Albert ushered them both into the house and out of the cold.

"So let me get this right. Rett found out that he had inherited a plantation in India and George, being the adventurous soul that he is, went along to help," chuckled Pip, revelling in memories of his two friends' adventurous characters.

After a delightful visit in which Pip ingratiated himself into both of their affections, he took his leave, promising to return in a few days after his business was completed.

Albert commented that he thought him a gracious young man, charming and solid. Dolly had slightly different impressions and was too shy to voice them.

True to his word, Phillip Chase visited them again two days later. He asked Albert if he may take Dolly out for a walk. Dolly was elated. They strolled, talking like old friends. They walked around the old village and they went into the church, more to get out of the cold than to worship.

"This is a beautiful church, how old is it?"

"I think it dates back to the Norman Conquest," answered Dolly.

Pip put his hand on hers on the pew and she did not pull it away.

"You are freezing Dolly; let's get you back into the warmth."

"I think that might be best, I am rather cold, Pip."

As they walked back to the house Pip held her arm protectively.

"Are you coming back here again?" asked Dolly, not daring to breathe until she heard his answer.

"Wild horses couldn't keep me away," Pip smiled his dazzling smile and Dolly blushed.

"Will you come over Christmas?"

"I will be here on Boxing Day if my father will lend me the automobile. If he won't then I will walk, swim, run or ride a horse to get to you," Pip teased.

As they approached her house he stopped and turned to look at her.

"Dolly, I don't know if this is real but with your permission I would like to visit you again and get to know you more. That is, if your father approves."

"I should be delighted, Mr. Chase, and I believe that my father will not object to your visits."

That night Dolly dreamed of Pip's touch on her hand and looked forward to his next visit. Just as she was falling asleep she saw George's face smiling at her, and she had a fitful night trying to figure it all out. She was young but her feelings were real, so she tried to make sense of it all.

Mathew was angry. Anthony had deliberately avoided him by taking on extra shifts at the hospital. Mathew was supposed to be studying for his finals but found himself distracted by thoughts of Anthony. Neither of them had made it back to Cotters Marsh for the Sunday visits and Mathew felt lonely with thoughts about the approaching holiday. The hospital was making rudimentary preparations for Christmas and as yet neither he nor Anthony was on the rota to work on Christmas Eve or Christmas Day. Mathew was hoping that Anthony did not volunteer his time. As the hours crept by his mood did not improve. At long last, the door opened and Anthony entered their room.

"We have not seen each other for a while, Totey, is everything alright?"

"Of course, I just wanted you to have some space, especially no distractions for your studies," Anthony said lightly.

Mathew hoped this was true and went to cook them both some supper.

"Are you spending Christmas with your grandmother?" asked Anthony, partly because he was hoping this was true.

"No plans yet, Totey."

"I will be going home because I am too tired to take on extra shifts," Anthony sighed.

"Totey, are we alright? I mean is there anything wrong between us, you seemed to be avoiding me."

"Not at all, Mat, were you thinking there was?"

"Yes," Mathew's voice quivered with emotion.

Anthony went to him and they embraced. It was always Anthony who broke off when they embraced, but something was different, Anthony felt it. Mathew felt it. He did not pull away and Mathew lightly kissed his neck. Anthony dare not move because the sensations he felt were overpowering. Mathew caressed Anthony's back and moved boldly to kiss his face. Anthony did not move away and was shocked when involuntarily he moved closer to Mathew. After a very tender kiss on the lips it was Mathew who pushed Anthony away.

"Well, Totey, that was wonderful, thank you."

Anthony flushed, not with embarrassment but with pleasure. Mathew did not push him for more, he was happy that the relationship was progressing this well.

"Maybe I can ask my parents to invite you and your grandmother for Christmas. God knows we have the room in that big old house," Anthony suggested.

"Would you, Totey, I want to be with my grandmother but I also want to be with you," Mathew pleaded.

"If you do come, Mat, make sure you are more restrained around my parents, we do not want them to know us, the true us."

"I will be the pillar of decorum and respectability," laughed Mathew.

"And study fellow, otherwise we will become paupers."

"Your turn next year so be nice to me now, or I will make you suffer then."

They both settled down to a very pleasant evening. Mathew put on the phonograph and played some new jazz records he had been given to listen to by some of the other interns.

The friends decided that they would all visit each other on Christmas Eve. Dr. Preston agreed that they all meet at his house in the afternoon while he went to visit the sick in the village, and his wife went to prepare the church hall for the after service meal for the congregation. Joan had decided to stay at the convent after arranging for her mother to visit her aunt in town, for the holidays. Victoria had once again persuaded her mother to allow a visit because George and Everett were not there, and she promised faithfully never to be alone with Anthony or Mathew. Neither Victoria nor her mother understood the irony in this.

Mrs. Preston had prepared a small meal for them with some punch. She had asked the maid to stay in case the group wanted anything else. They all arrived at the house together. They settled into the parlour and removed their outer wear and boots. It had been snowing steadily for a couple of hours and they were thankful to have a roaring fire for warmth. Nan was awkward and cumbersome and she waddled to the largest armchair. Dolly waited on her, making sure she was relaxed and warm.

"The birth of your baby seems very close to me," remarked Anthony, and Mathew nodded.

"I feel so big and about to burst so I hope you are right," answered Nan, trying to place her very large belly in a comfortable position.

Victoria had brought them all gifts. For Nan she had brought some new boots.

"I do hope they fit Nan, we need you to be comfortable with walking the new baby."

This was particularly kind coming from Victoria who was not thought of as charitable.

"For you Dolly, I chose two of my very own favourite books, leather bound."

Dolly went over and embraced her. Victoria then handed Anthony a package.

"You must open this yourself," she said.

Anthony's gift was a brand new doctor's bag in beautiful brown supple leather.

"I don't know what to say."

"I know that at times this year I have been just awful to you all, but I do love you," Victoria confessed, "and for Mathew I give a new pair of gloves and judging by the tattered pair he is wearing, it is time."

They all turned to look and Mathew playfully tried to hide them.

"I will give Joan her gift later. I have chosen a bible that is etched in gold leaf, I think this is appropriate."

After everyone thanked Victoria, Dolly brought out her gifts.

"They are not as grand as Victoria's, but they too are given in love," Dolly explained.

Dolly gave Nan hers first, a full baby layette that she had spent months knitting for her. For Anthony she had bought a beautiful wallet she had personally hand painted. For Mathew there was a leather-bound journal, "To record your new patients," Dolly said.

"I have embroidered a shawl for you, Victoria and also one for Joan. I am sure that while she is a novice at the convent they will allow her to wear it," Dolly finished and Anthony stood up.

"Alright, so now it is my turn and I must say that I cannot top these gifts given by my very best friends. Mathew joined me in choosing these for you all. Dolly we have a small package for you, Nan an envelope and Victoria another small package. I will give Joan hers later. Oh! And I forgot I also have a gift for Mathew but he will have to wait until tomorrow as is our custom."

Dolly carefully opened her gift, which was a gold chain with a filigree pendant in the shape of a heart.

"It is beautiful Anthony, and Mathew, I am overwhelmed," Dolly gushed.

"Open yours Victoria," urged Mathew.

Victoria's hand was shaking with excitement and she revealed a cameo brooch similar to the one that Everett had given her, only not as grand. Victoria could not help herself and tears welled up in her eyes.

"Steady on girl, it is only a friend's gift," Anthony said, surprised by her reaction.

"It's not the gift, although it is very beautiful and thoughtful of you. It is that it brought back a memory I would be pleased to forget," Victoria answered.

Dolly knew why Victoria was so emotional because she had helped Everett choose the cameo brooch, knowing that he wanted it to symbolize a deeper relationship with Victoria, but it was not to be.

"Now mine," Nan said, hoping to lighten the mood.

Inside her envelope was a money bond that Anthony and Mathew had prepared for the child she carried. Nan gasped with surprise.

"As soon as the baby is born we enter the name here, see," Anthony explained.

"And then the bank will open an account in this amount here," continued Mathew. "The child will be started on its way."

Nan thought about the five guineas she had hidden for the baby and made a mental note that the child now owned fifteen guineas and together with Anthony's and Matthew's gift this was more than a year's pay for her. She hugged them both and then Dolly suggested they all had some punch to celebrate before they left for supper and the church services.

"I have something for you all," Nan spoke up, "I have worked on them with love."

Nan gave them all beautifully embroidered book marks and book covers with all their names on. She was hugged and kissed and thanked profusely as she shyly accepted it all.

The friends enjoyed the moment and Victoria had to leave, promising to see them in church later that evening.

"I will be going home with Dolly for supper," Nan said, "and will meet mam at the church later."

"Good. I am pleased you will not be alone in your condition," Anthony remarked, fondly hugging Nan once again.

After a light supper Albert, Dolly and Nan, wearing her new boots and shawl, made their way to the village church for the 10 o'clock service. The bells rang out to welcome the congregation as they all walked and chatted along the streets. Light snow was falling and the threatened storm had not yet arrived, and surprisingly it was not cold. Dolly and Nan spoke to various people as they walked arm in arm, followed by Albert, who stopped frequently to talk to his friends and neighbours.

The church was full and Nan and Dolly sat towards the back as was the custom for an unmarried woman in her condition. Albert joined Nan's mother Violet in the front pew. As the people piled into the church and were settling down to hear Reverend Simon's service, Marcus was searching the pews for Nan. He saw her and walked down the centre aisle towards her, smiling.

"Nan, why are you sitting way in the back?" he asked.

Nan looked nervously at Dolly, who was trying to think of a polite way of saying the congregation would not think it 'proper' for Nan to flaunt her condition. She and Nan shifted uncomfortably in their pew.

"It would not be… seemly," stuttered Nan.

"Nonsense," replied Marcus, "come with me."

He led Dolly and Nan by the arms through the centre aisle all the way to the front just behind Albert. Albert turned and smiled and winked at them. Nan heard the discontent from the congregation, and Dolly looked around at people whispering behind their hands. It went deadly quiet.

Bang! Whack! Reverend Simon thumped loudly on his pulpit and arrested everyone's attention. He glared at the congregation and started by saying, "Mary was refused succour at the inn…" What sinners they were to turn their backs on a young innocent girl with child.

Dolly looked around and saw the horror in the faces of some of the congregation. The Revered continued to chastise the soothsayers in the tone of his service and they were ashamed. Most kept their heads low and did not look at Nan. It was not until the Christmas carols at the end of the service that Nan realized she was sat across the aisle, along the same row as Victoria and her parents, and, John Hastings. She caught her breath and squeezed Dolly's hand so hard Dolly cried out.

"Sorry Dolly," she whispered.

A long hour later, after the service, the congregation started to leave the church to go to the village hall for refreshments. Nan, sitting on the aisle seat, sat there until the church emptied.

"Excuse me, miss, I think you dropped your glove," John Hastings eyes met Nan's and they twinkled with merriment, not a care in the world. He put the glove back in Nan's hand and walked away, talking amiably to those around him. Nan's skin crawled and she gripped the glove tightly and felt something there. In her palm was a five guinea piece and now she knew for certain who her baby's father was. She could not breathe, she could not think.

"Nan, what is it?" asked Dolly, "Are you unwell?"

Nan's next sound surprised her because she yelped out loud, not in emotional pain, although that was evident, it was a searing physical pain.

"I... I think... my baby," Nan tried to stand.

With that her waters broke and she cried out once again. This time others heard her and Anthony, Mathew and her mother rushed to her side.

"Child, what is it?" asked her mother, holding her as Nan tried to get up but could not.

"The baby, dad, what shall we do?" pleaded Dolly to her father, feeling faint herself.

Albert went to find Dr. Preston, who was just setting off to the church hall for refreshments. Marcus and Vicar Simon were also summoned and took charge, sending everyone to the church hall to eat, save Dolly and Nan's mother. Anthony and Mathew said they would wait outside while Dr. Preston evaluated the situation. Nan

156

screamed again, everyone wanted to help but did not know how. Dr. Preston came back in the church and Dolly and Marcus laid Nan down in the aisle of the church because she said she could not walk yet. They all gave Dr. Preston some privacy and only Violet stayed with her daughter.

"I am so scared, Anthony," Dolly confided.

"It is the most natural thing in the world," he replied. "Wait until it is you, Dolly," he teased.

"Never, I never, ever want to go through that, no never," she cried, adamantly.

"Wait and see," said the amused Mathew, who had seen and assisted in numerous births, "see Nan's face afterwards and tell us that again."

The wait was unbearable with the occasional cry from Nan inside. Dr. Preston joined them.

"Albert, you live the closest, can you go and fetch towels, sheets and blankets please. Nan is too close to move her, this little feller is in a great hurry to be born. We are moving her into the vicar's office as there is a fire there and a couch for her to lie on."

"I will go with you, Albert," offered Anthony, thankful for something to do.

"And me," echoed Mathew.

"Dolly, can you go and help Violet to keep Nan calm while I prepare for the birth, Marcus has already gone for my bag."

Dolly did not reply as she ran back to comfort Nan who was between contractions and asking what was happening. Violet was wiping her brow and was talking soothingly to her.

"A beautiful healthy child you will have child, I know it is hard but once you…"

She was interrupted by another contraction.

"Mam, I can't do this, Mam stop it, I can't do this."

"It will all be worth the pain, you will see," Violet soothed.

Dr. Preston, the Reverend and the two women half carried and dragged Nan into the rectory office where thankfully a fire had been stoked and it was warm. Dr. Preston asked for Violet and Dolly to remove Nan's lower garments and they did this without protest from Nan. Reverend Simon gave them a smock to throw on her and Dr. Preston examined her once again.

"No stopping this one, he has already crowned."

"What does that mean, is he alright?' asked Nan in a panic.

"Everything is just fine, Nan, nothing to worry about. As far as I can tell he has a head full of hair; that accounts for your heartburn," he smiled kindly.

Albert and co returned with the items and waited in the church for further news.

"Wager it's a boy," teased Mathew to no one in particular, "no takers, you have a 50% chance of winning."

They all laughed. Albert went outside to smoke his pipe and Victoria was walking quickly back to church.

"Mr. Marcum, is it true, has Nan gone into labour?"

"It's true, lass, but it may be a long one with it being her first an' all." He puffed on his pipe, "Go into the church luv, the boys are there."

Throwing decorum to the wind Victoria went to join Anthony and Mathew. They all sat waiting patiently, talking quietly about what the future had in store for a fatherless baby, even with their financial help.

"Come here, look at this," Albert called from the doorway.

The three friends walked out to see many of the congregation returning carrying parcels. They silently left them in the church vestibule and walked away.

"For the bairn," said one old lady, leaving baby clothes she had stored in her attic.

"Just an apology," said another, carrying a basket of fruit and vegetables.

Some waited on the outskirts of the village green for news of Nan's baby. One in particular was trying to be blasé and indifferent as he walked with Victoria's parents. John Hastings had a vested interest in this birth although he would never admit it to anyone.

"It's a girl," shouted Violet as the baby was born, "a sweet beautiful girl."

"This is Grace," whispered the tired Nan, "my daughter."

Dr. Preston wiped the baby and wrapped her in a towel and gave her back to Nan.

"Look at her curly blond hair," remarked Dolly.

"I know," was Nan's reply.

Dolly instantly understood that Nan knew who the father was and she felt a shiver as she remembered John Hastings' encounter with Nan only an hour before. Dolly shook herself and concentrated on Nan.

"This calls for a toast," the Reverend said as he produced wine glasses and wine, "if there is one commodity a Reverend has it is a supply of wine."

They all laughed and toasted the new child, whose name was Grace. Nan smiled and knew her daughter was loved by many people, and that made her happy. Marcus sat beside her and while everyone was admiring the baby, he was talking to Nan.

Victoria's father sent an automobile to take Nan and the baby home. Marcus wrapped Nan in a blanket and

159

carried her to the car. Dolly held the baby all snuggled up warm and when mother, child and grandmother were on board, Marcus accompanied them home. Dolly bent to kiss Nan and Nan whispered, "Happy birthday, Dolly."

Dolly had forgotten that Christmas day was hers and Everett's birthday. She thought of him in a foreign land and knew he was also thinking of her. Albert approached and wrapped a blanket around her shoulders.

"Happy birthday, luv. You and your brother were special gifts for your mam and me."

Dolly and her father walked home, both lost in their thoughts about birthdays past.

Reverend Simon sat down with his glass of wine and started to doze. He thought back to his twentieth year and the devastating relationship with Marie. She had been pregnant with his child but without discussing it with him she had a back street abortion and died. It was almost a year before he got his life back on track and he sighed sadly at what could have been. Simon Thomas was now almost forty and had recently been keeping company with the school mistress, Molly Arden. Keeping company is too strong a comment he thought, because they only met to discuss books, politics and such like. He enjoyed her stimulating company and was thinking that perhaps he should consider something more. Molly herself had hoped to speak to Simon after the service but she had just left for her home, alone as usual, as soon as she knew Nan and the baby were alright. She was concerned about Nan, but was disappointed not to have had a moment alone with Simon. Her friendship with the vicar was a lifeline for her. She enjoyed his company very much, a brief respite from the many lonely hours alone in her farmhouse.

Simon drained his glass and moved around the office, tidying up after the excitement of the night. He turned off the lights and started towards the rectory, hoping Marcus was not yet back from Nan's so he could retire to bed immediately. As he hurried past the green he saw someone sitting in the band stand smoking a cigarette.

"An exciting Christmas morning, sir," John Hastings said.

"Aye but all turned out well."

"Is the bairn alright?"

"Aye, Nan is too, she called the child Grace."

"You don't say, what a coincidence, Grace is the name of my grandmother," John replied, and Simon thought he detected a smirk.

"Peaceful this time of the morning," Simon continued.

"Yes, and I will be heading home now."

They both walked in opposite directions, but Simon was left wondering why John Hastings was so interested in the child.

Everett had retired early on Christmas Eve, even though George had urged him to stay and celebrate his coming birthday. Everett wanted to write a letter to his father and his twin. He needed them to know how much he was thinking about them and was terribly homesick these last few days.

December 24th 1917

Dearest father and Dolly,

I know you are both thinking about me as I am thinking of you. I would give anything to be home this holiday season and to escape from the infernal heat here in India. Don't get me wrong I am enjoying it most of the time, but I miss you both today. I know that it is probably snowing there and I envy you the cosiness of the fire and the comradeship of our friends. I understood from your last letter, father, that you are not going back to packing coal. I couldn't be happier and I am sure with so many out of work there, someone else will be glad of the job. George has had some bad headaches again, but will not let them stop him working. He has earned the respect of all around him, me included. The plantation will produce its first crop of tea soon, after a couple of years of neglect, so I do hope that the English continue to enjoy tea otherwise our profits will drop.

Dolly, I was at the market here last week when Baxter introduced me to another international trader who knew John Hastings when he was here last year, small world, isn't it. Today is our birthday and I am sure, like me, you are remembering birthdays past with mam. I miss her and both of you. Write soon as your letters warm my heart. Please send news when Nan has her baby. Love Rett.

Everett called for his houseboy to mail the letter immediately. Before he turned off his lamp George knocked on his bedroom door.

"Rett, are you awake? I wanted to talk awhile because I am worried about Nan."

"Yes, of course George, I will be in the study as soon as you have poured us a brandy."

George did as he was asked and sat under the ceiling fan to cool off. Everett joined him and they sat for a while in silence. Everett knew George had something on his mind and he waited for his friend to speak.

"Do you remember that merchant we met last week, the one who knew the Hastings fellow?"

"Yes, I remember."

"Well, I got to thinking, and later I made some more enquiries about him."

"Go on…"

"John Hastings came to India to buy some champion shire horses for breeding and while he was here he got into all kinds of trouble."

"Trouble?"

"Yes, Baxter found out that he was forced to leave India just ahead of the law."

"Goodness, George, what has that to do with us?"

"One of the things he was accused of was rape."

"Rape! What happened?"

"Apparently he tried to buy a young girl for sexual purposes and when he was refused by her father she was raped and threatened by him, at least that is the rumour."

"And now he arrived in Cotter's Marsh just before…"

"Exactly, I have put it all together. There is little wonder that Nan will not tell. The poor girl would not be believed."

"Do you think she knows who it was?"

"I think she is smart enough to have worked it out by now."

Everett contemplated this information for a few moments.

"I think we should write another letter to Dolly and my father, will you write to Nan?"

"I was thinking, Rett, that I will go home for a short visit; I will speak to Nan about it then."

"George, you will do something crazy if you go home. Let the law take care of John Hastings."

"I can't just do nothing."

"No, there will be a time, but right now Nan needs you to work here for her and the baby, I will inform Dolly of our suspicions and she will talk to Nan."

"Alright, Rett, we will bide our time, but I hope he does not hurt another innocent girl, or boy."

"Boy? I hope you are not saying what I think you are saying."

"Just rumours... but Baxter said he found out that Hastings visited boy houses occasionally, what a despicable person he is."

Everett called back the house boy and added another intense letter to Dolly.

Chapter 6

Dolly woke up on Christmas morning to the sounds of children playing outside her bedroom window. For a few moments she was hazy about last night's events. She stretched and thought she heard a sound. Yes, it was a sound she had not heard for months. Her father was whistling. He whistled a waltz that she remembered her mother and father dancing to, laughing and so much in love, oblivious to the watching twins in their happiness. Dolly smiled at the memory. She donned a robe and joined him in the kitchen where he prepared food.

"Dad, let me do that. Sit down and enjoy a pipe."

Dolly took over the preparations. Albert got up and fetched a parcel in brown paper.

"This is for you, child. It is a journal and I think you should record these days of your life so when you are old like me you will have not forgotten anything."

"Daddy, you are not old; you are young and much healthier now. Don't say you are old, you are my wonderful father who will dance at my wedding, and be there for the birth of all your grandchildren."

"So you will have children after all," he teased, "as long as they are not born in church."

They both laughed.

Later that day Dolly visited Nan but did not stay long because the new mother was obviously tired. Dolly barely recognized the infant with curly blond hair. She snuggled her little face to her cheeks and held her tiny hand.

"Look Nan, see how she curls her fingers around mine, look at her eyelashes, they are so long. What colour will her eyes be, I wonder?" Dolly gushed on and on, and Nan smiled indulgently because she had said exactly the same things when she awoke that morning. Violet brought them a cup of tea and fussed around her daughter and granddaughter. Just as Dolly was leaving Marcus arrived and she left him and Nan together. Dolly hoped that Nan had found someone who could love her as she deserved.

That night Dolly wrote her first entry in her diary;

December 25th 1917

This morning, Christmas morning, baby Grace was born…

On Boxing Day the village all gathered at the band stand in the village to sing carols and socialize. The weather was cold but the snow had stopped falling. The children skated on the ice dressed up in so many clothes, scarves wrapped round and around their necks, they could hardly move. Dolly and her father walked arm in arm, quietly enjoying the ambience of the day.

An automobile approached and Pip shouted to them to come over.

"I thought you would be here; want to go for a spin?"

"Not right now, Pip," Albert replied. "You two young people go off for a while, but come back by noon for hot brandy eggnog."

Dolly eagerly got into the car, looking around for her friends, hoping they would see her but they had not yet arrived.

"Where do you want to go, madam?" Pip joked, as he opened the door and helped her in.

"To the moon, kind sir, no, change that, to India please and be quick about it."

"I know you are missing Rett, but let us try to be happy today," Pip held her hand.

Dolly told him about the Christmas birth and he smiled.

"One day, young lady, that will be you holding a new life in your hands and you will be a wonderful mother."

Dolly blushed at the thought and she felt so happy she would explode.

The young people drove around the outlying lanes of the village until they came across the old Abbey that Dolly used to play in.

"Want to explore?" asked Pip.

"Oh! Yes please," answered Dolly.

Pip came around to her side of the car and opened the door for her. He held out his hand and she followed him into the ruins of the Abbey.

"Magnificent," Pip remarked.

"Yes, it is very ancient and has an interesting history."

"I was talking about you," smiled Pip as he pulled her close.

Dolly did not know how to react. Her feelings were betraying her and what was 'proper' and 'right' no longer seemed important. She felt the time-honoured sensations and feelings experienced by young lovers throughout history. Emotions overrode logic as she leaned into Pip's shoulder in submission. They stayed that way for some time and Pip kissed her hair and her cheek, and eventually after an agonizing wait he kissed her lips. Dolly returned his kiss. Pip was gentle and the lovers kissed again.

Dolly thought she would burst with happiness. Pip stroked her cheek and gently traced the outline of her eyes. As he passed over her eyelashes Dolly shuddered with ecstasy. Pip moved his exploring fingers to her neck and softly stroked her just above the neckline of her dress. His hands were cold but Dolly hardly noticed. She gave her senses up to the wonderful feelings Pip was awakening within her.

"Oh darling, I have wanted to hold you for a long time. I think I fell in love with you from the moment I saw your photograph."

Dolly's senses returned and she pulled away reluctantly. "Pip, this is too fast and I am afraid."

"We will take things slowly, Dolly, I will be patient," Pip smiled his dazzling smile and Dolly's head was a turmoil of thoughts.

Pip pulled away and for a while neither of them spoke. There was no need for words, holding Dolly's hand was enough connection for now.

"Let's go back now, it is past noon and poppa will be wondering where we are," Dolly whispered, reluctant to break the spell.

The young people drove the car back towards the village and Pip held her hand as he manoeuvred the car through the winding narrow lanes. The snow had once again begun to fall. They watched as the draft from their passing car whipped it up into swirls and clouds of soft white fluff. Dolly hardly noticed because her thoughts were back at the Abbey.

"The Abbey has always been special to me, but now I have another wonderful memory," Dolly blushed.

"The first of many I hope, my darling," Pip replied, as he moved slower through the drifting now.

"Oh! Yes, you make me so happy after such a dreadful year," Dolly snuggled closer to Pip.

They returned home to spend a memorable day with Albert. The men played cards and had a snifter of brandy while Dolly organized the kitchen. She went up to the room Pip would be using overnight and she blushed as she innocently turned down his bed. Later that night the lovers managed a brief goodnight kiss as they went to their respective rooms.

That night Dolly wrote her second entry in her journal and it began;

December 26th Boxing Day 1917

Today Pip came and we visited the ancient Abbey... and I think I am in love...

The following weeks passed pleasantly enough. Dolly busied herself with her father and baby Grace. The occasional visits from Pip became more frequent. His father owned a clothing factory and Pip was the general manager. His travels became centred on visiting Cotter's Marsh, to and from his destinations. Dolly's father enjoyed his company, and was delighted, but not surprised, when Dolly confessed that their friendship may become more romantic. Dolly missed her mother terribly and Albert tried to fill that gap for her.

Dolly talked about Pip to Nan when things settled down after the birth of Grace, but was hesitant to tell Everett anything yet. She knew why. George had expectations; they had a very informal understanding. After Dolly received the shocking letter from Everett about John Hastings she took a long time composing her reply.

February 29th 1918

Dearest Rett,

You may be surprised but I have already worked out who the father of Grace may be, and I think Nan does know, but as yet we have not spoken of it. I do intend to approach the subject with her as soon as I feel it is appropriate and in the mean time I will discuss the matter with Reverend Simon. If we are correct in our assumptions it will be very difficult to prove as you well know, but I will talk to some confidantes so we can be alert as to John Hastings' whereabouts as much as possible. I will write also to George on this matter as he must be very worried about Nan.

The baby is strong and healthy with a mop of curly blonde hair and ice blue eyes, she is very beautiful. Violet is the doting grandmother and it seems that dad is also spending quite some time there. This may not only be the attraction of a new baby and I know you will join me in wishing him well in any friendship that takes his mind from mam's death. We all miss her and the months have not lessened our pain. From your last letter it seems that you and George are doing a splendid job on the plantation and although I miss you both terribly, you sound content with your life right now. I will explain my letter after George has had a chance to digest what I am saying and no doubt he will share the information with you. Please understand that I wanted George to understand first, I owe him that much.

From your loving sister, Dolly.

Dolly sighed deeply. She took some time to gather her thoughts before she picked up a new sheet of paper and started to write;

My very dearest friend George, Dolly scrubbed this out and took a new sheet;

Dearest George,

In Rett's last letter he mentioned that you have once again been ill. I am worried that you are not getting the medical care you need. Your headaches are a result of your war injuries; you should get more advice about what you can do to ease your pain. Baby Grace is the darling of the village and I am sure she will love her uncle when she meets you. Although it has only been a few months since you and Rett left Cotter's Marsh, it seems a lifetime ago, so much has happened here. With the birth of Grace the village is a nicer place to be with neighbours dropping off the occasional gift of food and clothing for Nan. Rett told me about John Hastings and rest assured we are all keeping a close eye on Nan and the baby. Reverend Simon says that there was no proof at this time but he believes that Hastings could be capable of such a crime just by his seedy behaviour around the village. He told me that the night of Grace's birth he found Hastings hanging around outside long after everyone had left.

Dolly sighed and continued,

There have also been regular visits in the past months from Phillip Chase. I know he has written that he came just as you both went to India. He and I have been stepping out for the last month and I wanted to let you know personally. I know that we had no formal agreement between us but we were special to each other. Perhaps I have matured away from our childish crush and I don't want to presume that there was more to our relationship than there actually was. I am and will always be your true friend and will always be there for you in that capacity.

Your friend with love, Dolly

Dolly read her letter and cried. That night she wrote in her journal;

February 29th 1918

As much as one tries it is impossible to go through life without hurting others. Today I think I broke George's heart, I hope not, but my instincts tell me he had his hopes on a future as my husband. I feel sullied somehow and the love I feel for Pip is clouded in shame tonight. I hope tomorrow will be a brighter day for my heart. I hope that someday George will forgive me.

Victoria was in the parlour sewing beads on an elaborate evening shawl. She looked up as her mother came into the room.

"Mama, you are looking peaky, are you ill?"

"No child not at all, I am just tired I think."

"I heard you and papa last night and your voices were raised although I could make naught of what you were saying."

Lady Hastings was flustered because she had no idea her conversation was overheard, least of all by her impressionable daughter. She turned her face to the window away from Victoria and spoke in a controlled voice.

"It was nothing to worry about dear, just a small squabble about the tea dance list and protocol. Nothing to worry about," she turned away from Victoria so she would not be detected in her lie.

In truth there was a lot to worry about in the Hastings household. Sir David had been approached discreetly by a private detective from Grimoldsby town, about some illicit dealings to do with his brother John. Katharine had begged her husband to tell her the details but his reluctance to include her resulted in their first

172

altercation in years. David had looked very worried and John was on an extended trip to London so could not settle the matter. Katherine knew that gambling had been involved but her husband had managed to keep the lurid details of his brother's sexual misconduct from her.

The detective had been asked by the family of a young girl to look into her rape and to be secretive to save her reputation. John Hastings had been seen following her from her aunt's house on the evening in question and although there were no witnesses to the crime, the girl gave a good description which identified him. David had suspicions for years about his brother and had heard rumours about his sudden departure from India. He kept all these suspicions from his wife and when Nan was raped he could not help but wonder if it was John. He naturally feared for his own daughter who was now blossoming into a beautiful woman.

David had wanted to get Victoria away from the home as soon as possible and concocted the story about keeping her reputation intact. This satisfied his wife and he kept Victoria away from John successfully for a few months. However, John was due to return at the end of the month and if the detective had not located him by then he vowed to have a man to man talk with him, the outcome of which might result in him being banished from their home.

As if reading his thoughts Victoria innocently enquired about her uncle.

"Is Uncle John coming back soon?" Victoria asked.

"I think he may be back at the end of the month, why do you ask?"

"I was thinking about the afternoon tea dance and if he would be attending."

"I presume so, if he gets back in time. How many guests will there be?"

"I have asked everyone I know, Mama should I ask Joan?"

"I don't see why not child, she is still able to listen to music and dance, I am sure the nuns do not expect her to stop living while she decides what she wants. Ask her Victoria and she will decide."

"I will ask Dolly and the others to help me choose the music and Dolly asked me to give her some dancing lessons. May I ask them here next Sunday, Mama?"

"Yes, I will ask Mary to clear the summer house furniture so you will have some room. May I be included too, I love to watch you dance dear, you are so genteel."

"Oh! Mama I would love that and you can help me remember the steps."

The two chatted for some time and the sewing was temporarily put to one side while they made a list of formal invitations. On top of this list was Lieutenant Mark Gordon.

Mark Gordon had made several visits to Cotter's Marsh to see Victoria and they had been corresponding on a regular basis. Eventually, his letters were affectionate and personal. Victoria's parents held high hopes of this relationship. Mark Gordon was from 'good stock' and a suitable match for Victoria. Mark seemed to be hesitant to commit to Victoria in any meaningful way; however he did enjoy a very active physical relationship with her. Victoria was perturbed that he never once said he loved her when they made love, even though she thought she loved him.

His last visit to Cotter's Marsh had been in May, but of late his letters were not as regular and less affectionate. Towards the end of July his letters stopped altogether with no explanation. Victoria shrugged and dismissed the man, denying that she was hurt, but she did admit to being somewhat perplexed. One day she sat at her writing desk trying to write Mark a letter. After many attempts she gave up and started her needlework. She sat on the window seat not giving much more thought to Mark Gordon.

"It is his loss," she reasoned. "There are plenty of other fish in the sea."

Dolly was coming to see her that afternoon and Victoria could not wait to have some 'girlie talk' with her. As was normal most of the conversation revolved around Victoria but after a while they both took a stroll to the village to see Grace. Nan was working, but with Violet's permission the two friends often took Grace out for a walk.

"She has grown so much in the last months, I hardly recognized her," Victoria remarked.

"See her pushing to sit up alone, I swear Vicky she knows us now, almost as well as Nan and her grandmother."

Victoria seemed to be affectionate towards Grace but hesitated to hold her or change her when needed.

They pushed her carriage through the village. Victoria proudly pushed the perambulator. The girls stopped regularly to talk to people. Mrs. Martin was carrying a heavy load of washing to the wash house and Dolly helped her part of the way.

"Which one of you young 'uns will it be next?" she teased.

"Well, I heard Dolly swear she would never have children after she saw what poor Nan went through," Victoria answered.

"My, my Dolly child, this can't be true. I saw the way you looked at Mr. Pip Chase. Wedding bells soon then a brood of children's big as mine?" Mrs. Martin fell about with mirth.

"I soon changed my mind when I saw this little angel," retorted Dolly, giving Victoria a dirty look.

"Rightly so, rightly so, all bairns are to be loved. I loved each one of mine, whatever their names are…" she laughed so hard at her joke that she almost dropped her bag of washing.

"I'll love and leave you all, give my love to Nan and tell her to come and visit."

"We will Mrs. Martin," said Victoria, still smiling at their encounter.

Grace seemed to be loved by all who knew her.

The girls walked on past the church and almost to Dr. Preston's house, when Dolly froze. Walking towards them was John Hastings. As soon as he recognized them he doffed his hat, grinning.

"Good afternoon Miss Marcum, Vicky, I see you have Nan's baby with you today," and without a by your leave he picked her up and held her high in the air.

"Be careful uncle, she is still delicate," gasped the worried Victoria.

"Please put her back immediately," Dolly ordered sternly.

John Hastings glared at Dolly and smirked as he placed Grace back into her carriage.

"Well, she should be grateful her betters are taking an interest in her. The little bastard could be left in the poorhouse if we had a mind," he threatened, speaking with calm venom.

Dolly quickly pushed Grace away in her carriage and did not stop until there was a fair distance between them and Hastings. He just smiled and turned to walk the other way.

"What was all that about?" asked Victoria, as she ran to catch up.

"Vicky, I just thought it inappropriate that your uncle took liberties with such a young child."

"I do apologize for him Dolly; please let's not mention this to Nan. I did not know he was back here in Cotter's Marsh."

Dolly was only too pleased to let the matter drop because she did not want to alarm Nan, although she knew she needed to talk to her and clear the air about her suspicions. For the rest of the walk Victoria returned to the subject of the handsome Mark Gordon, not letting on that the relationship had cooled. Dolly was too distracted to talk about Pip, or that she was going to bring him to Cotter's Marsh's first Tea Dance the following week. The duo took Grace back to her grandmother and discussed fashion and music. Dolly was anxious to learn the dances of the day and spent a pleasant couple of hours practicing with Victoria. Sir David Hastings had purchased a new gramophone and records for the occasion and Dolly was transported away from her worries by the power of music.

David Hastings had been called away for most of that week and he had twice tried to talk to his brother about the detective. John had dismissed the notion that he could rape a young girl and told David he would go to see the detective after the dance and sort out this nonsense. Wanting desperately to believe his brother and somewhat reassured, David let the matter drop for the time being.

The day of the tea dance arrived and the Hastings summerhouse was full. Most of the guests were of

Victoria's age, but a few older people were acting as chaperones. Victoria smiled to herself as she saw the dowager Clarke sitting on the very chaise on which she had made love to Mark. Dolly enjoyed dancing so much that she was a sought after partner. Pip was also very sociable and mixed well with the entire roomful of guests, regardless of their age. Dolly noticed this and complimented him when they had a rare dance together. John Hastings was nowhere to be seen and Dolly began to relax. Nan and Joan spent a lot of their time talking to the older ladies and were not completely into the swing of things, for their individual reasons. They were occasionally asked to dance by Anthony, Mathew and Pip. Both Joan and Nan politely accepted and Dolly noticed they were both flushed with happiness by the end of the evening.

Reverend Simon and Molly were there but they just partook of the refreshments and were in deep conversation with Albert about farming practices most of the time. The young people dressed in their finery, trying to outdo each other. Victoria wanted to be the centre of attention and had bought a quite daring dress for the occasion. She was the centre of attention but not in the way she would have wished to be, much to her parents' chagrin. The afternoon passed pleasantly and Victoria and Dolly both enjoyed every moment.

The music was reluctantly stopped around ten o'clock and David Hastings thanked the guests for contributing to a wonderful dance. As they all said their goodbyes and made their way home, Victoria pulled Dolly to one side.

"Dolly, have you ever…?"

"Ever what?" she answered, distracted as she pulled on her gloves.

"You know Dolly, have you ever 'done it'?"

"Vicky, I hardly think this is the time for this kind of conversation. Why do you ask?"

"I have, and I liked it. I was just wondering if you and Pip had, that's all."

"Please Vicky, someone will hear you. The answer is no, and will be so until I marry," Dolly felt such a hypocrite as she remembered how she felt with just a kiss. She remembered how out of control her emotions were and how difficult it was to stop.

"I thought so too Dolly, but wait and see. When you are in the throes of love... tell yourself then to wait... I dare you," Victoria laughed merrily and she kissed Dolly goodnight.

In India Everett and George had accepted a formal dinner invitation from the local dignitary. There was quite a large British presence in the province and the two had made a lot of friends. The chums were sitting in the study smoking cigars and drinking a fine imported brandy. George was absentmindedly swilling his brandy around the glass, thinking about Dolly.

"When will this insufferable heat cool?" George spat out irritably, and took out his handkerchief to wipe the sweat from his brow.

"Baxter said that the monsoons are due in a couple of weeks and that should keep us busy on the plantation," replied Everett.

"It can't get here soon enough. Then we will have to cope with the humidity for a while."

Everett just nodded but his mind was also elsewhere.

The study was fashioned on the blueprint of the study at the Hastings house, and Everett had started a grand collection of books. In the short time he had been in India he had furnished one wall almost completely in many kinds of books, Art books, works of Shakespeare and the popular more modern works that he had found on his travels. His father, Albert, was happy to ship out his own small collection, and Everett enjoyed searching out English books in the markets. As a British colony, India was as much, if not even more, British than the British and this amused Everett. He had also taken to oil painting again, and the study was adorned with his talented works of art. Everett was particularly fond of making pictures using the workers on the plantation as subjects and these paintings were uniquely depicting the many colours of India. George said that he was almost ready to exhibit back in London but characteristically Everett denied his talent.

"Do you think Gita will be there tonight?" asked George.

"I should think so, seeing as she is the Chief of police's daughter. Have you ever seen such beautiful hair, and when she is in the full sari she is a dream catcher is she not?" Everett asked.

"Are you smitten, Rett?"

"Maybe but she would not want anything to do with me, a lowly country boy."

"You keep forgetting that this was in the past, you are now a rich plantation owner."

"Yes, I suppose you are right but I don't forget my past."

"Just don't wear it on your sleeve Rett, Gita knows a lot about the class system in England, she was educated there."

"I don't forget George. We are not as worldly as others believe we are."

Just then Baxter arrived. The car was brought around and the three men climbed in. It took quite some time to

180

drive off the plantation and small labourers' houses were springing up around the perimeter. The light was just fading and the flowers from the grove produced a sweet scent. George lit his cigar again and settled back and closed his eyes.

"Are you feeling unwell, George?" Baxter was concerned.

"No I am just fine, just a small irritation, nothing severe."

George did not sound convincing.

"We can abort this mission. It will probably be a bore anyway," offered Everett.

"Not on your life men, I am on my way to meet the girl of my dreams."

"I didn't know widow Gallagher and her facial wart was going tonight," Everett laughed. George playfully swiped him.

The letters between the siblings travelled to and fro for the next few months. These letters were often accompanied by a small painting Everett used to elaborate his letters, because, he said, he could not use prose the way Dolly could. In her many letters, Dolly always included a section for George about his niece's progress with amusing antidotes about her. Everett explained that he was stepping out with Gita and that she had been educated in England, and in many ways she was more English than they were. Albert did not know how to react to this news. Foreigners were still an unknown entity, although the war had opened the soldier's eyes to other cultures. Now travel was popular with the middle as well as the upper classes. Dolly received the news with glee and felt better about her own happiness now that her brother had met someone special.

Pip had become a frequent visitor and Dolly settled into a predictable way of life. Pip would visit for a few days but would then be away for months at a time on family business. Their intimacy was always controlled by Pip. He was gentle and firm. He was respectful and so frustrating Dolly wanted to scream. She often thought she was on a roller coaster of longing, excitement and then disappointment. She could not understand her feelings at all. There was a good reason not to become physically intimate before marriage, and yet she felt an invisible barrier with Pip even in their closest moment. Dolly shook off the negativity as soon as it crept into her thoughts.

"I love him and should be grateful he protects me," she thought, "But... oh I don't know, I am just being silly and looking for something that is not there. Maybe that is it? Is something missing? What is wrong with me? Pip is perfect for me." She shared these doubts with no one. How could she, they made no sense at all.

Things did not stay still in Cotter's Marsh. Dolly wrote to her brother about Molly Arden who had accepted a marriage proposal from Reverend Simon. Molly was to marry in a quiet church service in September. The whole village was abuzz with the gossip. Was she still a virgin, they wondered? Was the Reverend just looking for a housekeeper companion or a wife? Since his housekeeper had left to care for her own family, only Nan worked there. Molly wanted Nan to continue so she would be free for her inevitable duties as the Reverends wife. Nan was elated, she was educated by Molly and loved her deeply. Dolly too, could not have been happier for her former teacher, and offered to help with the arrangements in any way she could.

As the months rolled on, Molly looked as if she was a young girl in the first flush of youth. She was wearing more fashionable clothes and seemed to be constantly smiling. She told Dolly that she would be living in the vicarage as would be expected, and therefore she would be selling the farm and the ten or so acres of land. Albert was interested in the neglected farm. Dolly and Albert discussed the matter with Everett who assured them that they could now afford a larger home. Albert said he wanted to try his hand at farming which had been his dream for years. Everett was greatly relieved that his father had abandoned going back to the coal house.

By August of 1918 the transaction had been completed. The Marcums moved into the farm as soon as Molly was married in September. By November, Albert had already made some progress with a smallholding of livestock and planning the crop planting in the spring. Dolly had never seen him happier. He still saw a lot of Violet but they both seemed content with their friendship. Dolly knew he was happy and that made her happy too. It was still a working man's life, but now it was one of fresh air and productivity.

Soon after the move to the farm, Dolly sat on the edge of the bed. She looked out of her window to the fields below. A fox made his way along the hedgerow, trying to keep in the shadows. The sun was just rising and the morning chorus of the birds had started. Dolly turned back into her bedroom and looked at her reflection in the dressing table mirror. She sighed deeply. A lot had happened in the last year and she thought about her own marriage the following year. She had been a good daughter to Albert, kept his house, cooked his meals and generally looked after him to the best of her abilities at seventeen. Next year in the spring she would be doing the same things for Pip, her intended. They agreed to live at the farm and Pip would help both his family business and her father. So why was she melancholy?

Dolly sighed once again. It was not that she had any regrets of the past, nor apprehensions about her future; no it was deeper than that. Not everything was under her control. Rett and George were still in India; her father seemed very hesitant to become more serious about his relationship with Violet. Dolly still felt a tremendous responsibility for her father's happiness. She had received letters irregularly from George, even though she wrote to him every two weeks, the same time she wrote to her brother. She felt sad because she knew George was not doing well. He was having terrible bouts of migraine and had contracted a weakening fever three months ago which was lingering.

Victoria was betrothed to a new beau, although unlike Dolly, Vicky had had three beaux in one year. Joan had committed herself to becoming a nun and Dolly missed her terribly. Anthony was spending all his spare time with Mathew, and the group of friends only saw him briefly. The only bright spots it seemed were that Nan and Marcus were 'stepping out' after a long friendship, and baby Grace was growing stronger and more beautiful every day.

Dolly sighed once again as she scrutinized her reflection. She was unexpectedly pleased to see that she was filling out and was not so plain after all. Her hair was still long and it shone with health. Her breasts had developed and her waist was slim. Everything was in proportion to her five foot five inch frame. Pip seemed to think so and that was what was important. Dolly lay down on the bed again and daydreamed about her last meeting with Pip. They went out to the old Abbey. Dolly knew much about 'her place'. The Abbey was Anglo Saxon and originally an Augustinian abbey in 1132. In 1184 the Abbey became occupied as a nunnery until it was converted into a monastery where the monks stayed in residence for almost a hundred years. Dolly knew this from her studies but she was perplexed that she could find no date when it was turned back into a Catholic convent for the last occupants, another order of nuns. It had lain unoccupied for a hundred years. She surmised that it must have been the devastating plague, or another of God's pestilence heaped upon the unsuspecting people of those times. Dolly remembered her first exploration of the outer walls, which had been the resting place for the monks. As a small child she was amazed that these graves were not much larger than she was at the time.

She also knew much of the hardships suffered by the ancestors of the current Cotter's Marsh residents. She remembered reading about the devastating outbreak of smallpox in 1830, cholera in 1832 and typhoid, the most deadly, in 1887. Dolly often went to see the gravestones in the churchyard. She tried to imagine what life had been like only one hundred years ago. Theresa Cuthbert 1880 to 1889. Poor child probably died of typhoid. She was buried with an older sister, a younger brother and her parents, both in their thirties. There were almost fifty such headstones, what misery must have befallen Cotter's Marsh in those days.

Dolly shivered and sat up, trying to shake her sad mood. Although she could not fathom why she was apprehensive about seeing Pip today she dressed carefully for him, with a lover's pride. The unexpected cold snap seeped through any amount of clothing. Love does not feel the cold, she had concluded, but took along a warm blanket to cover their legs on the drive. She also took along a flask of hot chocolate and woollen hats and gloves. Pip arrived and they left immediately, eager for their time alone. Pip drove almost to the courtyard of the ruin. They walked up the steep incline and Dolly noted that this didn't seem to be an incline when she was younger. As a child she had just not noticed it. The lovers sat down on the massive stones that surrounded what used to be the main hall. They were protected from the bitter wind by two full, but crumbling walls and two half walls. A tree had grown on the inside and this gave them even more shelter.

"Here let me," Pip put a blanket around her and snuggled under it himself.

"This is my favourite place in the whole world," Dolly said.

"But you haven't seen the whole world," teased Pip.

He leaned closer and kissed her gently on the lips.

"No but I feel so safe here, I feel that somehow I am part of it all, part of history."

"And part of the future Dolly, don't forget our future. Will we live happily ever after just as our parents did? Will we have lots of children and grandchildren and will they all live happily ever after too? You will be a wonderful housewife and mother."

Something inside Dolly made her shudder at this innocent statement. Dolly looked up to see the sincerity in Pip's eyes, and as she did, he kissed her once again, only this time with more urgency. Dolly instinctively leaned back and he caressed her as she did.

"Are you cold now?" Pip whispered.

"No."

Pip caressed Dolly's neck and shoulder and she breathed deeply. He moved to caress her breast and she gave an involuntary whimper. Pip was more forceful as he unbuttoned her blouse and freed her. Dolly could not move, could not think, but gave herself up to the moment. Pip placed his lips on her nipple and played with it with his tongue as she squirmed in ecstasy. She was on fire, he was on fire. Later Dolly did not remember which of them stopped at that moment, it was probably Pip, she surmised, because it was always Pip who was the sensible one. She was sure that she wanted more, but did not know what that was, exactly. Pip stood up abruptly and walked a little away from her as he composed himself.

"It is fortuitous that we are to be wed soon, my love, because I cannot seem to restrain myself around you."

Pip kept himself turned while Dolly buttoned her blouse; he then held his hand out to help her up. As she stood he gathered her in his arms and held her close.

"I love you so, Miss Marcum."

"And I love you too, Mr. Chase."

The young lovers walked arm in arm back to the car. Unknown to them though, a new era was about to unfold.

Victoria was excited, her fiancé was due to arrive within the hour and they were to attend an opening of a theatre in the town. She hardly ever looked at herself anymore because everyone was constantly telling her how breathtakingly beautiful she was. Victoria wholeheartedly believed them. However, tonight she had plans and took great care with her toilet. Her relationship with Mark Gordon had been brief but pleasant and he seemed to lose interest in her after he had deflowered her. "His loss" Victoria reasoned, every time she gave a passing thought to him. Possibly as a rebound, she then had a brief affair with a much older man. Although he had the money to keep her in the manner to which she had become accustomed, he could not satisfy her in bed. Her present fiancé was totally besotted with her. He was just two years her senior but came from a very rich line of bankers and investors.

The first time they had made love Victoria fooled him into thinking he was the first, but they soon became sexually compatible and Victoria thought it was all so perfect. Robin Grant was not tall but he was well proportioned and had strikingly blue eyes. Victoria was not in love with him, although she liked him well enough, and reasoned she could amuse herself with lovers if she got bored. Robin was arriving on the early evening train and Victoria was to pick him up now she could drive the automobile.

"Darling, here I am," she shouted above the dim of the steam engine. Robin alighted with two suitcases. Victoria in her egocentrism thought that one contained presents for her. The second case was, in fact, only samples from the factory that Robin was taking to Newcastle.

"Here darling," she waved enthusiastically.

"I am so happy to be with you again," said Robin, dropping the cases and kissing her without giving a thought to decorum.

"I have the motorcar; let's get out of this din."

Robin put the suitcases on the back seat and offered to drive.

"Not on your life, I'm having too much fun," Victoria replied, driving through the winding streets of town far too quickly.

"Steady dear, I, for one, am too young to die," laughed Robin.

"Oh! You coward," Victoria changed gears noisily and drove on.

They drove for a while and when they approached Cotter's Marsh, Victoria stopped the car in a secluded place and they embraced passionately.

"Can't wait to get you alone," Robin whispered, biting on her ear.

"After dinner tonight we will go into the summerhouse, it is far too cold for anyone to go there in the evening," teased Victoria.

"The hours will pass too slowly," he said feigning distress.

They reluctantly drove back to the manor.

True to her word after supper that evening Victoria donned her boots and coat and invited Robin to take a walk 'to the village'.

The two lovers went directly to the summer house, where they passed a wonderful hour of lovemaking. They did not fully undress but managed to satisfy each other's yearnings. Robin was a caring and gentle lover, but Victoria wanted more aggressive lovemaking. She was smart enough not to let him know that at this stage in their relationship though.

"Oh, my love, please set a definite date for our nuptials. I cannot wait to make you my wife."

Victoria took some time to reply. Truth be told, she did not really want marriage, children and an end to her carefree days.

"Maybe we could consider sometime in the winter months, there is no rush is there?"

Victoria was still not satisfied sexually, and put her hand on him gently, then with more intensity. He soon became erect and ready for her.

"Please Robin, let's do it properly this time," Victoria was shameless in her need.

It was too much for Robin to restrain himself. As he entered her, he was immediately in ecstasy, fuelled by his unconditional love for her He started to move inside her, feeling the urgency of their combined desire. Victoria climaxed and groaned for more, but he abruptly pulled out as he too reached his pinnacle.

"What are you doing Robin, I want more," pouted Victoria.

"We have to stop now, darling, I do not want you to be with child."

Victoria sat up abruptly and glared angrily at Robin.

"You have taken precautions, haven't you?"

"Yes my love, but it is not foolproof and accidents happen."

Victoria face turned white. Out of frustration and unfulfilled desire, Victoria's mood changed, from loving and receptive, to cold and vengeful.

"Get out of my sight you... you stupid imbecile. If you cannot take care of me what good are you? I don't want a husband yet, let alone a bastard. Get out, get away from me now."

By now Robin was so shocked at her outburst that he froze on the spot. He arranged his clothing and bent down to cover her up. Victoria continued to rage at him and when he did not move she pushed him away. "Get out of here, out of the summerhouse. Leave me alone."

"Alright Vicky... my love, I am sorry, but I am sure you are safe. I did take precautions and I am sorry I led you to believe otherwise. We are to be married are we not? It is not so serious, please believe I love you."

Robin knew he was speaking to deaf ears as Victoria slammed her fists into the chaise in rage. He thought he had better give her some time to cool down. He did not want to return to the house without her, so he decided to walk towards the village. He left her crying and angry. He was confused at her change of mood and how easily she had turned on him. He only had a dinner jacket on and the night was chilly. He walked briskly in order to keep warm. As he walked he tried to decide on the best course of action and he hoped that he did not see anyone he knew.

After some time Victoria calmed down and pulled a rug over her to wait for Robin's return because, angry as she was, she did not want to return without him either. She felt tired after her outburst and closed her eyes. She felt the pressure of lips on hers. She responded to the kiss thinking she had gone too far with Robin and was about to make up with him. Only it was not Robin, it was her uncle John.

"Shh... you don't want your mother and father to know what you have been getting up to do you? I saw everything you little harlot... everything." John sneered and Victoria was stunned. John grabbed her half exposed breast and kneaded her roughly.

"No, Uncle John, please don't, you are my uncle, it is not right," whimpered Victoria, all her fight had dissipated. She had no strength left for a struggle and she was ashamed that her lovemaking had been witnessed.

"I want a little, just a little and it will be our secret," he hissed as he removed her breast from her bodice.

Victoria was very experienced with the needs of men by now and her mind was racing with all kinds of scenarios. "If I give him what he wants it will be over quickly, if I fight he will be punished but so will I, I am so afraid to be pregnant, what happens afterwards?" All these thoughts were jumbled up in her mind as her uncle prepared to have intercourse with her. He had roughly pushed her back onto the chaise and lifted her skirts and as he explored her and sought her womanhood with his fingers, he bit into her neck until she cried out in pain. He moved down to her exposed flesh and bit her lightly on the top of her thighs.

"Please Uncle John, don't, please don't hurt me. Stop Uncle John, please stop."

Victoria's protestations went unheeded as he entered her violently. Victoria buried her head into a cushion and bit down on her lip. She whimpered and tried to push him away but he held her tightly. He pounded her and held her down, bruising her arms in the process. It was over quickly and as he was pulling out of her someone entered the summer house.

"Get away from her," Robin yelled, pulling John off her and throwing him to the floor. He was not sure if the act had been with Victoria's consent or not so he looked at her for some guidance to his next actions.

"Robin, oh Robin, I am so sorry," Victoria cried.

Robin mistook the apology to mean that this encounter had been with her consent. He turned on his heels and walked away. He immediately packed his bag and without a word of explanation to his hosts he left for the train station. He did not know what to think. Victoria had showed a side to her tonight that he had never seen before. Her rage with him had been out of proportion to the circumstance, and then to walk into the scene... he could not even put his outrage into words. After about twenty minutes his love for Victoria calmed him. He rationalized that she loved him so much she was nervous about their future. He turned just as he got to the church and as he did so he heard an owl hoot a warning to him.

"Sorry fella, I was just wondering around. I will leave you alone to your hunting, good luck."

The encounter with the owl was the turning point for Robin, his mood lightened, and he wanted desperately to return to his love.

Victoria looked at her uncle. He had not yet stood up from when he was pushed to the floor by Robin. He sat up and leaned on the chair. The full moon shone accusingly through the summer house windows. It served to highlight the sinfulness of their coupling.

"It looks like you are on a bit of a sticky wicket," he smiled, "Get a grip, Vicky, your beau will not drop you in it, otherwise he will have to answer to your parents' wrath about your deflowering. It was him I presume…," there was a pause, "no? Then it must have been that cad Mark Gordon. If I had known sooner…"

Victoria stood up shakily and went over to her uncle. She slapped him good and hard.

"You little minx, I should give you another good fucking but I think you have had enough for one night."

John stayed where he was with a smirk on his face. He did not even cover himself.

Victoria walked slowly back to the house, too distraught to even cry. By the time she got there Robin had left.

Victoria wrote a long heartfelt letter to Robin, born out of selfishness rather than remorse. She did not like to be misunderstood, neither did she like the overwhelming feeling of helplessness she was experiencing. She cried often and kept isolated in her room for days after the incident. Her parents put it down to a lovers' quarrel and tried to coax her downstairs. She did eventually venture to the parlour when she heard that John had left for one of his adventures. A month went by and Victoria did not rally. She rarely left her room and ate so little her mother was alarmed. She looked so pale and ill that eventually the doctor was called.

He said that Victoria had gone through some trauma but would not reveal what that was. David Hastings was beginning to think that perhaps Robin had forced her to do something against her will and started to rant and rave that he would bring him to justice. Victoria cried and convinced her parents that Robin had been a gentleman. She told them that any misunderstanding had been her fault and that she had written Robin a letter of apology. This seemed to satisfy her parents and they tried to act as if life was normal but for Victoria life was anything but normal.

Robin replied a few weeks later and his letter was polite and cold. He said that he believed her, but was perplexed as to why she not reported her uncle to her parents at least. He understood that there would be a scandal, but if she was innocent as she had proclaimed then she should have taken the correct actions. Victoria did not know how to explain to Robin how she felt. She did not respond to his letter and sank deeper into depression avoiding everyone but her parents.

Chapter 7

The war was over in Europe; the sacrifices made by the British people would be etched into their memories forever. England had been irreparably scarred by the pain of death and destruction. The observable effects of war were only too evident with shortages of building materials that had to be used for the war effort and the parsimonious used the depleted supply of cloth in new sleeker and shorter fashions for women. However, the aftermath of war was seen more clearly in the psyche of the populace. Changes were made without complaints and the people acted together in unity in times of crisis. Women, who were hitherto working in the munitions factories, helping their men stay alive, now stayed at home. These same women were not now as content to be homemakers as they once were. The upper class still existed and made itself felt and until the 1920s they ruled exclusively in the political arena, but changes inevitably came. The country struggled to get the men employment. It was a slow, painful recovery.

New ideas struggled stubbornly with tradition. The traditionalists clung to the past and demanded respect though the power of money. The new idealists saw for themselves, not a life of subservience, but a life of possibilities to improve their station in life. That may well have been true for most of England, specifically the larger cities, but for those inhabitants of Cotter's Marsh the stability of tradition and class became their lifeline in times of unrest. The men knew the sacrifices of war were to retain their status quo, and therefore fought for England to remain unsullied by change. However, change was beginning to take place from within the country, not being imposed from without by foreigners. England was a place of unease and unrest. Cotter's Marsh began to feel this as surely as the chill of the North East wind.

Mathew had secured a position at the hospital as a paediatrician and Anthony had just passed his finals. They were on their way to Dr. Preston's house to celebrate.

"How does it feel to be the second Dr. Preston, Totey?"

"It feels just grand, Mat. I suppose I will be helping father from now on, it may mean that we see less of each other though."

"I am aware of that, Totey, but you must establish yourself as a doctor, you worked so hard for it. I have to work long hours and truth be told we hardly ever see each other now anyway."

"True, but we have to settle a date for a holiday in London, as we promised each other when I graduated. Do you remember?"

"Of course I do and we will write to your old professor. He said he would put us up there and show us the sights. A holiday in London will be something for us to look forward to, after all these years of study."

Mat put his arm around Anthony and looked around furtively before hugging him tight. Anthony, after checking that they were not being observed, returned the display of affection.

When they arrived at Dr Preston's there was a party in Anthony's honour. Anthony's mother had catered a grand affair with even a photographer to record the event. Victoria had made an effort to attend because she reasoned it would draw more attention to her if she missed it. Dolly and Pip were there, as was Joan who had a two month sabbatical before her final vows. Nan was also there with Marcus and she looked beautiful and very happy. Reverend Simon and his wife Molly Arden were also there. Albert was seated next to Violet, who had Grace on her knee. Grace was the centre of attention, of course. It seemed that the only people missing were Everett and George.

Anthony enjoyed being around his friends although it was all mostly small talk as he tried to be a gracious host. After some time he sat down on the sofa next to Dolly, exhausted.

"Well, doctor, are you pleased to go on to the next stage of your life?"

"I cannot believe how the years are flying. I only regret sometimes not going to India with Rett and Georgie. I miss them so much, have you had a letter from them lately?"

Dolly filled Anthony in on the latest news from the plantation and about Rett's interest in an Indian maid called Gita.

"Gita eh, well Rett must be truly over Vicky by now," Anthony chuckled. "I think by all accounts he had a good escape."

"Anthony!" Dolly acted shocked, "Vicky is our friend."

"Of course she is and will always be, but I think she is heading for disaster in her love life."

"That may be so, but who are we to judge?"

"True, very true dear Dolly. Are you happy, is Pip the right one for you?"

They both turned to look at Pip as he talked to Dr Preston.

"I think he is. We plan to marry soon."

"So I heard. If Pip is right for you, I am truly happy for you," Anthony kissed Dolly on the cheek.

"Is this what you get up to when my back is turned, you strumpet," teased Pip as he walked over to join them.

"Sir, you have caught us," Anthony feigned remorse, "we must have a duel at dawn, bedpans it is then."

Everyone within earshot laughed and the rest of the evening was as enjoyable, in part to Anthony and his sense of humour. No one noticed how down Victoria was as she made an effort to talk and occasionally laugh. However inside she was screaming with pain.

Albert was attentive to Violet's every need and at one point in the evening took over the care of Grace. Dolly watched him, fascinated. As he played and amused the infant she thought that this was how wonderful he was with her and her brother. Part of her was nostalgic for this demonstration of love from father to child.

Albert and Violet left after about an hour to take Grace home to bed.

"You stay Nan, and enjoy some time with Marcus," Violet said.

"Thanks mam. I really need to relax for a change."

Nan went back to dance with Marcus.

Marcus seemed to have made many friends in the village. He stayed at the vicarage and saw Nan daily. Their relationship was developing slowly and when he kissed Nan it was more like a brother than a lover.

Knowing that Dolly and Nan both had escorts home, Albert and Violet took the car back to her cottage. He helped Violet settle Grace into her bed. Grace was asleep before her little blonde curls hit her pillow. Albert then drove happily back to the farm. He re-stoked the fire and settled down with a pipe. He was startled by a knock on the door. It was a telegram and Albert's legs felt weak and his hand shook as he signed for it.

The telegram said;

December 1st 1918

On way home. Stop. George dead. Stop. Buried at sea. Stop. Please talk to Nan and his mother. Stop. Rett.

Albert read and re read the wire. George was dead? How, when? Buried at sea? Of course, the voyage was long. Albert knew they were heading home for Dolly's marriage in a few months, and Everett had asked Albert not to say anything so they could surprise everyone. Everett had written that George needed to see a specialist due to his increasing headaches but not to share this with anyone. Albert sat down and shook from head to toe. George dead?

He made his way slowly back to Violet's house. He was a frequent visitor, but she was surprised because he had left not an hour since. As always Violet greeted him warmly as he walked in. She saw his face and stopped in the middle of a sentence.

"Albert, what is it?"

Albert asked her to check that Grace was asleep in her cot and when she returned he showed her the telegram from Everett. Violet sat there for a long time before tears formed in her eyes and they fell unrestrained onto her cheeks. Albert sat close to her and as the realization hit her, her beloved son was dead; she reached for him and sobbed.

"No, No, No," she repeated over and over. They sat together in grief, until baby Grace cried her displeasure from being alone in her room.

"I'll go for her dear, just sit here."

Violet did as he bid and he brought Grace into the parlour and sat her on the rug with toys to play with. She stopped her crying and happily played without understanding the trauma that had unfolded around her.

"Nan..." Violet croaked, not able to get her words out.

"I know, she will be home soon otherwise I would go for her. I will stay with you until she hears the news."

Baby Grace giggled in delight as she found that she could put her toes into her mouth. The adults watched her without seeing, blinded by grief. Albert got a woollen jumper and covered Violet who was shivering as feelings came back into her body.

They heard Nan's voice talking to someone as she came into the house and Dolly and Pip were behind her. They stopped as if frozen in time, sensing something terrible had happened.

"Mam?" asked Nan.

"Dad?" asked Dolly.

"Sit down all of you," Albert ordered and they, robot like, did as he said.

Grace whimpered, confused at being ignored by her doting family. Automatically Nan rose to go to her.

"Not right now, Nan," Albert's voice was commanding.

Pip knelt on the floor to distract Grace with toys.

Albert took the telegram and played with it in his hands, not certain whether to show them or tell them.

"This is a telegram from Rett," he started, "He... George is dead, Rett said he died on the ship heading home to see a specialist and... and Rett said they had to bury him at sea. Rett is on his way home."

He watched as the two young women reacted. They reacted in the same way that Violet had, shock and disbelief. When they had processed what he said, tearing primal grief took hold. Pip moved up to sit near Dolly. Albert and Violet held Nan. Baby Grace looked on in her world of innocence, not understanding that she would never know her uncle George.

The days waiting for Everett to arrive were a haze of deep boned grief. The only thing Nan remembered was caring for Grace; her mother and Dolly took turns in doing that. The whole village was affected, even though they had lost many young men in the war. George had been a charmer and everyone loved him, including Dolly. Anthony and Mathew did their best to help Albert with the memorial service arrangements and took over when everyone was overcome with sadness. Reverend Simon and Molly were frequent visitors to the house and offered what comfort they could. Molly offered to take Grace for a night so they could rest but even through her fog Nan wanted to keep her baby away from John Hastings, so she refused Molly's kind offer.

Two weeks passed and Albert and Dolly met Everett at the train. This homecoming should have been joyous but it was far from that. Although Dolly noticed Everett's obvious grief she also saw how tall and handsome he had become. He sported a grand moustache, and was wearing white tropical clothing and hat. He was bronzed brown and looked much older than his years. As he stepped off the train he turned to help someone else step down onto the platform.

Dolly saw the most beautiful woman she had ever seen. She was dressed in a blue sari. Everett was holding her gently as she manoeuvred her way through the train station. He saw Dolly and his father and he waved to them but did not smile.

"He is hurting as much as we are," Dolly thought, as she clung on to her father's arm.

"Sir, Dolly, may I introduce Gita Rammed, Gita is my wife, and we wed just before we left India."

Albert looked shocked and then he smiled and welcomed her into the family. Dolly threw her arms around Everett and would not let go. Everett eventually prized her arms away and stood looking at her.

"Dolly, you are beautiful, you have grown, just look at you," Everett smiled at last and Dolly was relieved to have her brother back.

"I am sorry, Gita, I did not mean to be rude, welcome to our family," Dolly gave Gita a kiss on the cheek. "Everett will be a wonderful husband, just as he is a wonderful brother."

"I am so happy to meet you both at last. Rett has told me so much about you. He loves you very much."

They made their way to the automobile which Albert and Dolly had just purchased. Everett asked a thousand questions about the farm and when they arrived he did not recognize it. Molly had not kept it going after her parents died. She had just retreated into her own world, until Reverend Simon brought her back to life.

"Phew! What a difference, dad, I see you have bought some livestock; I hope your health is not jeopardized by all the work?"

"Not on your life, Everett, the fresh air is just what I needed. I just wish your mam had been here too."

They went into the farmhouse which Dolly had furnished with good taste. Dolly was an accomplished needlewoman and the furnishings were cosy and inviting. After being shown their room and given time for toilet, they made tea and sat down to talk. No one wanted to mention George but Everett began.

"He was sick for some time you see."

No one spoke.

"His headaches were severe and debilitating but he tried to do his work. George was respected by his workers and he has helped make the plantation a very lucrative business. Baxter is left in charge and when we return he and his family will return to England for a while."

Everett paused as he relit his cigar.

"Baxter knew before we left that George would not make it and he ensured George had put his affairs in order. His family will not want for a thing, George saw to that." Everett stopped and still no one spoke. He walked to the window and stared vacantly out. Not knowing where to stand, he seated himself next to his wife.

"Three days into the voyage George passed away. The ship's doctor said that he died in his sleep. We had to bury him at sea, you do understand?" Everett looked them both in the eyes and pleaded for their understanding, "He was dead too long to bring him home, you see that don't you?"

Dolly moved over closer and took his hands in hers.

"You loved him just as we did and you made the only decision you could."

Everett allowed a tear to escape and fall. Gita stroked his hair from his brow and said directly to Dolly, "Rett was his friend and did more than anyone would, in the end he was his nurse and cared for him as best he could."

She put her arms around him and he cried for a while into her shoulder. No one moved and they all waited for the moment to pass. Dolly was holding her brother's hand and she stroked it comfortingly.

The intense moment faded and Dolly said, "Rett, we have to go to see Nan and George's mam. You have to tell them what you told us, they need to know, no matter how painful it is. They will like to hear about how you took care of him, and that he did not die alone. And you will see his niece, Grace."

"You're right, Dolly. I will go alone, you don't mind do you, Gita?"

"No, my love, I will unpack and we will have a meal ready when you return, but take Dolly. You need her there with you."

Dolly turned and smiled at Gita and knew then that they would be friends.

No one remembered the memorial service clearly. Violet wanted to hold it before Christmas so as not to ruin Grace's birthday and christening. Reverend Simon was wonderful throughout. The pain they all felt at the loss of George overrode anything else. The only happiness that broke through the fog of grief was Grace, who was now a year old. She was starting to babble-talk and mispronounced things so adorably that anyone within earshot had to laugh. She was even-tempered and affectionate. Her christening had been postponed until George returned, but now arrangements were made. She had already been for a blessing from the church.

Reverend Simon understood the delay. Now she had to be welcomed into the church formally.

Christmas came and went and there was a belated party for Everett's, Dolly's and Grace's birthday at the farm on New Year's Eve. Pip was again away on business and did not attend. Dolly was disappointed, but reasoned he would be with her every birthday once they were married. Anthony and Mathew had been informed of George's death by a letter from Dolly. Mathew had been a rock for Anthony in his grief.

They had now returned from London and they were entertaining everyone with antidotes and descriptions of the big city. They spoke of street vendors, acrobats, musicians and actors. They related the stage plays they had seen and the vastness of the place and the multitude of people.

"It sounds as though you two will be moving there," Everett mused.

"That will be discussed, but no plans yet," replied Anthony, "Seriously, Rett, it is another world."

"We were enthralled by it all but actually moving there; that is a big decision," Mathew chimed in.

Everett realized at that moment that Anthony and Mathew were not just good friends, they were lovers. He did not know how he felt. He was angry at first, although he did not show it. He was quiet, thinking about how his friend's life would not take the same path as his. He knew about homosexuality. He knew that they were both headed for a life of hardship and heartache. In a flash he turned his anger to acceptance. This was his lifelong friend and he would be there for him, whatever his decision.

Earlier that evening, a light snow blew across the marsh. The tide was ebbing and the sand was being whipped up with the snow. Old Farmer Phillips was exercising his two working shepherd dogs on the beach, as was his usual routine at dusk. They were chasing after the sticks he threw into the outgoing tide, when they both darted towards the sand dunes. He whistled but they continued to run away from him. The light was fading quickly but he had no choice but to follow them. They stood next to what Phillips presumed was something washed up from sea. There was a light dusting of snow circling the outline of the mound. As he approached he saw that the mound was a dead body of a small child, and when he realized who the child was he vomited in shock. The two dogs were circling the body and whimpering as if they understood that this was a child. After he recovered somewhat from the shock, he left them to guard while he went to the nearest house to get help.

As the church bells chimed in the year 1919 everyone moved outside to hear the rest of the villagers celebrating. As they were all embracing each other and wishing each other well, an automobile drove up to the farm. Constable Bryan stepped out and asked that everyone return to the house. Dolly had a terrible feeling in her stomach. They all returned to the farmhouse, and speculated about this unusual occurrence. Constable Bryan accepted a hot chocolate and addressed them all. He cleared his throat,

"Ladies and gentlemen, I am sorry to interrupt your celebrations. Other bobbies have gone around the village with the same terrible news."

"What is it, man?" Albert could wait no longer.

"You are all familiar with a child called Samuel Green?" Everyone nodded. "Samuel was found dead this evening on the marshes. I am sorry to inform you that he was vilely assaulted before he was killed."

Everyone gasped. Dolly cried out and went over to her father for comfort as if she had been a little girl. The others talked among themselves in a horrified whisper.

"Who could have done such a thing?" asked Albert, his voice barely audible.

"Whoever it was, hanging is too good for him," answered Everett. The others nodded.

Everyone in the room was trying to process this news, trying to make sense out of unbelievable nonsense. A child does not die at ten years old.

"Little Samuel is dead?" Dolly spoke.

"Afraid so miss, murdered you can be sure."

"Murdered!" someone repeated.

"Who would do such a terrible thing?" asked Nan, and she shivered as she believed she already knew. She believed that any man capable of rape was capable of anything. Dolly had spoken to her about what had happened in India. Nan had said then that she was not surprised at any act that despicable man would do.

"Maybe it is time to share what we know, Nan?" Everett went over to her and she nodded.

"If you have any information that could help it is your duty to share it," the constable said.

Everett, Nan, and Dolly went into another room to tell the constable what they knew about John Hastings' activities in India, and Nan shared her suspicions about who was responsible for her own rape.

When the officer left Nan broke down and cried.

"I should have told earlier then Samuel would still be alive," she sobbed. Marcus put his arms around her, comforting her.

"I will take Nan and Grace back home now, she needs to rest."

Marcus gathered their belongings and prepared to leave. Violet wanted to stay at the farmhouse to talk to them because she had no idea why Nan had information concerning the child's death.

The rest of the guests left in a small group so that they all felt safe. At times like this they needed the comfort of each other.

"I will go and see the Greens now, after I see you back to the rectory, Molly dear. Marcus will you see she gets home safe?" the Reverend asked.

"I will take her right now, Simon," Marcus replied. They all left the warmth of the farmhouse and ventured into the cold night air.

Dolly told her father and Violet what she knew about the rape of Nan, and Everett told them what George had discovered in India. Violet was deathly white. Albert sat her down and gave her a brandy. She sipped it and gagged, but he made her sip some more. They did not speak until colour came back into Violet's cheeks.

"My grandbaby's father is John Hastings, is that what you are telling me?"

"I'm afraid so, my dear," Albert took her hand and rubbed it gently.

Dolly reached for a drink and Everett poured it for her. Gita sat quietly because she knew the story thus far and had asked Everett to inform his father. With the death of George it all was put to one side. When the information was shared everyone became silent. After some time Everett moved to stoke up the fire and was glad of something to do. This seemed to break the tension in the room.

"Albert, may I stay here tonight, in your guest room?" Violet asked, looking totally bereft of energy.

"Of course, my dear, I was about to suggest the very same thing." Albert was pleased he had bought such a large farmhouse, enough room for all his loved ones.

Anthony and Mathew had been quiet the whole time. They were as shocked as Violet at the news. They eventually made a move to leave.

"Do you want my father to come?" Anthony asked.

"No child, I will be fine, it is just the shock you see. First poor baby Samuel and then Nan. I will be fine, you boys head off home," Violet spoke quietly but decisively.

"Then we will see you in the morning," Anthony kissed Dolly, Gita and Violet lightly on the cheek. He shook hands with the men as if he needed contact with everyone at that moment, he needed reassurance that they were there with him. Mathew and Anthony donned their outerwear and left.

"We will retire too," said Everett, reaching out to Gita and giving her an affectionate squeeze as he helped her up.

"Me too," joined in Dolly, wishing that Pip was there.

Albert and Violet barely heard them as they were already talking quietly together.

"This was to be the evening we shared our plans with them, I want them to know that our friendship has turned to love," Albert said.

"We will wait, dear, others need us right now. Soon, it will be soon."

Albert sat with Violet until the house was silent and only then could she be led to her room to sleep.

Albert lay in his bed and did not undress. He still had on his Sunday best, although he had removed his shoes. He opened his bedside drawer and picked up the journal his comrade Peter Snow had written all those years ago, and for the first time in over a year he read.

It is hard for anyone to imagine that man is capable of taking another man's life. Today I killed someone's son, someone's brother and I have to go to my God with that guilt. Are we protecting our loved ones? If so then how do the Krauts justify killing us. Did I take the life of that man today just because I was ordered to do so? Was it only for an ideal I don't understand? How do my comrades find the strength to continue day after day knowing that at any moment they may die? Taking the life of another cannot ever be justified but I know in my heart of hearts that I will do so again tomorrow. I will do what I have to, to protect my own.

Albert closed the journal and cried for all the men he had killed, for Peter, for his wife, for George, and for little Samuel Green.

It was three a.m. in the morning and Albert could not sleep. He went into the farmhouse kitchen and found Everett already up and once again stoking the fire.

"Dad, can't you sleep?"

"I often get up in the night, son. Night is not always my friend. At night I feel my old bones."

"I know you have an early start with the livestock, is it too much for you?"

"Not at all, I have never been healthier; your mam would have loved this life."

"Yes, she was always worried about you working with the coal dust."

Albert poured himself a cup of tea, and a slice of bread and cheese. He sat next to Everett and they enjoyed the silence for a while. Each was remembering when Eleanor was alive and her serene presence.

"Dad, I forgot to give you and Dolly the photographs of the plantation. I also have painted you some miniatures to hang on the walls," Everett went to the parlour and returned with the parcel. They spent a pleasant hour looking at the photographs and Everett explained who the people were. He told of the influenza epidemic,

"Fortunately we were somewhat isolated on the plantation, so we were only minimally affected."

He told of the activities of Gandhi and how the people seemed to rally around him, and of the textile workers' strike, and of crop failures in parts of India.

"George had made sure that our labourers were well treated but even so our workforce was down when we left. Our yield was down but only marginally, we hope a better year next year."

He continued to show his photographs and Albert was enthralled.

"This one is when Baxter was instructing the labourers, he is a great foreman. This is Gita's brother Sanja, he is fourteen now and quite the little toff. This one is of the local market; our housekeeper goes there twice a week for fresh food."

Everett continued to tell his father about his life on the plantation until they both started to yawn. They both went back to bed with a feeling of a great love and understanding between them, not as father and son, but as two adults, as two friends. Neither of them mentioned the war.

Dr. Preston returned home after sun up and found that Anthony had not gone to bed.

"What is it, son?" he asked.

"Father, I was so upset about Samuel, and I wanted to tell you the news I heard last night about John Hastings."

"I know already Anthony, the law is searching for him, and he seems to vanish in an instant, and does not surface again until everyone's guard is down. Maybe I should have done more after Nan's rape and Victoria's breakdown."

"Father, what is it you know about that?"

"I can't say Anthony, but there should have been more that I could have done."

The man sat down and Anthony poured his father a large brandy.

Very early the same morning Anthony's mother Katharine came into the study and she had also been badly affected by the murder of Samuel.

"A voice like an angel," was all she could say last night; now she was more herself and was planning to go to the Greens to offer what comfort she could.

Mathew heard them talking and came down to join them. The housekeeper was asked to start breakfast because they were all planning on an early start.

"I have to return to the hospital this evening," Mathew said, "I will get grandmother back home and settled first. Thank you so much for your generous hospitality the last week. Grandmother loves to be with you all. I will go and help her down to breakfast."

"We loved having her here, Mathew," Katherine said.

Mathew left to go and wake up his grandmother who knew nothing of last night's events and Mathew wanted to leave it that way. The old lady had had enough tragedy in her life. Only his grandmother kept Mathew tied to the area. He harboured dreams of practicing in a large children's hospital and he had heard that Montreal, Canada was a leader in children's medicine. He saw no point in sharing this with anyone at this time. His relationship with Anthony was still fragile and his grandmother was alive and well. "A dream becomes even more potent the longer we wait for it," he reasoned. He was a patient man.

There was no time for Mathew and Anthony to say a private goodbye but Anthony said he would telephone him soon to arrange their next meeting. As the automobile drove slowly though the village, there was deep-felt grief in the very air. Mathew's grandmother was thankfully dozing for most of the way home. Mathew reflected on their holiday in London and smiled at the memory of the night that Totey had become truly his.

The sun was fully up before the farmhouse residents were up and around. Violet went to keep Albert company as he did his chores with the animals. Nan arrived in the kitchen to find that Gita had started the breakfast. The bacon smelled good but Dolly felt she could not eat a thing.

"Morning sis, wife," Everett playfully teased Gita.

"I will go to see Nan today," Dolly said. "She had quite a shock last night."

"We all did, I hope they have got the bastard," Everett remarked.

"The problem is that it is only suspicion at this time, no real proof," Dolly offered.

"What more proof do they need, the man is a pervert."

"That may be so, but in truth it is all rumour right now," Gita said, as she served them both their breakfast.

They all awoke from their inertia of grief for Grace's sake. A few days later, the afternoon of her christening was the start of the healing process. Nan was thankful that John Hastings had disappeared once again and the whole village turned out to name their Christmas baby. At the tea afterwards there was laughter once again in Violet's house. Albert saw her watching the people around Grace, and he stood at her side as she smiled.

"Well, my dear, it seems that life has to go on."

"It is hard but the pain is lessened when I am with my granddaughter."

Albert held her hand and Violet did not pull away. Dolly noticed and smiled.

That evening Albert stayed until everyone had left, and Nan had retired to her bedroom with the child.

He leaned over and kissed Violet gently on the lips.

"Nay Albert, what are we thinking of at our age?" she chastised, but with a smile.

"I am thinking I am with a beautiful caring woman and I want to be with her always."

Violet, for all her maturity, blushed like a schoolgirl with her first kiss.

"We had wonderful spouses, how can we forget?" she whispered.

"We will not forget but we need to go on, it is time." Albert kissed her again and she kissed him back.

"Are you ready, Vi? Will you be my wife?"

"Ask me in a few months, Albert, it is too soon after George... you understand. For now we must be content with just our love."

"In three months I want you to say yes, my dear, we may be older in years but I want to be with you and feel like a young man again."

Albert and Violet returned from gathering the eggs, and they were all happy to see the colour back in her face.

"My, what a lot of work on a farm," she laughed, obviously glowing in Albert's attention.

"You were a great help, my dear," Albert complimented.

"When are you two going to tell us your good news?" Everett asked.

"Is it that obvious, boy?"

"Obviously dad, and we are happy for you both, honestly. We want you to be happy."

"What is this?" Dolly seemed to come around from her daydream.

"Violet and I will decide in a few months, perhaps in the spring, dear, after we have recovered from the death of George."

"In love? You and Violet? I couldn't be happier, daddy. I want you to be happy."

"This is the good news we all need after the past months," Gita said as she went to hug Violet.

Dolly watched as her brother's wife kissed her father and she was glad she was part of their family. Dolly hugged them both too and then said she wanted to visit Nan. She wanted some air and therefore would take a walk.

"I will go with you now," Violet said and went for her coat. As they walked Violet asked if her union with Albert really was fine with Dolly.

"It does not mean we have forgotten them," Violet explained. "It is just that life has to go on, and I have grown to love your father dearly."

"I have seen your love grow from your friendship, and I really am happy for you both," Dolly hugged Violet and felt at peace.

Dolly had not seen Pip for more than a month because his father had asked him to go to France on business. He had corresponded with Everett and talked about their time in the war and George's sense of humour, but Everett did not share much of this letter with anyone. Dolly was upset that Pip had not made the memorial and seemed to be delaying his return time after time. After their last meeting, when they both went much further than they had intended, Dolly was worried that Pip thought less of her. She missed him dreadfully and tried to keep busy, spending her time with Grace. She spoke to Nan about her frustration with Pip.

"I just don't understand why he is still in Europe. He said that he had already transferred his father's funds to safer avenues. He does not seem too fazed about it all; our forced separation does not feel right."

"Oh Dolly, you are worrying for naught. Pip loves you. I think he tries to please his father at the expense of your relationship though, but I doubt whether it is intentional on his part."

"He should be able to say no to his father's wishes to be with me," Dolly sulked.

"I know, Dolly dear, but it will work out, just you see," Nan hugged Dolly and kissed her cheek.

A few days later Everett announced that they had to return to India soon, back to running the plantation. Although they had planned to stay for Dolly's wedding the news from the plantation meant they had to return as soon as possible. Baxter wanted to go to England to attend to family business and he was well due a break.

They had made arrangements to sail back to India at the beginning of March. Gita had made herself at home on the farm, although the Northern cold was not to her liking. She had spent many hours talking and helping Dolly. She asked when Dolly and Albert were going to India. Dolly said that she would one day but right now she had other things that required her attention in Cotter's Marsh. Dolly was not sure that Pip would want to visit India; he seemed so busy with his father's business. She doubted he would want that adventure. However, she kept those thoughts to herself.

Nan and Marcus were also planning to wed in a few months, silencing the tongues of village gossips. Anthony and Mathew were involved in their profession and working hard. Joan was living full-time now at the convent. Victoria was much more subdued than was usual, although she did make an effort to be around baby Grace as much as possible.

The winter of 1919 was brutal. Temperatures reached an all-time low and Reverend Simon increased his home visits to the village elderly. The church hall was heated daily to allow them some warmth, and this became a comforting destination for a lot of the old and infirm. Old Marge Sedgwick became the life and soul of the group, playing the piano and singing. Dolly got into the habit of dropping by every day to comfort and talk to her neighbours. Some decided to stay there overnight on occasion and the stronger males in the village brought in supplies of wood for fuel. Farmer Phillips popped in just to check on everyone and stayed for his third cup of tea, everyone understood the man's pride would not allow him to admit he needed help. His two dogs lay near the wood burning stove and refused to move. The village rallied around and supplied hot drinks and food.

Suddenly old man Clark started to tell a story about the hardship of his youth and somehow they were all comforted about their present situation.

"It is quite a gathering," Reverend Simon said to Marcus.

"Maybe this is what the village needs, a meeting place," he replied.

"Could be, but for now let us get these people through the worst winter in years." Simon went off to talk to Gladys Smith. Marcus wondered around providing food and blankets where they were needed.

"Young Marcus, I haven't seen you around much just lately, has young love changed you?" teased Margaret Gordon, smiling her toothless smile.

"Not on your life, Maggie, I am saving myself for you," Marcus laughed as he kissed the top of her head.

"Go on with yer', yer' cheeky monkey," she retorted, also laughing.

Joan had been sent from the convent with two sisters to assist in any way she could. After old man Clark finished his tale Joan started to sing. By the second verse the whole room joined in and Reverend Simon stood in the background with tears in his eyes.

"You know Marcus; we are witnessing a miracle of the human spirit. Nothing gets the English down, they rise to any occasion and face adversity with song. The war depleted them somewhat but their spirit survived. Just look at them all. I am so proud to be an Englishman."

"With a bit of the Scots," Marcus added, referring to his own ancestry.

"Of course, Britain is, and will remain great because the people are great."

He went into church to pray. Marcus did not follow him.

Victoria was sick, very sick. Her mother was frantically trying to placate her with promises of holidays abroad, more tea dances, new clothes and even a new car but nothing worked. The news about George devastated her and she did not respond even to Dolly's coaxing. She attended the memorial service and the christening, because she was Grace's godmother, but her heart was not in it. Dolly commented on her quietness but Victoria just said she had a cold.

Katharine Hastings tolerated her daughter's dark mood for another month before she lost patience with her. David Hastings was perplexed when nothing seemed to bring his daughter out of her doldrums. In desperation Dr. Preston was called once again and the news sent Victoria into hysterics.

"Pregnant, did you say pregnant!" her mother cried.

"I am afraid so, I am sorry but the only thing I can see to account for her malaise is that she is with child," Dr. Preston announced as he closed his bag.

"That can't be, she is not married," her mother carried on, stupidly.

"I will leave her with a tonic and will return tomorrow when you have recovered from the shock."

The Hastings house was in shock and Victoria's parents presumed that the child was Robin's. They insisted that she write to him to come at once. Victoria wrote him a long sorrowful letter explaining her predicament and she received a reply stating that he was to visit her the following week. He insisted she meet him alone and she made arrangements to go to town to the local hotel where they would be assured some privacy. She made excuses to her mother that she was taking a trip into town to buy some clothes because she no longer fit into hers. She insisted she go alone and as her mother was relieved that Victoria was getting out of the house, she let her go.

When Victoria entered the lobby of the hotel she was devoid of feeling. She had cried away any semblance of being human. Robot-like she made her way into the tearoom and selected a seat as far away from other patrons as she could. It was almost two o'clock and there was no sign of Robin. Victoria ordered tea and waited. At ten minutes past two Robin joined her. There was no sparkle in his eyes and he also looked drawn and ill.

"Vicky," he said, gallantly kissing her cheek.

"Thank you for meeting me," Victoria whispered.

There was an awkward silence while she poured Robin a cup of tea. As she handed it to him her hand shook. Robin put his hand over hers to steady it. Tears welled up in her eyes and she swallowed hard to stop them.

"I obviously received your letter about your pregnancy, and I am truly grateful that you admit that you are not sure if the child is mine or not." He coughed to clear his throat. Robin was hurting.

"Robin, I am so sorry. That night in the summerhouse my uncle had watched us make love and took advantage of me, you must believe me. Robin please, please believe me," Victoria's voice tapered off into a hoarse whisper.

"I do believe you now, Victoria but I am confused by you not telling anyone. I do understand that you would have been subject of a scandal and we would have been scrutinized about our own behaviour, but he cannot just get away with it," Robin paused. "Victoria, I should

220

have stayed that night instead of running away, like you, I was also confused and did not know what to do."

"I just wanted to die."

"I know, and I was a coward. I should have brought him to justice myself, but I was not sure of the circumstances. I thought you had welcomed his advances. Forgive me."

Victoria reached out for his hand and she was still shaking.

"Robin, I honestly don't know if the child is yours or not. I pray that it is yours."

"Let's get out of here and go for a walk in the park," Robin pleaded.

A short while later they sat on the park bench. The weather was pleasant but they did not notice. Neither had spoken but Robin offered Victoria his arm as they walked.

"What do your parents think, are they very angry?"

"They presume the baby is yours, Robin, and I am too much a coward to let them believe otherwise. John is papa's brother, it would kill him, or he would kill John. Either way they must not know."

"Good, then all is not lost."

"What do you mean?"

"What I am saying, my silly goose, is that we will marry and I will accept the child as my own."

Victoria looked at Robin, trying to read his eyes. She kissed him on his lips and hugged him tight.

"I think this meets with your approval," he laughed for the first time that afternoon.

"Oh! Robin, I love you and we would have been married. I am so sorry there was doubt about what happened. We can be married right away, my parents will arrange everything."

"I will write to your father and take responsibility for the baby. We will wed as soon as it can be arranged. However, I need to get you as far away from your uncle as possible. You will come and live with me and my parents until we can buy a house for ourselves."

At that point Victoria would have agreed to anything to escape the predicament she was in. It was only later that she realized she would be moving away from her friends and family. She was getting the consequences of her selfish actions and she had to live with them.

The next day, greatly relieved, Victoria confided in Dolly about her condition, but not about the rape by her uncle. She explained that she was to marry Robin in his home town in three weeks and would be living there permanently from now on. Dolly was not surprised at Victoria's news because in the last year or so she had gained an unsavoury reputation. Dolly was pleased that her marriage might help to stabilize her and give her the attention she craved. She told Victoria that she was sad not to attend her wedding, but she understood the circumstances and wished her happiness.

Dolly and Pip had twice changed their own wedding plans because of circumstances and the new date of April would mean that Everett and Gita would not be there. Dolly was sad about this but marrying any sooner would be disrespectful and inappropriate. Everett and Dolly had discussed this and Everett had purchased a camera for Dolly to get some pictures taken so he could see.

They were all in the farmhouse kitchen preparing their dinner. Dolly and Gita were rolling dough for the pies.

"All I need to know is that you will be happy as Pip's wife," Everett said.

He had not seen Pip since he arrived home in December, although they had exchanged letters, and Pip was not to return until after they had gone back to India. Dolly told Everett that Pip had made a vague promise that they would take a trip to India just as soon as they could. Gita wanted Dolly to see the plantation. She wanted to be a hostess and return their hospitality.

"You will see the markets, the richness of the land and the new interesting cooking spices. You could bring them back home and cook Indian dishes. In fact I will cook you all something special this very week."

Dolly smiled and informed Gita that she was not a good cook but was willing to try.

"No, Dolly had her head in the books. I remember when mam tried to get her to make bread once and what a mess it was," he laughed at the memory.

"But she can now, she makes the most wonderful bread," Albert came to her defence.

Dolly threw a piece of dough at Everett and he chased her around the kitchen table.

"Just like old times." Albert loved the horseplay.

An uneasy calm settled on the village. There was no sign of John Hastings and Victoria never mentioned the murder in her letters to Dolly, although Dolly had told her. The letters contained only the news of her pregnancy and how wonderful her marriage to Robin was. Dolly was a little irritated at Victoria's self centred-ness but realized that this was her way and she was not likely to change. The Hastings had fled to Bath for an extended period and the village settled into a semi normal routine.

The day of Everett and Gita's departure at the beginning of March was very emotional. Everett seemed eager to get back to the plantation and was happy his father and sister had loved ones to care for them.

"I am holding Pip to his promise, Dolly. You are to visit us soon."

Dolly felt that now her father was to remarry, his need for her was less. A visit to India was possible if she could persuade Pip to take the time away from his family.

"When the time is right, maybe next year, Rett, maybe next year," Dolly smiled happily.

"By then you will be an aunt," Gita teased.

"Oh, I do hope so you two."

Albert and Dolly said their final goodbyes at the train station and they both stood on the platform until the train was out of sight.

"Well lass, he looked well. He needed to come home after George's death, they were as brothers."

"Yes dad, I feel sad but at the same time happy. Rett has a wonderful wife."

"And we will be married in the next year, both of us. Who would have believed it?"

He took his daughter's hand in his and they went back to the farm. When they arrived home there was a letter from Pip

February 12th 1919

My dearest love,

I am afraid my stay here in France will be a little longer than expected. My father has many stocks and bonds in various establishments after the war, and there are some shady dealings here that I have to get to the bottom of. I have advised him many times to not speculate abroad but it seems he has not listened. I hope I can salvage his fortune here in France.

In the meantime I am desperate to hold you in my arms once again. My dreams are for you and about you. I want you at my side for the rest of my life as my wife. We have such a wonderful future together. I love you and cannot wait for the months to go by to our marriage. My family is eager to meet you. My father is a stickler for convention, but mother is easy to love.

If Rett is still there, tell him I will whisk you away to India some day. My heart is enclosed in this letter, keep it safe.

Your betrothed, Pip

Dolly held the letter close to her heart as she went to her room to read it again and again. She kissed it tenderly before putting it into her bureau drawer with the rest of her treasures. She knew it was time to talk to her father about his own upcoming nuptials.

"Dad, when you marry Violet, is it still alright for us to live here too?" Dolly held her breath for the answer.

"My dear child, hush, you are my daughter and this is your home. Another person living here will not change that. Thank goodness the farmhouse is large enough for all. You and Pip have a home here, of course you do."

"I was wondering if Violet was leaving her house for Marcus and Nan?"

"I suppose so; I never thought that far ahead."

"Then it will all work out splendidly."

"Come here and give your old daddy a hug."

Dolly did as he bid and for a few moments she was a child again in the comfort of her father's arms.

Chapter 8

Early in April there was great excitement. Great-aunt Daisy was paying them a visit. Albert was so excited he could not tie his shoes, and Dolly had to straighten his collar on his jacket. Pip was also due to return home in two days and Daisy wanted him to meet her benefactor. One of the guest rooms was prepared and Dolly and Nan had a wonderful time choosing linens and setting it up just right. Violet shared that she was a little nervous to meet Daisy and Albert reassured her that she was a very genteel lady who would love her.

The day arrived and the tea table adorned with the freshest bread and cakes. The butter had been churned by Albert from his very own dairy cows, and the bread and cakes made from his own crop of wheat. He was very proud of the use to which he had put the children's inheritance. Dolly, too, was proud of her father and wanted to tell her great-aunt Daisy that, although they missed mam deeply, they were now happy, in part due to their improved circumstances.

This time Daisy arrived in a brand new automobile. The driver wore a chauffeur's livery and went to assist her out of the car. He was to stay at the bed and breakfast in town. Daisy was dressed exquisitely and she was using a cane for support. Albert heard her arrive and went out to meet her. He gave her his arm and they chatted amiably as they walked to the farmhouse. Dolly hovered at the front door fighting the urge to run up to the old lady and hug her. They greeted each other with a brief kiss on the cheek and went into the farmhouse parlour.

"Sit down, sit down, Albert, don't fuss," Daisy waved for him to sit.

"Well, Dolly dear, you have blossomed into a beautiful young lady and you are to be wed soon, it seems."

"Yes, great-aunt, Phillip, Pip, will arrive on Friday; he has been in France on business."

"My dear, you are absolutely glowing, this is a love match I see." Daisy smiled a disarming smile, but Daisy did not miss the fleeting dark cloud pass over her eyes.

"I will get the tea," Dolly left the room.

"Albert, I see that you are an honourable man and you have made something of yourself. The farm is a viable business, by all accounts."

"Yes it is and I really love the work."

"It shows. Eleanor did choose a good husband after all."

"I miss her, Daisy, so much."

"I know that when our loved ones die we never recover fully, but you are still a comparatively young man, what is it 42, 43?"

Embarrassed, Albert laughed, "Let's leave it at that, Daisy, even old men have secrets."

As they were both laughing Dolly returned with the tea.

"Am I missing something?"

227

"Bless your heart, child, not at all. Tell me about your young swain, is he handsome?"

They passed a very pleasant hour and then Daisy asked to go to her room. Dolly hoped that she would be impressed by her work.

After Daisy had rested Dolly went up to see her.

"Great-aunt Daisy, tell me about mam when she was young."

"Sit here girl, beside me. I have brought you some mementoes from your mother and grandparents. You resemble your mother in looks, but I think you take after your great-grandmother in temperament. If I read you right, you feel that your life should be one long adventure, no?"

"How did you know that was how I feel?"

"You show impatience with the mundane and keep looking for greener grass, is this not true?"

"Yes, but it seems that fate has other things in store for me."

"Not for much longer, child. Soon you will be someone's wife. Does he share your need for adventure?"

"I think so, although to be honest it has never been talked about in that way. He has promised to take me to see Rett in India next year."

"Be careful, dear, that you are compatible with this love of yours. Some men want their wives to follow them. You are not a follower, just be sure. I do not know your Pip so I cannot give you advice. I know what it is like in the first flush of romance, how much you both want to be together. There is much more than physical intimacy, Dolly, to the making of a good match."

"Oh, great-aunt, you sound just like mam talking to me of such things. She knew how I felt and understood my restlessness."

They talked for a while before Albert called for them to come down for their supper.

The next day Dolly received another letter from Pip, once again apologizing for delaying his return. Dolly was shocked at her reaction. Gone was the adoring woman, waiting patiently for her love, and in its place came a demented, angry unrecognizable person. Dolly tore up the letter in anger and frustration and stamped around her bedroom as would a two-year old in a temper tantrum. After some time her head cleared enough to hear laughter coming from downstairs. She knew that her father and great-aunt had plans for the day, which left her free to feel the intrusive emotions of abandonment. She flung herself on her bed, fully expecting tears to fall, but they did not. Her head was spinning and eventually she heard her father and great-aunt Daisy leave in the automobile. Dolly stood up and tidied herself because she needed to get out of the house as soon as she could, to feel the wind in her face and to try to control her negative reactions and feelings towards Pip.

The April winds blew, and Dolly welcomed them. She was too angry to have a definite plan and eventually she found she had walked into town. The anger within her dissipated and she was left feeling quite numb. She made her way to the book shop, reasoning that she would get the same comfort from books that she had all her life. The shop appeared quite empty and the shopkeeper just nodded and went back to his own reading. Dolly scanned the shelves, trying to decide which subject would clear her mind and take her pain away. "India, that's it, I will read about India to be close to Rett," she thought, picking up an illustrated travel book.

From behind the book stacks a man started to speak in a soft voice, with a heavy French accent:

I will make you brooches and toys for your delight

I will make my kitchen, and you shall keep your room.

Dolly stopped what she was doing and impulsively replied;

And you shall wash your linen and keep your body white

In rainfall at morning and dewfall at night.

The French accent continued:

And this shall be for music when no one else is near,

The fine song for singing, the rare song to hear!

That only I remember, that only you admire,

Of the broad road that stretches and the roadside fire.

"Robert Louis Stevenson," Dolly smiled, as she identified the narrator in the next aisle. He was a handsome middle-aged man with slightly greying hair and a small moustache.

"S'il vous plait, Pierre Gravel, at your service Madame, and you are?"

"Dolly Marcum," Dolly stuttered.

"Pleased to make your acquaintance, Miss Dolly Marcum," Pierre gave an exaggerated bow, "you are very well versed in 19th century poetry, how refreshing."

Dolly blushed and was thankful for the schoolhouse library.

"What is a beautiful young lady doing out on a cold day like this?"

"I might well ask you the same question," Dolly replied.

"Touché, my dear. La bouche sourit mal quand les yeux sont en pleurs."

"I understood some of that sir, but what business is it of yours if I have tears in my eyes?" Dolly smiled, not at all offended by this fascinating stranger.

"Excusez-moi. I was so taken with you that I forgot myself," his words were polite but his eyes were sparkling with mischief. Dolly found him both fascinating and dangerously irresistible.

"Would you be so kind as to accompany a poor stranger in town to a local tea shop? I will just purchase these books and then was only to go along to my lonely hotel room. The company of such a beautiful cultured lady such as you will be the highlight of my trip."

Dolly was flattered and still quite angry with Pip so impulsively she said yes. At the tea rooms the two became acquainted. Pierre told her that he was a novelist promoting his new book, The Death of the Poet in English Culture. Dolly asked him so many questions about his writing that in the end Pierre good-naturedly changed the subject.

"Enough about me, my dear, I can see a sadness in your eyes. Please confide in a lonely stranger."

"Nothing to tell, really, Pierre. I suppose I am sad because my wedding has been postponed once again." Immediately Dolly wanted to withdraw the words. She was shocked she had confided in a stranger.

"That is not all is it? Il n'y a pas de verites moyennes, there are no half-truths, my dear, none that help anyway."

"Well, I think I am a little angry too." Now Dolly blushed.

"Mmm," was his reply, and Dolly carried on opening up her heart to this stranger. Dolly shared about missing her twin and the trauma of the last year.

"I miss my friend George and am still grieving. We once had something of an understanding when we were children."

"I can see where all the young gentlemen would be bowled over by your beauty."

Dolly was quite aware of Pierre's exaggerated flattery but she was so hungry for attention that she continued.

"Pip did not even come back to see Rett and his new wife, although they fought together in the war. His family seems to be his priority and that has me worried about our future together."

"Well, he is a cad that is all I can say. To leave such a beauty unattended for..."

"Five months."

"Five months must mean that the gentleman in question has lost his mind."

They both laughed and Dolly found Pierre so easy to talk to that she quite lost track of time. Pierre offered her a lift home and Dolly gratefully accepted, not giving a care as to what was 'right and proper'.

"Please Dolly, will you spend the day with me tomorrow? I am returning to France and I cannot bear it if you say no."

Dolly agreed to meet him the next day at ten in the morning at the same book shop.

That night Dolly felt no guilt, only excitement at the prospect of learning more about Pierre. She still was not asleep when she heard her father and great-aunt Daisy return from the theatre. She did feel she should go downstairs but felt that she wanted to enjoy her moment.

"What a difference a day makes," she thought, as she slipped into a wonderful sleep, the best she had experienced for months.

At breakfast the next day her father told Dolly that he had introduced Violet as his intended and Daisy was happy for them both. Daisy gave Dolly a lift into town and Dolly made some excuse about meeting a school friend for a day's shopping. She said goodbye to her great-aunt, who was returning home. She genuinely loved Daisy and knew that Daisy loved her.

"Goodbye dear, and make sure your young man treats you well, I am so sorry to have missed him. Maybe I will come for your wedding."

Daisy felt sad as she waved goodbye.

In the tea shop she saw Pierre before he saw her, and Dolly marvelled at his good looks. He was reading a newspaper and when he saw her he smiled and his eyes shone enough to light up a room.

"Miss Dolly, I cannot tell you how honoured I am to have your company. Would you like some tea or would you prefer to leave and explore the countryside?"

"Perhaps we should go now if we want to travel because storms are brewing in the North Sea and they can be brutal for the uninitiated."

"I think that I have seen those storms in France and we always curse the English for sending them to us."

The two left and started off driving around the town and some of the local sights. They visited the quay, and watched the fishing boats weigh anchor. They went to the park lake to see the Canada geese. They were so comfortable with each other they ventured further away into the countryside. They drove up to a small country pub where the roaring fire was a welcome interlude. Pierre had a beer and Dolly, unaccustomed to drinking,

233

just had a sherry. The innkeeper brought them some sandwiches and they did not stop talking. Pierre had been recently divorced and his marriage had fallen apart when his wife lost a child.

"No amount of caring and love could mend her broken heart. She pushed me away and eventually left me for another man. Raconteur tout serait impossible," Pierre broke into French trying to convey his pain. Dolly understood his meaning that it was impossible to explain everything that he felt at the time. "I am over it all now but I felt a double loss of her and the child so deeply that I did not write anything for many months."

"I can still see the pain in your eyes, Pierre," Dolly put her hand over his and he held her fingers gently.

"Let's get out of here. I am becoming far too morose for such an occasion," Pierre took her by the hand and they got back into the car.

They were many miles away from home, but it did not seem to matter to either of them. Pierre continued to drive when the heavens opened. He drove the best he could in the lightning and thunder, then he decided to take shelter in the dirt track next to an old barn. The two sat there for a while then they decided to make a run for the barn.

"At least we can wait it out more comfortably, and dry," Pierre reasoned.

They ran, laughing like two schoolchildren. Pierre forced the door open, and they went into the dry barn. For a while they watched the storm circle around through the half open door. Pierre explored further inside and found a wood-burning stove.

"This must have been for the baby sheep or calves if the snows came early," Dolly explained.

"Well, I think that my baby lamb could use some warmth right about now," Pierre replied affectionately.

After several attempts Pierre was successful at lighting a fire and before long they were warming themselves. Dolly removed her headscarf and coat, shaking off the rain and putting them on a wooden bench. Pierre came over to her and felt her hands. In turn he put each finger in his mouth and touched them with his hot moist lips, teasing them with his darting tongue.

"Ma cherie, you are freezing."

"No, I am warming up just fine, Pierre," Dolly replied breathlessly, trying to dismiss his familiarity.

It was too electric to ignore. Pierre was too close to her and Dolly shivered, not with cold but with longing.

"Dolly, ma cherie," Pierre felt it too. He held her head tenderly in his two hands and kissed her so sweetly that Dolly thought she had died and gone to Heaven. His lips gently brushed hers like the wings of a butterfly. She found that she was responding to his second kiss, which was more intense, and Pierre pulled her closer.

"Dolly, are you alright? Please tell me if you are not sure about this. I feel so attracted to you, you are exquisite," Pierre waited, holding his breath. "You are so beautiful."

Dolly could not help herself. After almost a year of unfulfilled longings, here was a man to whom she was unbelievably attracted.

Pierre continued to kiss her, each kiss holding more urgency than the one before. He laid her down on the barn floor and Dolly submitted to his caresses. He stroked her long black hair and kissed it. He kissed her neck and caressed her shoulders. He gently took her hand and again sucked on her fingers one by one, he kissed her in the palm of her hand. Dolly was caught up in the emotion. Pierre unbuttoned her blouse and to her surprise Dolly assisted him. He stood up and quickly removed his own clothes and joined her again. He removed the last of their clothing, at each movement kissing her body tenderly.

Dolly gasped. This was the first time she had seen a naked man, and the first time she had been naked in front of one. Momentarily she covered herself and Pierre sensing her hesitation, placed his jacket over her. He continued to caress her and Dolly was in a turmoil of emotion. Some primal instinct had reduced her body to a quivering pleasure-seeking organ, out of her control. At every new place Pierre kissed and caressed, he checked that Dolly was in accordance with events. He kissed her thighs and she felt his moustache as he moved about her mound of Venus. She gasped as his tongue found her secret place. He did not linger there long because he wanted to make love to this untouched, fascinating creature. He moved back up to her breast and Dolly felt she was about to explode.

"Pierre," she whispered as he straddled her in preparation to enter her.

"Pierre, this is..."

"I know, love and I will be very gentle with you. Here, put your arms around me and feel my manhood wanting you, loving you."

He pushed himself into her, and sensing her tenseness he stopped and waited for her to relax again.

"Dolly, my darling, je serai poet et toi poesie; I'll be the poet, and you, poetry. Just relax and feel my desire for you," he continued to croon to her in English and in French, until Dolly thought she would burst with longing. He pushed again, entering her secret place, loving her as no man had done before.

Dolly felt as though Pierre had split her in two. He stopped while she recovered from the initial pain. Slowly he started to move inside her and Dolly began to relax as he moved to and fro, transforming her from a child into a woman.

Pierre kissed her neck as she began to learn the dance of love. Before long Dolly felt herself moving in unison with Pierre. She had sensations she had never dreamed of and never wanted him to stop. She whimpered in ecstasy, throwing her head back and exposing her neck to his lips. Then as he brought her to a climax she screamed a little scream as she buried her head in his shoulder. Pierre stopped and kissed her on her lips.

"Dolly, is this alright with you, you are not hurt? I could not bear you to be hurt."

"Yes…I think so, I am not hurt."

Pierre did not stop for long, and continued his movements as he reached his own goal and, as he felt his climax approaching, he pulled out of her and sighed as ecstasy engulfed him. Dolly knew she was in love with him. He stayed perfectly still for a while and Dolly could feel his heart beating fast and then more slowly. He seemed to be at peace as he lay in her arms. After some time, slowly he moved away from her. Dolly knew that she had changed, that for the rest of her life she would remember this moment.

"My baby lamb, are you alright, I am sorry, did I hurt you? Dolly, speak to me," he kissed her lips tenderly. Dolly opened her eyes.

"Pierre, I am too happy to talk. Do you feel it? Do you realize that I will remember this moment the rest of my life?"

"I do hope so, cherie, I do not intend to let you go, ever."

They lay together in the aftermath of love. There were no intruding thoughts about any life outside of the barn.

Eventually it was Pierre who broke the spell.

"The rain seems to have stopped."

"I will love the rain from this day on," Dolly smiled.

They roused themselves and dressed. Dolly started to return to reality. Although she had no regrets she was unsure of where to go from here. Pierre, sensing her dilemma said, "Dolly, I have to return to France tomorrow, but may I write to you?"

"I would like that very much, Pierre. Will you ever return here?" She waited, holding her breath.

"We will see how things progress, my love. Let us take some time. You need to know your true feelings for your fiancé, and I need to get over my loss."

"I understand that, Pierre."

"I want you to know, Dolly, that you are a bright light in my dark world."

As they drove back to town Pierre held Dolly's hand and they said little as they basked in the feelings of satisfied lust. Pierre drove Dolly home and, as she was getting out of the car, he handed her "a package".

"This is my latest book, Dolly. I would be honoured if you would read it and let me know your thoughts."

Dolly was elated. She knew he really did want her to write to him. He kissed her hand and drove away. Dolly stood in the farmhouse driveway and watched as the car became a speck in the distance. There was, thankfully, no one home and she went straight to her room to open the parcel. As she did so a sheet of paper fell to the floor. She picked it up and she read it.

My dearest Dolly, whatever happens between us today I want you to know that I have feelings for you far stronger than is prudent after such a short acquaintance. Maybe that is what love is? I am still hurting from my recent loss, so please have patience with me and I hope we will be more than just friends with each other in time,

Your new friend, Pierre.

Dolly realized that he had written this message to her the night before and had included his mailing address in France. She held the letter close to her heart while she opened his book and read.

It was after midnight when Mathew returned from the hospital. Anthony was his weekend guest. He was waiting up with a drink of whisky, waiting for his lover's return. Mathew looked as white as a sheet and Anthony helped him off with his coat.

"It looks as if you need a drink and a hot bath, Mat."

"That would be wonderful, Totey, thank you."

Anthony ran the bath and as Mathew lowered himself into the healing hot water Anthony refilled his glass. He took it to Mat and saw that he had his eyes closed. Anthony knelt beside him as Mat started to explain.

"A young boy is in the hospital and he is unconscious. He is a small child, about eight years old. His name is Nicholas Brown."

Mat opened his eyes as tears escaped down his cheeks. "Totey, he was sexually assaulted and tortured to within an inch of his life."

Although shocked at this news, Anthony did not say anything; he just stroked Mathew's hair. He softly kissed his neck. It took a few minutes for Mat to continue.

"He is so little and now, even if he recovers, he is damaged for life. I have seen some things, Totey, but

239

this is the worst I have ever seen. That poor child had been bound and tortured..." Mat took a gulp from his glass, "Why Totey, why?"

"Some sick son of a bitch. Could it be the Hastings fellow?"

"The police are searching for him but he is still out there."

Mathew finished his bath and donned a robe. They both went into the kitchen to refill their glasses.

"Were there any witnesses?" continued Anthony, after a while.

"Apparently the child was in the park with his four-year old sister. She told the police that a 'nice man' asked them both to show him where the lake was, but she didn't want to leave the swings, thank God."

"Was she able to describe him?"

"Remember she is only four and her description did not match John Hastings, but he could have disguised himself. Oh! I don't know, Totey, the world is so sick at times. A young boy, disfigured and ruined for life, it might be a blessing if he dies."

"I don't think his parents would agree though, they would want him to live no matter what."

"A young couple were walking in the woods and they discovered him naked and tied by his hands to a tree, it appears they disturbed his attacker. The police said that the couple heard footsteps running away. A few minutes sooner and they would have seen him, the sick son of a bitch."

"Shush Mat; try not to think about it. You are a great paediatrician and surgeon and if anyone can save him it is you."

"I have to change and get back there, Totey. They are running more tests. They are trying to match blood

240

types. I need to get back to operate. I just came home to change, and steady my nerves."

"I understand. I will come with you for a while and keep you company."

"Totey, what would I do without your love?"

"Oh I don't know, there are a few nurses of both genders that would fill the gap."

Mat threw a wet flannel at Anthony and they laughed. This was just what Mathew needed to lift his mood, he had an important job to do.

John Hastings was drunk. He staggered down the alley in the worse part of town. He was clever enough to have removed all trappings of his station before venturing on the streets. Last night he had visited a whore house, but remembered none of the details and today he was set on even more seedier pursuits in the docks area. He was on the prowl for excitement and he knew where to find it. As he stood relieving himself against the side of the building he heard voices approaching. Slyly he drew back into the shadows, and drunk as he was, he did not move.

"Come er' luv, gimme a bit of luvin'," a male voice growled. John smiled because he loved to be a voyeur. He expected to see some action. He hid further behind a pile of scrap metal and boxes, discarded at the side of the building. He quietly started to button his fly but thought again and exposed himself as he anticipated some sexual excitement. He had difficulty steadying himself and he leaned against the wall.

In the half light he saw a large man wearing a sailor's uniform, and an earing in his ear caught the glow of the moon. John could see he was covered in tattoos.

John tried to keep his breathing shallow to avoid detection.

"Don't be shy my dear, just give me some loving and I will see you're alright", the big sailor cajoled.

"That's good, be good to daddy, here like this…"

John sniggered under his breath. He stayed as still as he could while at the same time pleasuring himself. He had a clear view from his vantage point. The big sailor turned and his partner was now facing John. The youngster was less than eighteen years old. John got so excited that in his drunken, compromised state, he fell sideward into the scrap heap.

"Who's there?" the big sailor shouted as he pulled up his bellbottoms. He recovered quickly and headed straight towards the sound, the young boy followed, equally alarmed. They found John on the ground trapped between the wall and the scrap pile.

"Get him Gregg," the younger one said, as he followed him towards John.

Gregg pulled John to his feet and they both assaulted him unmercifully. John was too drunk to defend himself. He was a puppet passed between the two sailors as they punished him. The last punch threw him backwards, back into the scrap pile, and a shard of metal pierced him between his shoulders. The sailors quickly left the alley and joined the others on the quay. They mingled and, keeping their cool, they joined their ships as if nothing had occurred.

It took nearly two weeks before John Hastings was found, but without any identification the authorities could not inform his family. The investigation by the authorities into his death was only half-heartedly carried out; believing as they did that this was a sexual quarrel in the seedier part of the London quay.

Dolly received three letters at the same time. Grateful that her father was working she hurried up to her room to open them. The first letter she read was from Pierre.

April 16th 1919

My dearest baby lamb,

This is my third attempt to write to you and I thought that perhaps the madrigal by John Dowland will only begin to address my growing feelings for you,

Come away, come, sweet love,
The golden morning breaks,
All the earth, all the air
Of love and pleasure speaks,
Teach thine arms then to embrace,
And sweet rosy lips to kiss,
And mix our souls in mutual bliss.
Eyes were made for beauty's grace,
Viewing, rueing love's long pain,
Procur'd by beauty's rude disdain.

I cannot stop thinking about our short time together and I truly believe that through you I will once again learn to live in this mundane world. My pain of loss is lessened and I can only hope that your decision includes me in your future life.

Love Pierre.

Pierre's letter brought a smile to Dolly's lips and she lay down on the bed, clutching his letter to her heart. She daydreamed about the rain and the barn and almost forgot the letter from Pip. Dolly sighed in her confusion and opened Pip's letter.

April 19th 1919

Darling Dolly,

At last my father's business is concluded and I am on my way back to you. We can now make plans for our wedding. I was so sorry to have missed Everett but I will be there in time for your father's marriage to Violet. Europe is still devastated in the aftermath of war and I will be pleased to speak in English once again. I am getting tired of speaking either French or German, although in business in Europe it is an asset. I will arrive on Tuesday next week, around the 26th.

I love you, Pip.

Dolly felt very uncomfortable. She was no longer sure she wanted to marry Pip. She had presumed she would come to their marriage bed a virgin and now everything had changed. She briefly thought that Pip had never quoted poetry to her, neither had he been a great reader. She was also shocked when he said "to speak English once again"; she was not aware he spoke any other languages. She realized that they knew very little about each other. The third letter was from India and addressed to both her and her father. She ripped it open and Rett wrote:

March 1st 1919

My dear father and Dolly,

Gita is having a child. We are thrilled and can't wait to be parents. We are hoping for a boy but if we have a girl we won't be too disappointed because we intend to fill this big plantation with lots of little Marcums. Thankfully Gita's family is here to help her. Since we returned, Baxter and his family have returned to England for six months, I have been working long hours. I hope one day to see you here, at least for a visit, I miss you both.

This will probably be the last letter you receive before your wedding, father, so may we both wish you and Violet all the very best. You need the comfort of a sweet woman and Mam would be happy that you have her. Don't overdo the farm work, dad, because you need to take life a little easier now that the finances are better. The plantation is doing well and we are assured of a good life, so enjoy it both of you.

Love, Rett and Gita.

The news that Everett was to be a father brightened Dolly's mood and she ran to tell her father. Albert was busy in the barn and Dolly blurted out,

"Daddy, you are going to be a grandfather, Gita is having a baby, isn't it great news?"

Albert stopped what he was doing and swirled Dolly around in glee.

"A grandfather? Maybe Violet doesn't want to marry an old grandfather?"

"Dad, you are not old and you forget that Violet is already a grandmother."

"So she is child, well, well, well, a grandfather eh!"

Albert and Dolly strode arm in arm back to the farmhouse to toast the future new addition to their family. Dolly completely forgot to tell him that Pip arrived on Tuesday.

Later that night Dolly was staring into the fire. She was daydreaming about getting on a ship and travelling around the world, India first of course. As her father handed her a cup of tea she suddenly remembered Pip was coming. She sat upright,

"Dad I forgot, Pip will be here next Tuesday." She paused. "I am a little confused and I don't know what to do about it. I wish with all my heart that Mam was here."

"Child, I do too, but I am here, and maybe if it is too delicate to talk to me, Violet will help."

"Of course, I will talk to Violet; she is so kind and understanding. I wanted to talk to Nan but she seems so busy with Marcus and Grace. They are planning to marry in the autumn. I don't want to spoil her happiness; God knows she needs to be happy after what John Hastings did to her. You must know by now, daddy, that I am having second thoughts about marriage at this time."

"Could this have anything to do with a certain gentleman from France?" Albert smiled.

"How… oh of course, poppa, it is not a secret. I have someone who writes to me, someone I met in town one day. His name is Pierre."

"Pierre? Must be something if he has captured my daughter's interest," he teased, squeezing her hand. "Does Pip know?"

"I think he senses something and I don't know what to tell him. It isn't that I don't love him but right now I am confused."

"Take your time, poppet," Albert used her childhood nickname, which he hadn't used since her mother died. She sat at his feet and he stroked the top of her hair.

"Whatever you decide, luv, there is no hurry."

Dolly sat there in silence, watching the embers of the fire dart and splutter little sparks which looked like dancing stars.

The next morning Violet came to the farm with little Grace. Nan was working so they had a habit of spending time at the farmhouse and Albert popped in to see them between chores. After breakfast Albert left to see to his livestock.

"Violet, may I talk to you about a personal matter?" Dolly asked.

"Of course, child, I will soon be family and if I can help in any way I will, you know that."

"You see, Pip is to come back on Tuesday and he is expecting to pick up where we left off last November, six months ago."

"And you are not sure?"

"Exactly, I am not sure now. I was before he left but I seem to want something different now."

"Or someone different?" Violet asked astutely.

Dolly was shocked at Violet's understanding of the situation. She started to sob and Violet put her arms around her.

"Come on child, it can't be so bad. If you need more time to decide then take it. God knows Pip has taken his time."

Dolly blew her nose.

"You see, six months ago I thought Pip was all I ever wanted. I am beginning to realize that we don't know each other well. I didn't even know he spoke French and German, how pathetic is that?"

"You need more time, child. No one will rush you."

"I have met another man, a Frenchman who is a famous novelist and quotes poetry to me."

"And this you find romantic, and more to your liking, I see. What I do know, Dolly, is that you are a worldly girl and your father worries that you would not be happy unless you experienced more of the world."

"Yes and Pip is so, so ordinary. Oh! Violet, I sound so ungrateful. Pip does love me but I think we see our future together in different ways."

Violet comforted Dolly and baby Grace crawled up on Dolly's knee. They both laughed as Grace kissed her cheeks.

"Grace, you are a blessing to us," Violet said.

Dolly took her little hand, and they left for the barn.

"Let us go and find the baby chicks, Grace."

Pip arrived as planned and settled into the farmhouse. They had no time to talk privately until the next day. Dolly suggested they walk into town to buy some supplies for her father's wedding. As they walked Pip held her hand and occasionally pulled her close to him.

"I am sensing something, Dolly, something has changed. Talk to me, my darling, I am very nervous."

"Pip, I don't know how to put everything into words, every time I formulate a phrase it sounds wrong… it has changed Pip. Not that I am saying we will not marry but I do need more time to get to know you more."

"I knew it, my love. I know that six months apart is too long. I am devastated that you are having doubts. When I was away from you I missed you and wanted you to be my wife more than anything, but you must be sure that this is what you want too. I don't want to lose you."

Pip stopped walking and pulled her close. He kissed her gently on the lips and Dolly responded. She did not feel the overwhelming desire she had felt for him in the past, or even close to the desire she felt when Pierre kissed her, but she still loved him, she was sure of that.

"Thank you, Pip, for giving me time, maybe if we get to really know each other more it will all work out."

"I will stay for a week and will win back your heart, just wait and see. I will stay until after your father's wedding and then I have to return to give my father an update from Europe. He has papers still to sign."

"I understand, Pip, and look forward to the next week with you. Maybe we will sort out why I feel this way… Pip?"

"Yes, my darling?"

"Oh never mind, it will wait." Dolly genuinely meant it when she said she loved him and she held his hand as they continued into town. Later that night she could not sleep, and felt she was a coward not to have been honest with Pip. It was such a mess.

In her journal she wrote,

April 29th 1919

Today my life seems surreal. I wish that I were two people. Pip does not deserve a wife who has been unfaithful and yet my relationship with Pierre is not the whole reason I am unsure about marriage to Pip. I know I love him but I want Pierre. There now, I have said it. In Pierre's arms I am alive; I need that passion in my life. How is it possible to be sad and happy at the same time?

Albert and Violet were wed on May 1st, May Day, and it seemed the whole town was part of the celebrations. The maypole was up on the village green and the Morris dancers entertained. Violet looked beautiful in her cream dress with a garland of flowers in her curly grey hair. At the insistence of Nan she wore a little rouge and did not look a day over thirty. Albert was a nervous groom, constantly asking Dolly if he looked alright. "Dad, you look so handsome, I would marry you myself," Dolly laughed.

Marcus was honoured to be asked to walk Violet down the aisle. Nan was her bridesmaid, wearing a modest beige suit and carrying spring flowers.

Reverend Simon conducted the ceremony and Marcus preached the sermon. The village needed a happy event after all the tragedy and they made the best of it. The men were getting drunk and singing old songs and the women were dancing up a storm and chatting happily to each other. The children were running around the maypole and playing, enjoying the warm spring weather after the harsh winter. Dolly kept herself busy away from Pip, not avoiding him exactly, but making sure her father's wedding ran smoothly. Nan and Grace were to stay at the farm that night and Violet and her father were to spend their first night at Violet's house. The villagers had great fun decorating the outside with streamers and balloons.

After the exhausting day Nan, Pip and Dolly were enjoying a moment of peace around the fire. Marcus was back at the vicarage as he had taken over Simon's place for a couple of days.

"Any news on John Hastings?" Pip asked.

"Mother heard from the detective that they found a body in London that may be him. Dolly, I did not want to spoil the wedding telling you this, but since Pip asked..."

"It's alright, Nan. How do they know it might be him?"

"Well, his landlady in London reported him missing after he did not return. He owed her rent so she looked in his room and realized he had been missing a while. Apparently there were photographs and other forms of identification in his room and they are looking for a match."

"Are you alright, Nan?" Dolly asked.

"Absolutely, I hope it is him that is dead. I will breathe easier that he will not return for Grace. I am watching her closely, thinking he will take her."

Dolly remembered his actions in the park but thought it best not to share this with Nan.

"Does Vicky know?"

"I shouldn't think so, it was only two days ago."

"She will know when they report it to his brother. I hope she will not be too stressed at the news, she is how many months pregnant?" Nan asked Dolly.

"Seven or eight, I believe."

The trio talked for some time and baby Grace was sleeping on the couch.

"I will go to bed now," Nan said as she picked up her daughter.

"Goodnight, Nan," said Pip.

Dolly got up and gave Nan a kiss and gently kissed Grace on her forehead.

"She is an angel, everyone's child."

"Yes and for that she is blessed," Nan went up the stairs to bed.

"Are you tired, Dolly?" Pip asked.

"A little."

Pip came closer to Dolly and put his arms around her, but he did not try anything further.

The news had indeed reached the Hastings at their hotel in Bath. The detective wanted identification and David Hastings explained that John had three rather distinct scars on his body. He also had a birthmark on his right shoulder that turned out to be identical to the one on the corpse, so confirmation that it was his brother was made. David Hastings excused himself when the detective left and went for a walk. He did not know how to feel. He seemed devoid of an appropriate response. A year ago he would have grieved but today there was some relief that John could not hurt anyone else. He turned a corner and almost ran into Robin and Victoria.

"Oh my! Your mother and I had completely forgotten you were arriving today," David stuttered, never the diplomat.

"Papa, that is so unlike you. You look ill, what is wrong?" Victoria was alarmed.

Robin took Victoria's arm and they all went back to the hotel. As they entered the room they saw Katherine in tears.

"I am sorry, it was such a shock," she started to explain.

"What is a shock mama? Papa?"

"The detective has just left and I… we had to identify Uncle John… you see, Vicky, he has died."

David went over to his daughter and led her to sit down.

"Oh! I see," was all Victoria could muster.

"Good riddance," Robin announced, banging his hand on the desk.

David and Katherine looked shocked, so Robin looked at Victoria. "May I?"

"They should know now," Victoria said in a whisper.

"Know what?" David asked.

"Sir, the baby that Vicky is carrying is, in all probability not mine, there is no gentle way to say it."

Victoria started to cry and her mother went to her.

"What is this nonsense, Vicky?"

"It's true. One night in the summerhouse after Robin and I had a little spat, Uncle John came in and…and…"

"No, no you would have told us," her mother said.

"I couldn't because Uncle John said he was watching Robin and I being… being intimate."

"Oh my God, so he raped you?" her father realized.

"But the child could be yours, Robin?" asked her mother, hopefully.

"Perhaps, we both pray that it is mine. No one will ever know but due to the circumstances of John's death we wanted you to know his true character."

252

"Oh, I think we already knew his true character, but there are some things he was accused of that I find hard to believe, such as young children, that is not his... shall I say 'taste?'"

David went to pour them all a drink. He rang for tea for Victoria.

After a sombre supper together David announced that they were returning home to Cotter's Marsh. Victoria had cheered up a little and asked if she and Robin could come and visit them.

"Child, you are our daughter and now that the baby is coming soon we both want to see a lot more of you... both," her mother said, only now realizing just how much Robin loved Victoria.

"Have you found a house yet, Robin?"

"No sir. I was thinking that perhaps we will find some land and build one to our liking. Victoria is constantly talking about how she would furnish it, and a nursery, aren't you dear?"

"I can't wait to get started; it will be some time before we can do that though."

"Why don't you both take a wing of the manor house for your own apartments while you decide?" David proposed. "Your mother and I speak of it often."

Victoria put her arms around him and kissed his cheek. "What do you think, Robin, could you bear to live in a small village again?"

"Whatever will make you happy dear, all I want is for you and the baby to be around loving people."

"Then it's settled, you will be home in time for the birth," said her delighted mother, all gloomy thoughts of John dissipated as they planned for the new baby.

Anthony was getting quite a name for himself as the village doctor. His father was only too willing to give up

253

the limelight to his son. It was Anthony who went on home visits while his father was based in the surgery most days. Everyone loved Anthony. He was called to Nan's house one evening because Grace had a fever. After examining her he reassured a worried mother and grandmother that the fever would soon pass and the child was going to be fine.

"Stay for a while, Anthony," asked Nan. "I miss you."

"Life is so busy, Nan, I barely have time for my family. I would love to stay for a while, you were my last visit today."

They settled down in the kitchen near the fire and Nan poured them a brandy.

"Are you excited about your wedding, Nan?"

"Oh, Anthony, I never thought I would be worthy of someone's love after what happened to me."

"Marcus is getting a gift in you and a bonus gift in Grace."

"He seems to be very attached to her."

"But?"

"It's just that... oh, never mind it is silly."

"Come on, Nan, I have known you long enough for us to be honest with each other."

"Well, he doesn't try to be more than friends, you know, he doesn't try to be intimate."

"Perhaps he respects you and is afraid to push things intimately after your trauma."

"I thought that might be it."

"But you love him?"

"Yes, he is the sweetest and kindest man." "Then I am sure it will work out. Watch him after the wedding though, you may not be able to handle all that affection," they both laughed.

"Anthony, while we are being honest with each other, what about you?"

"What do you mean, Nan?"

"I think you know, you and Mat, are you more than friends?"

Anthony got up and poured himself another brandy and he reached to refill Nan's glass but she gestured no. He sat down again and took a swig.

"The answer to that is yes, we are more than friends, does that bother you?"

"Are you happy, is that life the life you want?"

"Yes and yes."

"Then I am happy that you are happy, although to be honest I wanted to see you married with children. Does anyone else know?"

"I think my father suspects but we don't talk about it. Nan, when we were in London there was a freedom that would never be possible in Cotter's Marsh."

"Are you serious about moving there?"

"Well, I don't want to leave here and Mat has agreed that we should take two or three holidays a year and then he can cope the rest of the time."

"I like Mat and we all see how much he cares about you."

They were interrupted by Violet, who had come to stay overnight because of Grace being ill.

"What was that about Mat? Is he coming soon?"

"No mam, we were just chatting, just like old times. I miss our talks."

"Then fight to keep your friends dear even after you marry. My friends were a great comfort to me."

"I have to go now ladies, thank you for the drink and fire, they were most comforting," and he turned to wink at Nan. "Everything in its own time."

The weather was hot. The summer was full on and everyone was struggling to keep cool. The parks were full of people picnicking near the lakes and children were playing in the water, to the distress of the resident ducks. Mat was sat on his usual bench as Anthony approached him.

"Lunch old boy," he said chirpily.

Mat did not smile with his eyes just with a slight movement of his lips. Anthony gave him the sandwiches and sat beside him.

"Oh dear, I see we are distracted, what is it?"

"Hello, Totey, thanks for the lunch. I need this." Mat started to open the food.

"So what is the dark mood about?"

"How well you know me."

"Well, it's been a while now, so yes I do know you, especially your 'front office smile'."

"Another young boy was just brought in to the hospital, too late I'm afraid."

"What? But John Hastings is dead!"

"Yes, and he was dead when the other child was attacked as well."

"How is that child?"

"He survived, but at what cost. He will live that trauma for the rest of his life."

"And the one from today?"

"Found in the east end of the marshes by a fisherman, half submerged in the sea. He couldn't have survived that brutality."

"God help us, we thought it would all stop with Hastings' death."

Dolly was on the marshes. She loved being outdoors in the summer months. Her correspondence with Pierre continued and he talked to her in his letters about his healing process and his life as a writer.

I can be a writer anywhere in the world, my baby lamb, and if I had you at my side we would fly together on the wings of love.

Corny, yes, she thought, but so much from his heart that she wanted desperately to see him again. Dolly sat on a rock and looked out to sea. The gulls were noisily diving for fish and the breeze caressed her. She was transformed to a world apart from the mundane, a world that, although exterior to her, was also part of her. She pushed her long hair up into her hat and languished in the sun, closing her eyes. She was sad and lonely for Pierre.

"Plus le visage est serieux, plus le sourire est beau. So this is where you have been since the cold of winter," said a French accent.

Dolly nearly fell off her rock in shock and Pierre put out his arms to hold her.

"My baby lamb, are you not happy to see me?"

"I... I... how did you get here?"

"The usual way, ship and car," he teased.

"Pierre, I have missed you so much," her words stifled in a passionate kiss. He held her close and eventually they sat down on the rock. He removed her sun hat and kissed her face.

They made love there on the deserted marshes and afterwards Pierre asked her if she had settled anything about Pip.

"I am such a coward, Pierre. I told him half a truth and he said he would wait patiently until I was sure."

"And are you sure?"

"Up until this moment I did not know my own mind. Yes, my love, I am sure."

"Baby lamb, will you do me the honour to be my wife?" Pierre was so emotional he struggled to find the words in English.

"Yes... yes... darling Pierre, from the first moment you recited poetry to me I was to be your wife."

They embraced and kissed once again but Dolly stopped another intimate encounter.

"Pierre, we will be seen. I am out of my mind with love."

"Me too, baby lamb."

"What of you? Pierre, are you over your loss?"

"I was sure that I was over my loss, long before I asked you to marry me. I have been waiting for you to break away from Pip."

The lovers went back to the farmhouse. Albert was out in the barn but Violet was there.

"Ah, the mystery man," she smiled.

Pierre bent to kiss her hand and Violet made a display about being honoured and became giggly.

"Well, Dolly, I see what you mean, how can you resist such a charmer?"

They waited for Albert to return and Albert was just as gracious as Violet had been.

"All I can see, young man, is the look on my daughter's face. Anyone who can bring that much happiness to her is alright in my book."

Pierre had booked into the hotel in town and it was thought to be more prudent that he not stay at the farmhouse.

"I will write to Pip tonight so there will be no misunderstandings," she told them all.

"I will take my leave of you now, and perhaps you will all join me tomorrow for Sunday dinner at the hotel?"

"Do you mean all of us, Nan and Grace included?" Dolly asked.

"I don't think Nan will be joining us, she is going on a picnic with Marcus," Violet intervened.

"A picnic, what a wonderful idea, perhaps we should do that instead so we can enjoy your changeable English weather," Pierre winked at Dolly and, remembering the rainstorm, she blushed.

"That sounds wonderful, Pierre, we will be honoured to join you."

"Good, then I will make arrangements for the food and will pick you up at noon."

"Make it one so we can go to church," asked Violet.

"One it is."

Dolly saw him to his car and he gave her a sweet kiss and drove slowly away.

"I don't want to go...," he shouted and Dolly laughed.

However, that night she was not laughing when she sat down to write a farewell letter to Pip. Of late their correspondence had been less frequent and rather stilted, but Dolly knew that the slightest encouragement from her would have been enough for him to marry her. It took many hours to write and she used almost a whole writing pad until she had the best combination of caring and rejection. It was two in the morning but she still wrote in her journal,

July 1st 1919

Today was a day that I had to put my own needs before another's. Pip is a good man and yet I have broken his heart. He did nothing wrong and yet I turned away from him into the arms of Pierre, a foreigner, a man who challenges me intellectually and who is far from predictable. The woman who eventually becomes

Pip's wife will be a very lucky woman. Tonight I will spend thinking about Pip and our love for the last time. I will indulge myself in self loathing and then when the sun comes up I will be truly and totally for Pierre.

Chapter 9

Two days later Dolly was walking arm in arm with Pierre. They were headed to the market to buy some things at Violet's request.

"Dolly, Dolly, it's Vicky," shouted a voice from over the crowd; Victoria appeared large as life with a belly proudly displayed in front of her. Almost running to keep up was Robin.

"Don't run, Vicky, it's so bad for you," he panted as he caught up.

"Stuff and nonsense, I didn't want to miss you Dolly."

After a heart-felt hug introductions were made. The men shook hands and then let the ladies walk ahead while they lagged behind talking politics.

"When is the baby due, Vicky?" asked Dolly.

"Anytime now," she beamed.

"Well, it certainly suits you being pregnant. Are you having an easy time?"

"The baby is no trouble at all, apart from the incessant heartburn," Vicky laughed.

"I am sorry we did not attend your wedding, Vicky, was it fun?"

"Not really, mama and papa were furious under the circumstances, but Robin is so sweet and has won their hearts."

She had not told Dolly any other details about how and by whom the baby was conceived.

"Are you staying here now?"

"Yes, we are converting a wing at the manor house. I am so excited and you must come and help me Dolly. How are Nan and Grace? I have written to them and the trust is set up for Grace but our letters seem to be 'polite', for lack of a better word."

"Yes, I understand that. Nan was very upset when you left and she once told me she felt abandoned, first Rett and George and then Joan becoming a nun, and then you running off to be married. She needs stability around her, I think."

"I will make it up to her. We now both have a child so that should help her to forgive me."

The foursome spent a pleasant hour and went to the tea room to rest, due to Victoria's condition.

"Tell me how you met," asked Victoria. Robin rolled his eyes.

"Only a woman would ask that, Pierre. I really don't understand the species, do you?" they all laughed. Victoria did not ask what had happened to Dolly's engagement to Pip and she made a mental note to ask Dolly when they were alone. They all seemed to get along well and when they separated Dolly asked to be informed the minute the baby came.

"Any day now," Robin put a protective arm around Victoria.

"Can't wait to get my figure back and go dancing again," she said. Dolly noted the pained look on Robin's face.

After they had left, Pierre and Dolly remained in the tea shop and Dolly explained the relationship between her and Victoria.

"A social papillon, I mean butterfly. She seems quite self-centred, although I can see you are good friends," Pierre remarked.

"Pierre, you are so astute. Yes, Vicky is self-absorbed but in a crunch she comes through. She set up a small trust fund for Grace, she didn't have to, she genuinely wanted to."

"Petite lamb, I am not criticizing your friend, merely making an observation."

"I know, Pierre, but I do so want you to like my friends."

Pierre reached across the table and held her hand.

"If you have chosen them as your friends then I will adore them, my sweet," and he smiled his wonderful smile and kissed her hand.

Gita went into labour and Everett went into panic. The house staff were all running around with no direction and although they were all briefed on what to do, they forgot, due to temporary insanity.

"Go and get her parents," Everett at last started to take charge.

"Rett darling, I have hours yet, please calm down."

Briefly Everett was back in the trenches in France, not having a clear direction to go and being frightened beyond reason.

"Gita, what can I do?"

"Nothing dear, just leave it all to the midwife. The doctor must be..." she went into a contraction and Everett held her, she pushed him away.

"I will get the doctor... no I will send Timir for the doctor, that's it and I will ask the house staff to boil

263

water," he left Gita who hadn't heard a word through her pain.

An hour later things were calming down. Gita's parents had arrived, and her mother took charge while her father took Everett into the study to wait. They watched as people went to and fro around them, ignoring them and everyone seemed to know what they were doing. At one point the cook brought them some food but neither of them touched it. It was nine hours later when the doctor came in to tell Everett that he had a son. He paused and added, "And a daughter." Everett lost the use of his legs and thumped down on the large leather chair.

"Congratulations, dad," Gita's father shook his hand enthusiastically.

"And congratulations to you too, grandfather."

"So I am, so I am."

After the women had finished their work Everett was allowed in the bedroom to see his beloved wife. She was propped up on many fluffy pillows with a fresh pink nightdress on, holding two bundles in her arms. Everett stood momentarily at the door thinking that she had never looked more beautiful or been so loved.

"Gita, I love you so much. We were all so worried, are you alright?"

"I couldn't be better, Rett, are you pleased?"

Everett answered her with a kiss. He looked at the babies and laughed as they resembled little old purple people.

"They will fill out, I promise," Gita laughed along with him.

"What shall we call them?" Everett asked. "We only planned on one name."

"What about after your mother?" Gita suggested.

"I think that is a great idea, and the boy can be named after your brother, Sanja. Eleanor and Sanja it is. Wonderful, wonderful."

Gita's room filled up with visitors and after some minutes her mother asked them all to leave her to sleep.

"You too, Rett my boy, let her sleep, she has done a marvellous job today. The nurse will take the babies to the nursery. Go... shoo."

Everett kissed his wife and the foreheads of his children and went back into the study. The men did not sleep right away but talked about politics, the textile strikes, and the growing movement for independence from British rule.

"Keep your workers happy, son, they will work for you if you are fair."

"That was what Baxter said before he left. He should be back next month. I feel overwhelmed at times. George's death really affected us and Baxter's absence is felt at ground level. The crops are doing well though, and this year should be a bumper year."

"Make sure you prepare for the lean years, then."

"I have every intention of that sir, now I have children. Did you hear that, 'children'," they both laughed and talked of more pleasant things.

That night before he actually went to sleep Everett wrote to his father and sister telling of his good news.

The screams at the manor could be heard throughout the house. Victoria did not take well to childbirth. She struggled and did not listen to the doctor or nurse as they tried to guide her through her contractions. Robin was at a loss how to help her. As he approached her she threw her arms out and hit him right in the eye.

"Get away from me you... you."

265

Poor Robin left the bedroom and sulked in the kitchen. The kindly old cook gave him a cup of tea and tried to reassure him that childbirth affected women a different way.

"Eeh, master Robin don't take it so hard, Missus will be her old self again soon."

"I know, Madge, but I can't help her."

"The doctor's there and that is who she needs right now."

Robin picked up his cup of tea and went to the study, where he found David and Katherine, her parents.

"Well, me boy, it's time."

"Yes. I don't know what to do."

"Sit here and talk to us, Robin dear," Katherine patted the couch.

The hours dragged on and Katherine went to see how things had progressed. When she came back she said that Victoria did not want anyone in the room except the medical staff, she was visibly hurt.

"Everyone deals with childbirth differently," offered Robin, mimicking the cook.

"Yes dear, I know, but she is having a difficult time."

"Sit here, dear," David patted the seat next to him, "and don't worry, they know what they are doing."

"I suppose so, it's the waiting that is hard."

"What names have you picked out?" asked David, trying to lighten the mood.

"Well, Vicky likes Edward for a boy and if it's a girl she wants to call her Anne."

Katherine noticed he didn't say 'we'. They continued to wait for another four hours until the screams ceased and the doctor came into the room.

"Well, son, you are the proud father of a daughter."

They all stood up and joyfully congratulated each other. The relief was short-lived, however, as the doctor continued,

"Unfortunately Victoria will not be able to have children again. To have another child will result in her death. There was internal damage that will heal this time but she will not survive another pregnancy. You have a healthy daughter, though."

They all stared at the doctor and then at each other. Katherine was the first to react. Tears ran down her cheeks and she went over to David for comfort.

"History repeats itself, David. That is the same thing that we endured, and now my beautiful daughter is suffering the same fate."

"There, there dear, we have enjoyed having the one child, although we did not intend to spoil her so," he smiled.

"No more children?" Robin asked.

"I'm afraid not."

Katherine went to him and put her arms around him.

"But you have a daughter, Robin, a daughter," and she hoped that it was his daughter and not John's, and she also knew that Robin was thinking the same.

"Would you like to see your wife?" the doctor asked.

The child was wrapped up in a pink blanket and was in a bassinet at the side of Victoria's bed. She was sleeping soundly. Robin kissed her, trying not to disturb her. Robin gently looked at the baby. He stifled a sob as she had the beginnings of blonde curly hair.

"Babies change rapidly, she has baby fluff right now, all babies have this, it means nothing," lied Katherine as she looked over his shoulder and caught his gasp.

"She is beautiful," he whispered.

"Just like her mother," David added.

They left Victoria to sleep while an army of nurses fussed around. Robin retired to his room for a while and wept.

Pierre had to leave once again for France and Dolly was beside herself with worry. They decided that they would take one last picnic before he returned. Dolly was getting dressed appropriately for the inclement weather, when she looked out of her window. Coming up the drive was Robin, alone and in a great hurry. Dolly ran downstairs and opened the front door just as Robin reached it.

"Hello Robin, this is a pleasant surprise. Why didn't you drive? How are Vicky and the baby?"

"Dolly they are fine, I wanted to clear my head and before I knew it I was walking up to the farm, well..., can I talk to you for a minute?"

"Of course, please come in."

Dolly took him into the study where Pierre was reading a book and, sensing that Robin needed privacy, Pierre excused himself. Dolly asked Robin if he wanted a drink even though it was morning.

"Yes please Dolly; I think I will have more courage to talk then."

Dolly poured him a glass of port and they sat down.

"I cannot stay with Vicky, she is breaking my heart," his voice faltered. "You see, Dolly, she has not bonded with our child." He emphasized 'our', "and every day she is becoming colder, I really don't know what to do. I tried talking to Katherine but she says it happens sometimes to new mothers, I cannot take much more. I feel so disloyal talking like this but you are her friend."

"And yours too."

"Thank you Dolly, that is why I ventured to talk to you, please help us before I just have to leave."

"I don't think I can help much, Robin, but I will go to see her after Pierre leaves in the morning."

"Pierre is leaving?"

"Yes, he has to see his editor and will be in France about a month."

"I can see you love each other very much; I only wish that Vicky felt the same way about me as I do about her."

"She will learn to love you, Robin, you are a good man."

"I want to care for her and Anne, I really do, but she pushes me away."

"This will pass, Robin."

"I do hope so, I will make sure I will not be there in the morning so you will have time to visit."

Robin left and Pierre came into the study to ask Dolly if she was ready for the picnic. Dolly's mood was quickly elated as he put his arms around her and nibbled on her earlobe. Dolly giggled and turned around to kiss him.

"We are so lucky Pierre; we are so much in love."

When Robin returned home the first thing he heard was Victoria screaming orders at the baby's nurse.

"I told you to come for her after half an hour, more than an hour has passed, and there you are, strolling in as if you have just remembered. Take the child to her room immediately, she has done nothing but cry."

"Maybe she is hungry, mam," the nurse replied,

"That is what I pay you for, and don't even try to suggest that I put her to the breast again, it is disgusting and painful, and besides I have no milk. Take her back."

"Mam, you have to let her suckle to stimulate milk…"

"Get out, get out," Vicky shouted. The nurse picked up Anne and went to the nursery; she almost bumped into Robin who was listening outside the door.

"Vicky darling, you must learn how to care for our baby," Robin said, going to the bed and taking her hand.

"You think I don't try," Victoria started to cry.

"It's not that you don't try, dear, the nurse is helping you. I know it is all very tiring but please be kinder or the nurse will give her notice."

"You are on her side, how could you. You want me to just be a mother and I am still young, I deserve a life."

"Yes dear, that will come, but right now Anne needs you."

"I don't care, and don't touch me," she pulled away her hand. Robin sighed, not knowing how to help his petulant wife. Eventually he left the bedroom and went to the kitchen. The cook was preparing their meal and he poured himself a cup of tea.

"Still in shock is she?" the cook asked.

"Yes, I do believe she is," Robin answered, ignoring the impertinence of the cook, today he needed a friend.

"Should be up and around by now, she needs to get on with life, that she does."

"I know, Madge, and we are being patient with her."

"Too patient, if you ask me."

"Please cook, keep those opinions to yourself. If Sir David hears you I won't be able to speak on your behalf, their daughter comes first."

"More's the pity."

Joan was allowed a letter a month from 'outside' and Dolly had written to her with the news. She wrote about the twins for Gita and Rett, about her plans to marry Pierre and finally the birth of baby Anne. Joan was happy that her friends were all experiencing the positive things in their lives, but her own mother was very sick with cancer. She wrote back to Dolly asking for Anthony to care for her mother as she knew no other doctor that would be so caring, not even his father had Anthony's empathy for the sick. Joan put Dolly's letter in her cell and made her way down to the main building. She bumped into Sister Josephine who said that Mother wanted to talk to her. Joan quickly went over the reasons she might be summoned but could not come up with any.

"Sit down, my child."

Joan sat but stayed upright at the edge of the chair in anticipation of what was to come.

"There have been some developments abroad, my dear, and there is a request for some daughters of God to go to Africa as missionaries."

Whatever Joan was expecting, it was nowhere near this.

"Mother?"

"We have asked Sister Josephine and Sister Mary and they suggested that you would be an ideal candidate as you are fresh and open to new ways to worship the Lord."

"Yes Mother, but I am not worthy."

"Just what I expected you to say. Child, you are as worthy as any one of us and your youth will help the other two who are now in the middle years of their lives. Will you agree to go?"

"Of course, Mother. I would be honoured to be chosen."

"Good. I will make arrangements. You will be allowed to go and see your mother, she is sick is she not?"

"Yes, she has cancer."

"Then you must spend the next month with her while we arrange things, will this be alright for you? You will be always wearing your habit to remind you that you are a bride of Christ."

"Yes, thank you."

Joan went home. Sister Josephine gave her and her bicycle a lift as she was going into town for groceries. The convent grew a lot of their own food but once a month they needed to replenish supplies. Joan took out a small case from the car and smiled at Sister Josephine, who had been a good friend to her.

"I will be back soon. I am looking forward to the next chapter in all our lives; I just wish my mother was not so sick."

"Enjoy the time you have together and when she goes to a better place, be happy for her."

The friends waved goodbye and Joan turned to go into the small humble cottage that had been her home before the convent.

When she walked into the dimly-lit room she saw that Molly was trying to get her mother to drink some soup.

"Joan," her mother cried happily.

"Joan, we are so happy to see you," Molly said.

Joan went to her mother and kissed her tenderly. Joan was shocked at the change in her. She was still comparatively young, in her early forties, but looked old and very tired. Her skin was translucent and parchment white. Her cheeks were sunken and her lips were so pale that they appeared to disappear into her face. However, at the sight of Joan her eyes sparkled and she smiled in happiness.

"Molly, thank you so much for caring for my mother. I will be home for a few weeks, but please continue to visit."

"Wild horses couldn't keep me away, your mother has many more recipes to share with me, haven't you, Nancy?" She laughed, bent to kiss her cheek. She left mother and daughter alone.

"How are you child? Are you happy?"

"Yes, mam, it was a good decision. The only problem is not seeing you."

"I know I am very sick, Joan, but why did the Mother allow you to return home?"

"We will talk later. Right now you need to drink this soup."

"Bossy," laughed her mother.

That night as Joan knelt to pray she changed her plea from making her mother well to ending her mother's pain on earth. Rather than feeling sad she felt happy that she was able to help make her mother's last few weeks more content.

The next day, reluctantly, Joan left the house to buy groceries. Molly had come by and said she would stay with her mother, who mercifully was sleeping. Joan walked to the church first and Reverend Simon was outside sitting on a bench, reading.

"So wonderful to see you, and congratulations on your marriage," Joan said, as she approached.

"Joan, errr... Sister Joan. What a wonderful surprise," Simon got up and hugged her.

"Don't let me stop you, sir. I hoped to see you here to let you know that I made the right decision for me."

"Yes, I can see, you have a peaceful countenance that is rare, Sister. Are you home for long?"

"Just a month. I am to be sent to Africa on God's work but my mother knows nothing of this."

"Sister Joan, you have grown up. I know your mam is very ill and we will do everything we can for her."

"I know she is loved and I will stay as long as I can, although if God wishes it she will be called to Him very soon."

"Yes, I think you may be right, dear."

Simon blushed because he called a nun 'dear' but it was so hard to think of a child he had seen grow up, become a bride of Christ.

Joan ignored his faux pas and continued on her way to the shops.

She was hoping to meet her friends who had no idea that she was home. Dr. Preston was the next person she saw and, throwing convention to the wind and ignoring her nun's habit, he hugged her and kissed her cheek.

"My, my child, you look quite splendid. Anthony will be thrilled to see you, although we wish it was under better circumstances."

"Yes, and I would love to see everyone too, but right now I'm afraid I must hurry and get back to mam as she will soon be awake."

"I will give everyone the news that you are back, and they will come and visit you, I am sure." Dr. Preston waved as he walked quickly to his next appointment.

Joan concluded her shopping and as she arrived back home she heard her mother ask Molly where she was.

"I'm here, mam. I just got you some good bacon and eggs. I have become a great cook lately."

Molly and Joan's mother laughed.

"I don't think bacon and eggs are considered a gourmet meal," Joan saw the humour and laughed herself.

"Lord above, child, you do my heart good to see you," her mother smiled.

In the town police station Detective Terrence Smith threw his uneaten sandwich into the dustbin. He sighed and sat down to go over the files once again. Two dead children, one severely injured and now a seven year old boy missing for two days. What were they missing?

"Don't you ever sleep?" asked Timothy Downs, bringing Terry another cup of tea.

"What are we missing? We must be missing something. No one can kidnap these children in broad daylight without making a mistake."

"I know, Terry, but we need a break in the case, the bastard is slippery, more than slippery, he is depraved."

Terry loudly slurped his tea and picked up a paper.

"It says here that there was no connection between these children, that it was purely by random chance. That I find hard to believe. There must have been some connection between the little bairns and their killer."

"The boy that survived, Nicholas Brown, remembered nothing of his attack and I for one am loath to question him again, the little mite."

"I know, Tim, but he may remember something that will save the missing child. Do you want me to go?"

"No, it's my job, but I will take Susie Talbot with me and go out of uniform if that is alright with you?"

"Go ahead, but be gentle."

"That's a safe bet, mate."

Tim went in search of Susie and found her in the canteen talking to another detective who had been brought in to the case from Scotland Yard. Tim walked over to them and Susie put down her cup.

"I will be taking Susie to question the boy, sir, if that is alright with you?"

"Go ahead with caution, he has been through hell and back," Jack Dobbs replied.

When Dolly got to the mansion it was well past ten in the morning and Victoria was not yet up. Katharine Hastings showed Dolly into the study and went to tell Victoria that her friend was here. Dolly heard Victoria shout something and Katherine came back into the study.

"It seems she is unwell today and can't see you, Dolly. Forgive her, she has had a hard time."

To this day Dolly doesn't know what possessed her. She marched up the stairs to Victoria's room and flung open the door. The occupant was shocked into silence as Dolly went to her bed and pulled back the covers.

"Now I will only say this once, Victoria. Stop acting like a child and get out of this bed and back to living. You are not the only woman to have had a baby and I daresay you will not be the last. We are all sick to death of your childish antics. There is a helpless infant in the nursery who wants her mother, and you have a wonderful loving family who care about you. Stop the blubbering. There is naught wrong with you that a spanking wouldn't cure. Old as you are, you are a selfish child right at this moment and we will no longer tolerate it. Do you hear?"

Victoria did not protest and with the help of Dolly she dressed and went downstairs without saying a word. Her mother was in the hallway and after the initial shock of Dolly's words she rejoiced that someone had put her daughter to rights. Once in the study Dolly was still fuming that her friend had responded so negatively around those who loved her.

"Have you seen Anne?" Victoria asked in a small voice.

"More to the point, have you seen Anne this morning? It is ten o'clock and someone should be caring for her…"

"The nurse…"

"Her mother," Dolly retorted, wanting to shake Victoria violently. Victoria started to cry.

"Don't turn on the waterworks, you have work to do."

Dolly almost frog-marched her friend to the nursery, where the nurse was just about to change the baby.

"Get to it, Victoria, she is yours for life."

Victoria looked at her tiny daughter and moved towards her. Tentatively she started to change her nappy. Dolly signalled to the nurse to leave the room with her and leave Victoria alone with Anne.

"Eeh, miss, are you sure?" the nurse asked when they started to go down the stairs.

"Quite sure," answered Dolly, with more certainty that she felt.

In the study she sat and waited with Katherine for Victoria to make the next move. After some time they heard her come down the stairs. Katherine moved to help her but Dolly held her arm. Victoria walked into the study with Anne in her arms. She was smiling.

"Dolly dear, I would like you to meet my daughter Anne," and she placed her in Dolly's arms.

"Isn't she the sweetest child you ever saw?" Victoria gushed. Her mother was dumbfounded.

"Absolutely Vicky, and she looks so much like you. She is beautiful."

Victoria flushed with pride. Dolly spent a pleasant couple of hours with them all, and no one mentioned what had happened that morning. Victoria was back, selfish and self-centred, yes, but kind of heart and Dolly was relieved that she had now realized she was a mother.

Anthony was working many hours and even with his father's help he could not keep up with the demands on his time. He had just come back home at three in the morning after attending one of the Martin children who had the croup. Dead tired he fell asleep without even removing his boots. His father came into his room to talk to him and stopped at the door to observe his son. Anthony was no longer a boy. He was still shorter than average, but he was stocky and even with a three-day-old beard he was beautiful in his father's eyes. Dr. Preston stood there praying that his son would be able to resist his homosexual tendencies and lead a happy rewarding life with a woman, not to mention having children. Yes, he knew about Mathew and he liked him very much. He knew that if it wasn't Mathew it would be some other man that attracted his son. He was no stranger to this side of life. In the army he had encountered relationships between men and had the philosophy then of 'live and let live'. Now though, it was different. This was his beloved son, it was different. He moved to the bed and removed Anthony's boots. They dropped to the floor with a clatter but Anthony did not stir. Anthony's mother came into the room.

"Is everything alright?" she asked, concerned.

"Yes, he is exhausted. He needs a break, dear, and we will discuss it with him in the morning."

"I think you are right, let's put out the lamp and go to bed, it will soon be daybreak." Dr Preston took his wife's hand and they left Anthony to sleep.

The next morning Anthony was up and about early. He was sitting in the garden when his parents called him.

He smiled and kissed his mother as he joined them for breakfast.

"So things are busy in Cotter's Marsh, son?" his father stated.

"Yes dad, more than I thought possible."

"That is because you have many more skills than I, son, you have become proficient in your trade to be sure. I am proud of you."

"Thank you, that means a lot to me."

"You are so tired and overworked, my dear, we are worried about you," his mother remarked, frowning and looking concerned.

"I am fine mam, don't worry."

"I have a proposition, son. How do you feel about expanding the practice? The population here is growing and there is a demand for more services. We could use the present clinic and bring in another qualified doctor, even a nurse to help, what do you think?"

"Dad, that sounds great, is this feasible now?"

"To be sure, son, I have made enquiries and there are many changes in the medical field, enough to warrant expansion, if you are agreeable."

Anthony put down his knife and fork and went over to his father. He hugged him like he did as a child and kissed his cheek. Dr. Preston blushed, but Anthony could tell he liked this spontaneous show of emotion.

"We will discuss it again tonight, son, after the surgery."

Suzie and Tim left the police station and walked to the home of Nicholas Brown. Susie was experienced in interviewing children, and this was her first time seeing this child. Tim had spoken to him before and prepared Susie about his attitude and visible scars. Nicholas's mother was very reluctant to allow them to talk to him, but knew that another child was missing. Nicholas was sat playing with a train when Susie saw him. Even though she had been prepared she gasped when she saw his facial scars and deep purple scar on his throat.

"Hello Nicholas, remember me? My name is Tim."

"I love trains," said Susie, sitting on the floor not too close to him.

Tim sat down and Mrs. Brown offered them tea. To get her out of the room they both acquiesced. Susie asked if she could see the train, and Nicholas handed it to her.

"This is the place they put the coal to get it moving," he whispered.

"You seem to know a lot about trains."

"My daddy is a fireman. He used to be a stoker on the steam engines. Once he took me up there and I pulled the whistle."

"What fun," replied Susie, thankful the child was talking.

"Is he, how exciting, and are you going to be a fireman?" asked Tim.

"Maybe, when I get better."

Susie picked up a drawing that he was in the process of colouring. One half was recognizable as trees and swings but the other was scribbled on angrily. She asked him if she could draw with him and he moved to the table and gave her paper and crayons.

Susie was interrupted by Mrs. Brown returning with the tea.

"He don't remember nothing, yer know."

"I presumed that was the case," soothed Tim. "We are here just to check up on him. The whole station cares about what happened, you know."

"I know, they have been kind, everyone has been kind," she started to weep silently.

Susie continued to draw and Nicholas picked up a crayon and started to draw the same picture. After he had finished Susie started to draw shapes on her own drawing and asked the boy to imitate them.

"This one is a square," she said and he repeated the square.

"What do we know that is the shape of a square?" she asked.

"A table," he replied, happy for her attention.

"And this is a triangle."

Nicholas repeated the exercise until Suzie drew the shape that had a major reaction. Nicholas threw down his crayon with a look of horror. He ran to his mother and his mother comforted him.

"You should go now," she said sharply to them.

"I am sorry we have upset him, Mrs. Brown, but we have to try everything."

They left the house and Tim asked Susie what had happened.

"Something very significant, I think. We will explore the possibilities back at the station."

Joan was reading to her mother and did not notice that she had fallen asleep. Molly was coming up the path and she went outside to greet her.

"How is she, dear?"

"Not too good today, she slept barely at all last night."

"Do you want a break, Sister; I will stay for a while?"

"Thank you, I will take this opportunity to go and visit my friends."

Joan took her wrap and walked off down the lane towards the farm. She had not gone far when an excited, "whoa there, where are you off to?" made her turn around. Anthony dropped his bag as he swept her up in his arms and swung her around in glee, completely disregarding her habit.

"Tony, oh Tony I have missed you all so much."

"Come, Sister Joan, you are happy aren't you?"

"Very happy, Tony, but I miss you all."

The friends walked further and as they arrived at the farm Anthony kissed Joan on the cheek.

"I will have to run, I have a patient to see, but if you are still here afterwards I will join you," he said as he walked quickly away.

Dolly saw Joan's arrival from the kitchen window and she ran out to meet her and waved to Anthony as he left.

"I heard you were home for a while Joan... Sister."

"Oh, come here Dolly, and give me a hug," Joan reached out and Dolly rushed into her arms.

They both cried a little at their long overdue reunion. Dolly took Joan inside and she continued to prepare some homemade bread. Violet and her father were around the farm doing chores so the friends had time to catch up on all the news.

"So you decided that Pip was not the right one after all?"

"I loved him, in a way, but once I had met Pierre everything changed."

"Like a lightning bolt?" laughed Joan.

"Exactly, like a lightning bolt."

"And what of Victoria, how is she with the new little one?"

"She is content I think, but she does not have much enthusiasm for mothering. Robin is distraught because this will be their only child."

"I see. What does God have in store for her now, I wonder?"

They talked for some time before Albert came into the kitchen for a drink. He was taken aback at the sight of a nun sitting in his kitchen but as soon as he realized it was little Joan he went up to her and kissed her.

"My, my you look splendid in your garb," he said.

"Thank you. I just wish I could have come for a visit under better circumstances."

"Yes, how is your mam?" asked Dolly, putting the last batch of bread into the oven.

"Not well, I'm afraid. Reverend Mother allowed me to return for a month before…"

"Before what… Joan?" Dolly was alert. She had a feeling she would not like Joan's answer.

"Before I go to Africa."

"Africa," they both repeated together.

"Yes as… as a missionary, although I know I am totally unworthy."

"Nonsense Joan, eh! Sister, you are the most worthy person I know," replied Albert.

"Africa is so far away. Will you stay there long?" asked Dolly, wiping her hands on her apron.

"I don't know. They need help and three of us are assigned there, I don't know for how long."

Just then Violet came into the kitchen, to see where Albert had got to.

"Joan, Joan my dear," she exclaimed going over to her and hugging her. "What a lovely surprise. Now I know what happened to Albert," she smiled.

They talked for a while and Joan asked that they not tell her mother about Africa.

"I fear she is dying and I don't want to worry her," Joan said.

"We are so happy to see you dear; of course we will not share this information with her." Violet answered for them all.

The bread was ready and Dolly removed it from the oven. They were all enjoying the hot bread and jam when Anthony arrived. He was caught up on the news and they spent a half hour longer, lingering in the comfortable kitchen filled with love. Eventually Joan took her leave, and Albert and Violet went back to their chores on the farm.

Anthony stayed behind for a second helping and as he watched Joan walk down the road he said, "I have a terrible feeling that when Joan goes to Africa she will never come back."

"Don't be a soothsayer, Tony, it's not like you. You are the optimist among us."

"Maybe I have seen too much of life, Dolly, too much misery. I can no longer believe in a merciful God."

"My goodness, Tony, where is all this coming from?" asked Dolly, quite alarmed.

Anthony smiled, "Oh it is just a bad day, the Martin boy just died and I am usually defeatist after a death."

Dolly went to put her arms around him.

"When are you seeing Mathew?"

"Next week and I hope we can come to some arrangement. Father is expanding the clinic and wants to engage another doctor. I am hoping Mathew will consider it. I know he wanted to work in the larger hospitals but I miss him Dolly. Does that sound terribly sinful?"

Dolly smiled and kissed his cheek.

"You are a wonderful man, Tony, and deserve to be happy; God knows that is difficult at times."

Victoria was dressing to go out for the first time since the birth of Anne. She fussed over her figure and complained that since the pregnancy her hair had lost some of its lustre. Robin hovered around her trying to find comforting words that would find his way back into her heart.

"Vicky darling, you look wonderful. Your skin has a glow that will be the envy of everyone tonight."

"But my fat is still there and no one will envy that," she pouted.

"They do not have a bundle of joy in the nursery," he countered.

She looked up at him and smiled.

"Have I been a perfect shrew to you, Robin?"

"Not perfect," he laughed and surprisingly she joined in.

Later that evening, after they had returned from the dinner party, Victoria allowed Robin to share her bed once more. He came to her tentatively, expecting that at any moment she would lose her temper with him. He slid beside her in the bed, hardly daring to make a sudden move for fear she would reject him once again. This night though, she did not push him away and seemed quite contrite about her treatment of him.

"Robin, thank you for being so patient with me."

"I love you, and there is nothing you can do to change that. We need to talk about Anne and our future."

"Yes, I know, and I wanted to ask if you would consider staying here at the manor. Anne would grow up with her grandparents and in a small safe village."

"I don't know how safe it is here. First Nan, then you and the children, God help us: those little children hurt, and killed."

"I know, but I would like to be close to my friends and they can be your friends too."

"I know my poppet, Dolly particularly cares about you so much and I quite like her fiancé, Pierre."

Robin stopped talking and kissed Victoria on the lips. She took some time to respond but her need for intimacy took over and she kissed him back.

"Enough talking darling, I want you, it has been so long."

"I want you too Robin, so much," and she playfully pushed him back on the bed and covered him with kisses. Robin was so happy to have his wife back.

Nan almost ran up to the farmhouse. She wanted to see Dolly and tell her that she needed company to shop for her wedding dress. Dolly arranged to go with her to town that very afternoon. Dolly was happy to drive her new car and Nan could not contain her excitement.

"What colour should I wear?"

"White of course," answered Dolly.

"No Dolly, that would not be right. I am sure even Marcus would disapprove of that."

"Alright then, maybe a cream or ivory. What about trimming with blue, or pink if we can find the material?"

"Let's just look around and maybe the perfect dress will be in the shop today."

They went around from shop to shop. Eventually they were tired and so they decided to stop and have refreshments in the tea shop. After they had ordered tea and crumpets Nan became very serious.

"Dolly dear, can I be candid with you?"

"When have you not been candid, Nan? Ever since we were little I could always count on you to say it as it is," Dolly smiled.

"When you are with Pierre, what does it feel like?"

"My dear Nan, I feel as though there is no other person in the world, like no one could ever exist for us but each other, it feels like..." Dolly stopped and looked at Nan. "Nan, why are you asking, is it not like that for you with Marcus?"

"Well, I know it is for me but it seems different for Marcus, colder, kind but... oh I don't know. Here I am rambling on with my vivid imagination and he probably feels every bit the way I do."

The duo continued their quest. Nan found an unusual pale blue dress that she matched up with a hat and gloves. The fashion was still favouring dour-looking clothes but, as Nan said, this was her wedding day and she wanted to look happy and bright.

"You will be a beautiful bride, Nan. Marcus is so lucky to have you."

"After we are married Marcus said he would adopt Grace and become her true father. I pray she never finds out who her father really was."

"I second that Nan, and you deserve all the happiness in the world. Let's get back and show Violet your dress."

Mathew returned from the hospital to a very excited Anthony. He barely had time to put his bag down before Anthony was explaining what his father had in mind.

"Could you do it Mat, could you live in the village and be partners with us?"

"This is so unexpected, Totey. Let me unwind for a while and we will look at the pros and cons of the situation. This has really caught me by surprise."

Anthony busied himself preparing food while Mathew went to change. After he had prepared them both a scotch he went to join Anthony in the kitchen.

"So, tell, what brought this sudden decision from your father, Totey?"

"Well, I think he realized that I was overwhelmed with all the work and he knew that he did not have the more modern skills to deal with it all. He is great in family practice but lacks the knowledge that I have... we have to care properly for the people."

"I see... go on."

"Well it occurred to him that if I was not to be worked into an early grave I had better get some help. He suggested expanding the practice and after we talked I asked him if I could approach you. He has misgivings, of course, but he also is aware that wherever you are, I will be close to you. He thought that if you were willing, he would gladly consider it some more."

Anthony ran out of breath and Mathew looked at him long and hard.

"Do you know how difficult it would be to keep our relationship private, Totey?"

"Yes, but this way is also hard, Mat. I see you so rarely and then we are both so overworked; it is not the kind of quality time we deserve. Please don't say no. At least think about it."

"How long are you here, Totey?"

"I have to return tomorrow afternoon."

"I will tell you then. I am happy at the hospital and this would be a big change for me... for us."

It seemed interminable, waiting for Mathew's answer. Anthony could hardly contain himself from pushing him, persuading him or even pleading with him. Somehow he managed, and waited until Mathew was ready. After a restless night they made love. Anthony felt so happy in Mathew's arms. He felt that nothing could ever get through his bubble. They had a lazy morning, reading the newspaper, cooking breakfast and Mathew was the first to rouse, and get dressed, and then they talked.

"Totey, I have given a great deal of thought to what you proposed yesterday. I need to explain how I feel about what the future holds for me."

"Go on," encouraged Anthony, not liking where this seemed to be heading.

"I came into medicine to learn new ways and new techniques. I love doing research and I suppose I want to be a pioneer in paediatric surgery, make a difference in some way, and explore un-chartered territory... Oh! You know what I mean. I have spoken about it many times. Grandmother is very old now and when she passes I wanted to apply to Montreal, to do children's medicine. I know this is in the future, but I feel you are settled into small village life and that worries me. I don't see you leaving your family, now or in the future."

Anthony's heart sank. "I hope you are not saying what I think you are saying, Mat?"

"Totey, I love you and would like nothing better than to spend every day of the rest of my life with you, but I would feel that I had compromised my own desires to practice medicine in the way I had hoped. Please say you understand."

"I do understand, and I have known your ultimate goals, but I wanted you close, I suppose I was selfish."

"Not at all, Totey. You are so happy being a family doctor and therefore that is where you will do the most good. We need not rush things and don't forget we have a trip to London to look forward to in the autumn."

Mathew went to Anthony and put his arms around him.

"What do you say we get some fresh air and go for a walk in the park, I'll let you feed the ducks?"

Anthony playfully swiped Matthew and they laughed. Anthony knew in his heart that things between them had changed and they were no longer on the same path.

Pierre wrote to Dolly that he was on the way back to her and she couldn't wait to meet his train the next day. Violet was in the kitchen and saw how Dolly was beaming.

"I think I know why you are so happy, Dolly, Pierre is on his way back, isn't he?" she smiled, and tweaked Dolly's nose.

"Mam used to do that. She said she did it because I looked so full of myself."

"And she was right."

They both laughed and Dolly got on with helping Violet prepare supper.

The next day Dolly dressed with care. She was taller now, and her figure was fully that of a woman. She still wore her hair long but now it was more stylish. She went out to start the car when she saw Joan running up the drive.

"Dolly, oh Dolly, I have just been for Dr. Preston because Anthony is in town. Mam died last night." Joan looked pale and Dolly told her to get in the car.

"Have you found the doctor?"

"Yes, he said he would go to the house right away."

"Come on, I will drive you home. I have to pick up Pierre at the train station and then I will come right back."

"Oh Dolly; I would be grateful if you would. There is so much to do now, and I really don't know where to start."

"Never mind, dear, I will be back soon. I will go and get Molly too."

Dolly dropped Joan off outside the cottage and she went to get Pierre. For once the train was on time. Even the terrible news she had just received could not quell her pounding heart at the sight of Pierre. He pulled her into his arms and kissed her as if he would never let her go.

"Je t'aime, je t'aime, je t'aime, I love you, I love you, I love you," he shouted, as he swung her around, almost knocking another passenger off his feet.

"Excusez-moi, I am so sorry," Pierre apologized.

"It's alright mate. Looks as though you two are in luv. Good on yer!"

Dolly and Pierre laughed.

On the way home Dolly explained about Joan and she asked if Pierre wanted to be taken straight to the farmhouse while she went for Molly.

"I will not let you from my sight, little lamb," and he took her hand and kissed her tenderly. Dolly drove around to the vicarage and it was Nan who answered the door. She explained what had happened and Nan left a note for Molly, and she accompanied Dolly back to Joan's cottage.

"Pierre I am so happy to see you again, but it is unfortunate that the circumstances are so sad."

"Yes, Nan, I know. Even when we expect death it is a shock, is it not?"

They all arrived at the cottage and they saw that Dr. Preston was there. He joined them all downstairs and said he would inform the undertaker and Reverend Simon.

"Thank you, doctor, mam is at peace now," Joan said and she kissed the rosary around her neck. "Mam will be buried in the church, the same church she was married in and I was christened in. She will be with pa now and I can rest easy."

"That's right, Sister, you have only two weeks before you go to Africa. It is as if your mam knew you needed to grieve her before you go."

Joan could not prevent tears from falling on her cheeks and Dolly went over to sit her down.

"I will prepare some refreshments, Joan," Nan said as she busied herself preparing tea.

The Reverend came at the same time as Dr. Preston was leaving and he went to see Joan. They both retired to another room to say prayers and the others sat around trying to think of how to ease her pain.

"She is a brave woman to go to Africa," said Pierre at last, relieving the building tension, and they all then discussed what that would be like.

"I know I worry about Rett, but Africa is so… so foreign," Dolly said, trying to make sense of it all.

"What about India, that is foreign too, Dolly," offered Nan.

"Yes, but Rett said in many ways it is more British than Britain."

"That is why Africa needs her more," comforted Pierre just as they returned from their prayers.

The undertaker arrived as Joan and Reverend Simon came back to the group and this is when Joan gave way to her grief. Dolly held her gently while Nan took them to her mother's room. It was all over in a couple of hours and Dolly insisted that Joan spent the night at the farm with them.

"I really appreciate it, Dolly, but mam is here in this cottage and I need tonight to say goodbye."

"Then I will stay with you," answered Dolly and Pierre looked stricken but recovered well.

"Of course, Dolly must stay, she is your friend and she loves you. Please accept her help," Pierre pleaded.

"No, dear Dolly, Pierre, thank you but I will be fine. I have God to comfort me. I promise that I will be alright. Now go, Dolly, and spend time with your handsome fiancé, I am sure he wishes you all to himself," and she smiled through her tears.

They all took their leave, promising to be there early the next day and Dolly took Nan home to the farm where Violet had been caring for Grace.

"Please stay tonight, Nan. It seems ages since we spent time together," pleaded Dolly, putting her arm in hers.

"I think I will Dolly, Marcus is away for a few days. He often goes on religious retreats so he will not miss me."

It was late at night before the lovers had any time alone. After the last sounds from upstairs were still Pierre put down his drink and went over to Dolly.

"I now have the privacy to do this thing as it should be done," Pierre went down on one knee.

"Dolly, my little lamb je t'adore; will you honour me by being my wife?"

Dolly gasped as he produced a beautiful engagement ring.

"I know you wanted to use your mother's ring that you have been wearing, but I wanted to give this to you as a token of my love."

Dolly flung her arms around his neck and the sudden force sent him toppling over with her on top of him. She showered him in kisses and he said, "I take it that is a yes?"

"Yes, yes, yes my love, I will be your wife."

They broke apart and struggled to rise. They knocked over a small table in their efforts. Albert, hearing the commotion, came into the room just as they recovered their feet.

"Am I interrupting?"

"No, daddy, we are officially engaged and we must set the date as soon as possible."

"I see, you two need to be together, it seems," he smiled a sly smile remembering his own courting days to her mother. "I will talk to you in the morning, goodnight to you both and I couldn't be happier."

Dolly heard him chuckle as he made his way to break the news to Violet.

"Oh Pierre, we are so happy and yet there is so much sadness around us."

"That's as may be, my petit lamb, but life goes on and you are my life," he kissed her passionately. At last she broke free and they remembered where they were and that he had to go up to his own room.

Susie and the rest of the police force were hard at work. They had put a list together and were in the process of elimination. They had gathered all the known criminals that were known to have a religious fetish. One person of interest was a young man of twenty-three who sported a tattoo of thorns on his head. He had been convicted of lewd and lascivious behaviour and had served prison time for it. After two days of questioning it turned out that he could prove he had actually still been in prison when Nicholas had been so brutally attacked.

One by one the detectives methodically interviewed any person who had the slightest sexual inclination towards children. It was a mammoth task involving three counties, and five detectives were brought in to assist Terry from Scotland Yard.

"We're gonna get this bastard, and I won't retire until we do," announced Gary at the morning briefing. Gary was to retire at the end of the month.

"Just a matter of time now, Susie gave us the piece of evidence that will bring him to justice," Ted said, chewing on his pencil.

"How many are waiting to be interviewed?"

"Four. Stan Osborne, forty-two with three counts of child sexual abuse. Barry Timmons, sixty, just out two weeks prior to the first attack. Joss Jamison, thirty-nine, one account of child sexual abuse and three of lewd and lascivious behaviour, and the last for today is Billy Marsh, fifty-one, buggery on a minor, two counts, he has been out for two years. That's the lot," Tim finished, and handed the documents over to the others.

"My sister is having her kid baptized so I will be going to London for three or four days, chaps, get the bastard locked up before I return, OK?" Tim ordered, before he left for a well-deserved rest.

Every one of the twenty-three people assigned to the case had a personal commitment to find the culprit. Susie had gone back to talk to the sister of Nicholas but when shown the photos of suspects she only giggled, she was only four years old after all. Nicholas was no more help, so it was back to the drawing board. They were about to widen their search to the neighbouring counties and Scotland Yard put every available officer on the case. The top brass wanted this killer as much as the foot officers did. Susie was a thirty year old woman who had lost a sister to a paedophile when she was just an infant. The repercussions on Susie's family were to haunt her for the rest of her life. She wanted this bastard, and she wanted him bad. She was thankful that at this time she had no children of her own. She felt that she had seen too much of the depravity and low life. Christ! She lived it daily, why would she even consider bring a child into this world.

Chapter 10

Dolly was walking home from the market early in the morning. Pierre was still asleep at the farm when she left. She had heard his snores through the wall and it seemed to her that she was sleeping next to him. She smiled the smile that only lovers in love do and was daydreaming about the day they would sleep in the same room.

"Hey there, Dolly, wait for me," Nan called and hurried to catch up.

"Nan, where are you going this morning in such a rush?" Dolly asked, delighted to see her friend.

"I was just at Reverend Simon's and he asked me to check out how much rubbish needs carting away in the village hall. He knew Marcus was due later today so he wanted us to have supper with him and Molly later," she explained breathlessly.

"I will come with you, Nan, because it seems ages since we were alone to talk."

"That would be wonderful, Dolly. Do you want me to help you carry your parcels?"

"Thank you, Nan, I have bought some fish for supper tonight."

The friends continued to chat while they made their way to the church hall. They walked the long way around the churchyard and took some time to visit Eleanor's grave. Dolly placed a flower on it and both girls lingered there, talking about how much Eleanor loved the children, how she had encouraged the friends to visit and how they all confided in her when out of sorts with their own family.

"Do you remember the day when we were all playing at your house, Dolly, and Anthony ran to tell your mother he was growing kittens?"

"I remember that day, Nan, how funny that you do too. We must remind Tony of that, Mathew will find it very funny."

"Yes, and when your mother asked him how he was going to do that he produced...," by now they were both in stitches laughing, "A pussy willow branch."

"Stop Nan, we are in the cemetery after all," Dolly tried unsuccessfully to stop giggling herself.

They recovered somewhat and continued towards the church hall.

"I forgot to get the key," gasped Nan.

"Don't worry, we can break in like we always did as children," Dolly declared.

"Dare we?"

"Why not? That is, as long as the back door to the stage has not been repaired," Dolly replied.

The co-conspirators arrived at the hall and crept around the back, stifling giggles as if they were ten years old once again. Dolly arrived first and using a stick she pried open the rusty lock. It gave way with remarkable ease.

"See nothing has changed, scaredy cat," Dolly teased.

Nan moved closer and by habit looked around to see if they had been spotted.

"All clear," she pronounced and that resulted in another round of stifled giggles.

Dolly pushed open the weathered door and they were successful in gaining entry into the hall. Dolly stopped in her tracks and Nan bumped into her.

"What is it?" she whispered.

"Shhh."

They were both silent for a moment. Nothing. Nan walked closer and stopped just as Dolly had done.

"I hear it, Dolly."

"Yes, so do I. It must be a fox, or something trapped and frightened."

They both heard a guttural cry that they thought must be from a trapped animal behind the stage, what else could it possibly be? Slowly they came closer, no longer laughing but a little alarmed. The stage door gave way to a hard push but the entrance was blocked by a curtain. They both thought that was strange but they quietly went into the back of the stage. They heard the groans again, louder this time and Nan gripped on to Dolly's arm.

"Let's get out of here," she whispered, taking a step or two back.

"No, I want to see what is making the noise. If it is a wild animal we will go for help, whatever it is we cannot leave it trapped here," Dolly whispered to Nan.

Dolly continued slowly and quietly toward the sound. There were three steps leading down to an inner room where the broken furniture was stored. Each step creaked a little and Dolly took her time descending, not wanting to spook the animal. As she got further she was shocked to see long eerie shadows dancing from the dim light of a lamp.

"Dolly, let's go," whined Nan, afraid now and already turning for the door. Dolly pulled her back as they got to the last step and turned into the small alcove of a room.

Nan screamed and almost fainted. She screamed once again and her own voice shocked her into action as she ran out to summon help. Dolly stood still, transfixed by the horrific sight in front of her. In the dim light of the lamp, Marcus was stark naked from the waist down and as he turned, Dolly's eyes, now accustomed to the half-light, focused on his silver crucifix that reflected brilliantly in the light. It took a moment for her to see the knife he had in his hand. He moved to one side and although Dolly saw the horror before her, it did not register. Tied and gagged was a little boy, blood streaming from the many cuts on his naked body. The child's eyes caught hers and she whimpered in response, just as he was doing. Dolly stared at Marcus as he processed the intrusion into his depraved, private world. Marcus smiled grotesquely, and crumpled to the floor, babbling something, Dolly did not hear what. He rolled into a foetal position and cried for his mother. He still held the knife. Dolly was still, as if she had turned into a statue, she even remembered watching a spider crawl across the floor, until Albert's voice broke through her horror.

"Dolly, oh Dolly, come outside we are all here now. It is over." He took her by the arm and pulled her outside. Charlie was just behind, followed by the constable.

Pierre was also running up the path around the churchyard and he took Dolly from Albert. The men's eyes met briefly and Albert said, "Its bad, Pierre, get her away from here."

300

Pierre tried to guide Dolly to leave the place but she stubbornly stood trembling where she was. He held her close and she did not speak.

Albert ran back inside and assisted the constable and Charlie to get Marcus unarmed and handcuffed. There was no resistance from Marcus. He was still babbling and acting like an infant. Dr. Preston arrived before the ambulance and he went to help the child. He was shocked at what he saw. The inner room had been set up as a torture chamber and the child was cut numerous times, but alive, he was alive. Dr. Preston covered the boy up with his coat and released the rope around his wrists and ankles. He slowly removed the tape on his mouth and the child started to cry.

He carried the whimpering child outside just as the ambulance arrived, and the detectives were not far behind. Marcus was still naked, bound now and he lay on the grass, the madness in his eyes far removed him from anything considered human. Nan was there watching the whole scene and she calmly went over to Marcus and spit on him. Violet gave Grace to Molly and ran over to Nan.

"I am alright, mam. The little boy... the little boy?" no tears would come.

Reverend Simon covered up Marcus and shook his head.

"I had no idea, I had no idea."

Molly, with Grace in her arms, moved her away from Marcus. The detectives soon pulled Marcus from the scene and took him off to answer for his crimes.

Susie was there shortly afterwards and said to her colleague, "The cross, look at his cross. That was what Nicholas remembered, that is what he drew. We were looking in the wrong direction. We did not think a real vicar could do such a thing. Thank God he was found. We would not have looked in this direction for many more months. God knows how many more children he would have killed or injured." Tears were falling down her cheeks and she swiped them away with her hand. Police don't cry.

"But you understood the clue from Nicholas. You were smart enough to explore his feelings through drawing. I think your future with the force is assured, Susie."

"No, Mike, I think this is the last for me. I have seen too much of the seedier side. I will think about my future in a different direction."

"That will be a great loss to the force, Susie. Think long and hard. You have a gift and you were on the bastard's track even if it was a matter of time."

Susie sighed but that night she had the first good night's sleep for many months.

Everett was sleepy this morning. The twins were colicky and although he and Gita had employed a nurse, they had both been disturbed by the intermittent crying throughout the night. Gita stretched in a provocative, kitten-like movement, that was tempting to a man just aroused from his sleep.

"Good morning, darling, are you ready to be up and about?"

"Mmm... although I am still sleepy, my head by far prefers the pillow, and my body prefers to cuddle up to my wife."

Gita laughed, "The pleasures of being a daddy, I think."

"And a wonderful pleasure it is... except..."

"I know darling, you are tired, having had little or no sleep last night. Do you have business early this morning?"

"Unfortunately Baxter isn't due back for another week, so I have to meet with the foreman and go over some things," he moved over to her side of the bed and kissed her.

"Try to sleep some more, the nurse will feed the babies. When are your parents due?"

"Not until this afternoon so I will do as you suggest and dream that you are here beside me."

Everett kissed his wife again, this time lingering, his lips teasing and inviting.

"Go, you naughty man...go."

Reluctantly he dressed and moved away from the sanctuary of their bedroom into the kitchen. The cook was preparing breakfast and he informed her not to disturb Gita for another hour. After fortifying himself on a hearty meal he went upstairs to say goodbye to the twins. The nurse was getting them bathed and ready for the day. At three months they were robust and beautiful. Everett almost burst with pride when he was with them.

"Still not sleeping through the night?" he stated the obvious.

"No sir, but they are thriving well, is madam resting?"

"Yes, she needs it. I will take my leave of you all now and be back later this afternoon."

Everett went to kiss his daughter Eleanor, who met his eyes with her own ice blue ones.

"What a charmer you will turn out to be," he laughed, and then moved over to his son, Sanja. Sanja was sleeping but as Everett bent to kiss him he opened his eyes.

"Sanja seems a much more serious child, doesn't he nurse?"

"I can't tell sir, they are both so adorable."

Everett mused that he was the fun loving one and his twin sister Dolly was the serious one. He left to go to his day's business.

Gita's parents spent the night and enjoyed their grandchildren. They brought the inevitable gifts for them; a new set of exquisitely embroidered clothes for both of them.

"I can see we have to watch you both very closely or we will have two spoiled children on our hands," laughed Gita.

Her younger brother Sanja was away at boarding school in England. Sanja was very politically minded and Gita's father, being the police chief, had wanted him away from all the unrest in India for the time being. After they had dined, Everett and Gita's father walked around the perimeter of the plantation to talk.

"It seems that as soon as we have peace in one region, another erupts into violence."

"What is the latest news on this area, are we in danger?" Everett asked, worried for his family.

"The uprisings seem to focus on the towns where they will get the most support. The English are sending another five hundred troops to stabilize this region, but keep your eyes and ears open Rett, have an evacuation plan ready if need be. The crop failures this year have added fuel to the fire. Last year's influenza outbreak seemed to subdue the most radical elements, but right now I can't be sure of anything."

"I thought the legislature was aimed at sharing the power with the British?"

"It was, and went some way to quelling the violence, but some factions want it all, no British rule at all. The textile workers' strike hurt the economy and led to more instability."

"I will consider sending Gita back to England with the children. She can supervise Sanja, too."

"That may be best, Rett. The sooner the better, although you have a job on your hands persuading her to go."

The next morning Gita prepared to go back with her parents to town. She needed to shop for more supplies for the babies and she planned to have lunch with an old school friend who had just arrived from England.

"I am so looking forward to seeing Carol. It has been four years and we were together throughout our school days, do you remember, dada?"

"Yes, she was the sensible one as I remember," he laughed.

"Yes, I liked Carol, why did she stay so long in England?"

"Apparently she lived with an old aunt, but her aunt just died so she became homesick, we have written to each other regularly. She has done well for herself and has become quite a leader in the women's movement."

"How exciting," said her mother, putting on her gloves.

"I see we have a feminist on our hands," teased Everett, smiling at his mother-in-law.

"I do see their point though, Rett. Women are as good as men in many occupations and should have the chance to prove it."

Their bantering was cut short as her husband was impatient to get back to his work.

"Are we ready? I have sent for the car. Get a move on dear, I have a meeting this evening," said her father.

"I will be back late afternoon, Rett dear. I will tell you all the news from England. The twins were sleeping when I went up to say goodbye."

They all piled into the little car and the driver was instructed to bring Mrs. Marcum back to the plantation before five.

"Yes sir," he tipped his hat.

The car slowly made its way the few miles into town. When they were on the outskirts they were slowed to a crawl by a throng of people.

"I didn't know there was a demonstration planned today," Gita's father sounded alarmed.

"Should we turn around, dear?" asked her mother nervously.

The crowd milled around them, seemingly quite peacefully.

"No, I think the protest march is moving towards the centre of town and we will keep to the perimeter."

The car continued to crawl along, the driver honking his horn to warn of their approach.

The crowd suddenly started to get ugly, pushing and shouting. A man on a megaphone was shouting for order but the crowd only became more agitated. They spilled onto the road and started to push the little car from side to side. Gita screamed and her mother grabbed her and they both lay on the floor.

"Sir, what can I do?" the driver was panicked.

"Get away, get away, leave us alone," shouted her father to the crowd.

He opened the car window further to try and gauge how large the crowd was.

This was a mistake because someone in the crowd recognized him as the Chief of Police. The rabble opened the door and pulled him to the ground. The women screamed again. The driver was also pulled out but he was allowed to run for his life. People were trying to tip the car and open the passenger side door.

Gita suddenly became calm. She disengaged her mother's terrified hold on her arm and struggled out of the car under her own steam, while at the same time covering her sobbing mother with the rugs and coats so that she was hidden from view. She heard her mother's muffled protests but she wanted to divert them away from the car.

The noise was deafening as the mob became more unruly. Shots rang out which excited them even more. They pushed Gita down onto the road next to her father who was being trampled as the mob pushed forward. She covered her head as blows came from faceless assailants. Believing the car was now empty it was left alone as they all gathered around the Chief of Police and his daughter. Someone threw a rock which hit Gita on the head. She was dazed but heard the shot that was aimed at her father's head. Briefly she looked through the legs of the mob and saw him lying lifeless not five yards from her. She screamed just as a bullet hit her. She was silent. Her last thoughts as she lay dying were of her children.

Realizing the enormity of their actions the crowd quickly dispersed. Gita's mother gingerly raised her head to look out of the car window to see her beloved husband and daughter slaughtered in the middle of the road. Grief overtook caution and she ran over to them. In minutes the police arrived with the driver who had gone for help, but it was too late. The driver sat on the side of the road with his head in his hands. Gita's mother was holding her husband and rocking him like a baby. A policeman gently took her up and back to the car. He motioned the driver to come over.

"Take her back to the plantation," he ordered. "We will come out there later to see her."

"Yes sir," the driver sobbed.

Gita's and her father's bodies were removed from the street. Order was restored in the town but not before ten people had been brutally murdered. The police came out in force to restore order, motivated by the murder of their beloved police chief and his daughter.

It took the two of them less than an hour to go back to the plantation, and Everett was working in the fields when he saw the car returning. His thought was that Gita had decided not to meet her friend after all; he was not in the least alarmed. He continued to work until a labourer ran to summon him back to the house. There he was informed that the world as he knew it was no more. His distraught mother-in-law was given a sleeping draught and put to bed. The nurse had double duty that night and amazingly, for the first time, the twins slept through. The driver could not stop reliving the nightmare and was eventually sent to the kitchen to rest. Everett prepared to go into the town to recover the body of his beloved wife and father-in-law. He felt an overwhelming need to laugh at the absurdity of it all. He could summon no rational thought. It was a nightmare, not real and he and Gita would say how strange it all was when he woke up.

Some days later it all seemed to sink in, his wife and father-in-law were dead. His children were motherless. His mother-in-law could not go home alone, it was too dangerous. Decisions had to be made.

Nancy's funeral was very touching. Joan sang a farewell to her and there was not a dry eye in the church.

Reverend Simon, trying to be strong for the village, gave a sermon about how wonderful Heaven was and how God took his daughter home to rest. In the churchyard no one looked at the church hall, or commented on the nightmare they had all gone through. The funeral tea was ultimately the farewell tea for Sister Joan. She was leaving for Africa in ten days. Dolly's wedding was the last time all the friends would be together.

"Please don't forget us all, Joan," Anthony pleaded, ignoring her habit.

"You are always in my heart," she replied.

The friends decided that they would all meet up one last time as friends, before she left. The villagers dispersed and there only remained Dolly and Anthony.

"Say Dolly, do you think this Africa deal will be too dangerous for Joan?"

"I don't think the convent will send the three nuns into a region where they would be at risk, do you?"

"I suppose not, I just feel we are all drifting apart, Rett in India, Joan in Africa. Where will our Dolly be tempted to go, I wonder?"

"Pierre talks about us travelling to see Rett in India, why don't you come with us?"

"India, my dear Dolly, my life is not many miles away from here," he laughed.

Three days later the friends met at Nancy's house, as Joan packed up her remaining possessions to go to charity.

"We still have the means to make you all tea, and I see Dolly has brought some food," she teased, knowing Anthony's passion for tea and scones.

Nan sat down and, although subdued, tried to keep up the friendly banter.

"I will worry about you all without my sensible influence." Joan looked at her friends and they noticed the tears of sincerity in her eyes.

"Now, now don't let this meeting be maudlin," Anthony chastised.

Mathew had come to see them all and Anthony told them of his father's decision to expand the practice. He also told of Mathew's decision not to take the job.

"Nothing remains the same," Nan said, taking a scone and squeezing lemon in her tea.

They all knew that she had lost much in the last month. Dolly got up and poured herself a cup.

"I can hardly believe all the changes we have gone through in so short a time."

Pierre arrived at the house and he settled in a chair next to Dolly.

"Excuse-moi, I was delayed mailing off my latest manuscript, forgive me," he pleaded exaggeratedly, his hand over his heart.

"How can we be angry with a man who sounds as romantic as you do," laughed Anthony, who received a kick in the shins from Mathew and they all giggled.

"Is it true, Pierre, that you are taking Dolly to India after your wedding next week?" asked Joan.

"I think that the truth is more likely to be that she is taking me. You all know my wonderful Dolly, and in the words of Pascal Blaise, "Les riviers sont des chemins qui marchent, et qui portent ou l'on veut aller, rivers are moving paths that take you where you want to go. In this case my river is Dolly." They all laughed.

"Oh Dolly, how can you stand it, he is sooo... French," blurted Joan, which made it all so much funnier.

They were interrupted by Victoria who apologized for being late.

"Children can be so inconsiderate," she offered as an excuse and this further amused the friends.

"Oh Vicky, you will never change..." said Dolly.

"What...what?"

"Nothing luv, just that you are always reliable and consistent," offered Anthony.

"Thank you Tony... I think." Victoria looked puzzled.

"Never mind, where were we? Oh yes, travel," Nan continued.

"Dolly, how are your wedding plans coming along?" asked Mathew, forgetting that Nan was supposed to wed Marcus that very week end.

Nan kept a smile on her face but they all knew she was hurting.

"Everything is in place, I believe, Violet and Molly are both taking charge."

"Oh dear, then we will have all the bells and whistles," teased Pierre.

"Joan, are you going to be there too?" Victoria inquired.

"Yes, it is fortunate to be the day before I return to the convent, I sail the following week."

It was a bitter-sweet meeting. They all bantered and teased for a while longer until they saw Albert running up to the door. He burst in looking as white as a sheet.

"Excuse me, Joan, Dolly, I have just got this telegram." He handed it to her with shaking hands.

To father and Dolly,

Gita and her father killed. Both babies fine. Letter following.

I will attempt to contact you by telephone.

Rett.

"No!" cried Dolly, and she passed the telegram to the others to read.

The group was as stunned as Albert and Dolly.

"They must have been in an accident," Joan eventually offered.

"Those poor children, how old are they now?" asked Mathew.

"Three months," Dolly's voice sounded far away to her.

"Dolly dear, we must go home," Albert took her by the arm and Pierre took the other one.

They were walking up to the farm when the post mistress called out to them.

"There was a call for you, Albert, from India, Rett said he will call back in fifteen minutes. He said he has a telephone at the plantation."

They all changed course and walked to the post office. There they sat, stunned, until the shrill ring of the telephone shattered their thoughts. Albert stood up and took the receiver.

"Rett... is that you Rett?"

The group could only hear Albert's side of the conversation, which was a little annoying.

"I see, I see, oh dear, yes of course. Wait while I get a pen, here is Dolly, she is here, wait I will put her on." Albert passed the receiver to Dolly, while he searched for a pen to write down Everett's number.

"I want to ask you something Dolly."

"Anything Rett," she was weeping now.

"I will be sending my babies home to you with Gita's mother; can you keep them safe for me?"

"Of course I will. Rett, you must come home, you can't stay there alone."

"Baxter is back now and we have loyal workers, we will ride out the riots, but my children have to leave. Timir will accompany them; he loved Gita and will protect the babies with his life. Can you handle them all?"

"Oh Rett! Of course we will, you know that."

"There is one other thing Dolly, Gita's brother Sanja is at boarding school in London. Can you go there and tell him the news that his sister and father are gone?"

"Yes, I will get all the information from dad, I suppose you told him the details?"

"Yes and I have sent you a letter, it should arrive there in a few days. Dolly?"

"Yes Rett?"

"I love you and I am sorry this will once again ruin your own wedding. Please go through with it, it is what Gita would have wanted."

"I will Rett, if you are sure. And when it is safe we will return the twins back to you. I love you, be safe. Goodbye."

Dolly gave her father the phone and he wrote down Everett's number, promising to get one installed at the farmhouse immediately.

"Now son, you be safe and please consider coming home to your loving family," Albert pleaded.

"Dad, I am needed here, I just worry about the children, take care of them and we will be in touch soon. Goodbye, I love you all." Everett put down the phone and sobbed.

Albert told them the details of Gita's death and they sat there in the post office in complete shock.

Violet was caring for Grace when they all went back to the farm. She had known something terrible had happened but Albert had not explained as he ran to find Dolly. It was a sombre evening for them all.

"Dolly, you will soon see your little nephew and niece. Please focus on this, my love," Pierre was beside himself with hurt for his fiancée.

"Yes, we must prepare a nursery for them," offered Violet, joining Pierre in his effort to comfort.

"We can put the nursery next to Dolly's bedroom, which, by the way, will soon be Dolly and Pierre's bedroom," teased Albert, trying to find something to hang on to.

"Rett asked that we not postpone the wedding and I agreed," Dolly whispered.

"I love him already. He is a man after my own heart," answered Pierre.

Nan came home and she stayed the night. Grace was growing and was a real beauty with her blonde curls and eyes as large as saucers. She was also blessed with a happy disposition. Violet gave her over to Nan, who needed to be busy.

"Come and watch me bathe her, and get her ready for bed, Dolly."

Dolly followed Nan and left the others preparing dinner.

"Dolly, what is to happen to those motherless babies?" asked Nan, not aware of the recent request from Everett that they be sent back to England. Nan busied herself with preparing Grace for her nap.

"Well, it seems I will be a surrogate mother of my brother's children. They will come with their grandmother, but I have no idea whether she plans to stay here. I know Pierre and I will be going to London tomorrow to tell Sanja the news. I have not met him but from what I understand he is a bright boy with a future in politics."

"I don't envy you the task of breaking the news, but I understand you cannot wait until his mother arrives, that would be unfair. How old is he?"

Nan laid down Grace and the little cherub fluttered her eyes at Dolly as she was pulled into sleep. Dolly kissed her tenderly on her cheek and pulled up her cover.

"I believe he was six or seven years younger than Gita, which makes him fifteen, maybe sixteen, I think. From what Gita had told me he wanted to study law."

"Is he to return here with you?"

"Yes, and I thank God every day we have this large house. Our family seems to get larger daily.

I don't know what they will ultimately decide though."

"I can stay at the cottage more when they all get here so that will relieve your burden somewhat."

"You are like my very own sister, Nan. I love it when you are here," Dolly hugged her and then she broke down. Nan hung on as she sobbed into her shoulder.

"Dolly dear, it will all work out, you will see. I will give you all of Grace's clothes she has grown out of, although I am sure the twins will have many of their own. We will make a nursery. Gita's mother can have the room we prepared for your great-aunt Daisy. Let us return to the people downstairs who love us."

The duo moved out of the bedroom and descended the stairs. Everyone sat around the table while Violet served the meal. Dolly went to help but Nan said for her to sit and she would help her mother. No one can prepare for such news and each, in their own way, was silently dealing with it.

Dolly tried so hard to feel only happiness on her wedding day. Arrangements had been made for Nan and Grace to stay at the farm. Pierre and Dolly were to have use of the cottage for a week in lieu of a honeymoon, given the circumstances.

Pierre was the ultimate in attentive grooms. How handsome he looked in his wedding suit. Albert gasped when he saw his daughter in her wedding gown. She had chosen cream lace and satin and she carried one single lily as her bouquet, just as her mother had done before her. As they waited to walk down the aisle, Albert turned to his daughter.

"Mam would have been so proud of you today, child. She would have approved of Pierre and how beautiful you look." He helped her pull the veil over her face. Dolly was unsure of her decision to present herself at the church as a virgin. When she discussed this with Pierre he had reassured her that their union was blessed and even if it was a little early, they were betrothed to each other. Dolly was grateful to hide her tears lest they be mistaken for anything but happiness.

Pierre stood tall and proud, with his best man, Anthony, at his side. Dolly knew that Pierre had grown up an only child and that both his parents were dead. That was why the loss of his child, and then his wife, had affected him so badly. He looked so alone and vulnerable standing there that she knew she would dedicate her whole life to caring for him. He held out his hand as she approached and Albert placed hers into it. He could not see clearly through the veil but was aware that before him stood his life's love, a beautiful vision of loveliness. The ceremony went smoothly with Pierre only reverting to his native French a couple of times in his nervousness, which helped relieve the tension.

Matthew was outside to take photographs as they stood on the church steps. Dolly and Pierre moved alone over to Eleanor's grave to place her bouquet and they rejoined their guests. The reception was given by Victoria at the manor and she had done a splendid job of it. Violet and Molly had surpassed themselves in the catering.

Pierre couldn't wait to get Dolly to himself. Their private time had ceased since the news of Gita's death. They had all rushed around preparing a nursery for the twins' arrival. He had only been able to passionately kiss her one time when they had gone for a late night walk four nights ago. He was pacing back and forth in the study when David Hastings and Albert joined him.

"Getting some peace from the ladies?" Albert teased.

"Not at all, I was just deciding whether to have a cigar or not, would either of you gentlemen care to join me?"

They all busied themselves lighting up and each chose a leather chair and sat back to enjoy. The sounds from the reception filtered through and they could hear Joan and Nan singing.

"They will all miss Joan when she leaves; God knows when the child will return from that Godforsaken place. Africa, why couldn't they just send her to Europe, she could do more there convincing the Germans to be more law abiding," grumbled David Hastings.

"We have to remember that they are not children any longer. I can hardly believe that the impulsive son of mine is now a father himself. Now this man here plans to spirit my wilful daughter away and make an honest woman of her," Albert reflected.

"An honest woman she may be, Albert, but I hazard a guess that she will always retain her spirit and wilfulness, and I have a lot to contend with," Pierre smiled playfully. "And if she doesn't behave I know where to go for assistance."

"From what I know of you. Pierre, you are hardly a pushover," the men laughed.

"Here you all are," Victoria came into the study. "I wondered where all the handsome men had disappeared to."

"Handsome indeed," answered her father," that means she is wanting something, mark my words."

"Papa, how can you say that, I always will think you are handsome, old yes, but handsome," and for that remark she earned a swat on the bottom from her father.

They all went into the garden where the guests had moved for some air.

Dolly was talking to Molly and Vicar Simon when Pierre saw her, he politely moved her to one side.

"If I don't have you to myself soon, cherie, I will burst in anticipation. Come now quickly."

Dolly giggled as they stole away from the group.
"Where to?"

"To our honeymoon. We will go directly to Violet's house and they won't miss us for some time. Quickly, my little lamb."

The couple sneaked away from the manor and used Pierre's car as a quick getaway. Victoria heard the car driving away and all the guests ran out to the driveway, laughing and complaining at their cunning.

"Let's continue with the reception," Albert announced, "and let the young ones enjoy the start of their lives together."

"Hear, hear," the group agreed and the party went on far into the night.

"The village needed this," said Reverend Simon to Molly.

"You are so right dear, some happiness at last. Too much misery cannot be good for anyone's heart," she turned and kissed him lightly on the cheek.

He looked into her eyes and read the message of desire and he felt very fortunate and loved.

Violet was helping the kitchen staff to clear the table until David Hastings asked her to leave them to it.

"You, my dear, are a wonderful woman; Albert is a very lucky man."

"What is this," teased Katherine. "My husband complimenting another lady within earshot of his wife?"

"My darling Katherine, everyone knows I only have eyes for you." David had a twinkle in his eyes that his wife knew only too well.

"Come husband and dance with your wife," she took him playfully by the collar and everyone around laughed heartily.

Chapter 11

It was three weeks later, with telephone installed; Albert tentatively called Everett at the plantation. He had great difficulty with the new machine, but was determined to speak to his son. The operator connected him after many aborted attempts.

"Hello... hello, is that you, Rett?" Albert nervously shouted into the receiver.

"Dad, I am so happy you called, have the babies arrived?"

"Yes, Dolly, Pierre and Sanja are on their way to the station as we speak. Sanja is anxious to see his mother. How are you?"

"Everything seems to be unnaturally calm right now. I miss everyone. Baxter has sent his family home but chose to stay here with me. He has been just great. Is Sanja returning to school?"

"I think so; after he is satisfied that his mother and the babies are fine."

"Good, he is needed in India and must get a good education."

"Pierre has taken him under his wing. They talk often of politics and poetry. Though for the life of me I don't understand what they say. Sanja respects Pierre's intelligence, and Pierre is impressed with the young boy."

"Good, I am glad. My mother-in-law will need a lot of understanding. She has lost her husband and daughter, and now she will be in a strange land living with strangers."

"I realize that Rett, and we will take good care of her."

"Dad, I will call you in a couple of days for news of my children. I love you all. I have your number now and can call you."

"Good bye son and God bless."

The little caravan arrived at the station just in time for the train's arrival.

"Mon Dieu, darn it, it's early for a change," Pierre grumbled as they hurried to meet it. Charlie followed them, as there would not be enough room in one motorcar for everyone and their luggage. The group waited anxiously as the passengers alighted.

They saw Timir first; he wore totally inappropriate Indian dress, complete with turban. He put some cases on the station and went back inside. Pierre and Sanja ran to help them.

"Mama," shouted Sanja, as she alighted with Eleanor in her arms. Sanja embraced them both.

"Go child, help Timir with the rest," she ordered.

Sanja went onto the train and emerged with his namesake in his arms. He passed the boy to Dolly as he went back to help with the rest of the considerable amount of luggage.

Dolly, restricted by the baby could only say, "Welcome." She managed to kiss Mimi on the cheek.

"You must be Dolly, I have heard so much about you," she said gracefully.

"You must be Albert. I am Gita's mother, Mimi. Please call me Mimi."

"Thank you for caring for my grandchildren... Mimi." Albert took the little girl from her as they walked to the cars.

"Yes, they are also my grandchildren. It was a joy and a pleasure."

Dolly looked at this woman. She was just as beautiful as Gita, but with an obvious sadness about her that Dolly fully understood. She wore a dark blue sari, made of a beautiful luminescent material. She also wore a jewel on her forehead which gave her an air of mystery. Dolly knew that she had been educated in England and was well versed in the English way of life. Still, Dolly said, "I do hope you will not be disappointed in the farm, Mimi. We do our best but cannot compare with what grandeur you have left."

"Think nothing of it child; I am happy to have got my grandchildren to safety. My own future is uncertain but theirs is here with you all, for now."

They made their way home. Dolly rode with Pierre, Mimi and the babies. Albert, Timir rode with Charlie. Thankfully Charlie had a roof rack to carry the entire collection of luggage.

Violet was waiting at the door for their arrival. She came to take the baby from Mimi, for which Mimi was very grateful. They made quick introductions as the troupe made their way inside.

"Mama, you look so tired, shall I show you your room. You must rest," Sanja offered as he assisted his mother to stand once again.

"Timir, please take my mother's bags to her room and she must rest," he insisted a second time.

"Come, I will show you where to go," Dolly started to climb the stairs.

When Mimi was settled Dolly and Sanja went back for the babies.

"It is time they had a nap too," Dolly said to Violet, who still held Sanja.

Later, as supper was being prepared, Sanja told Timir that he would share his room.

"No sir, that I cannot do," he replied, shocked at such a suggestion.

"Timir, this is England. We accept you as an equal. After what you have done for my brother, it is the least we can do for you," Dolly was genuinely moved at the man's deference.

"If I were you, Timir, I would think carefully before you cross my wife. She is a she-devil when roused," Pierre laughed.

"Sir?"

"Don't tease him, not until he understands us better," Albert joined in.

"Another thing we must do is get Timir into more suitable clothes. He will freeze in those," Pierre suggested.

Nan arrived after her work to collect Grace. She was invited to join everyone in a meal, which she gladly accepted. The twins slept a while, after which Nan and Dolly changed them, fed them and then brought them back into the heart of their family. Mimi also roused herself and joined them as they prepared to eat.

"I feel a little better. My, what a long journey that was."

Mimi gathered a twin in each arm and sat near the fire.

After supper they all gathered around to hear the latest news from India. Mimi cried when she related the horrific events that resulted in her husband and daughter's deaths.

"You mean you were there, Mama?" Sanja was shocked.

"Yes, my son. I am ashamed to say, I could do naught to help. Gita saved my life by hiding me. I knew I had to live for the twins, and my wonderful son."

Sanja could not look at anyone, he was crying, after all he was still a young boy who had lost both his father and his sister in one terrible afternoon.

Mimi gave the twins to Nan and Dolly. She went to her son and gathered him in her arms. She rocked him to and fro until he stopped crying. Rather than embarrass the child, the others entered into conversation.

"What do you want to do now, Timir, Rett said that you would not be averse to helping me on the farm?" Albert asked.

"Sir, if that would be to your liking, I would be honoured to work for you."

"That's settled then. Sanja will be returning to his studies soon so you may have the bedroom to yourself. My dear wife will provide you with your meals and I daresay she may get you helping her in her garden."

"Yes indeed, that sounds like a wonderful plan. I do declare that my dear husband has volunteered to do his share of the pots," retorted Violet, good humouredly.

Everyone laughed. Mimi and Sanja joined them once again.

"Anyone for a game of chess?" Sanja asked.

Albert took him up on his offer while Dolly, Pierre and Nan went for a walk.

Thankfully the twins slept like angels all through the night, so everyone woke the next day refreshed. Mimi, with Albert's help, called Rett to let him know everyone was safe.

The farmhouse was abuzz with visitors the whole day. Nan was at work as usual so Violet was taking care of Grace. Grace was absolutely enthralled by the two new babies. She wanted to touch and play with them constantly.

"'Or', 'J'," she tried to get her baby tongue around their names, poking them as she spoke.

After furnishing him with dungarees, Albert showed Timir around the farm. He was impressed at the man's knowledge of the land. Mimi stayed on the porch most of the day reading quietly. Sanja had been persuaded not to lose any more of his education and was preparing to return to school the following week. Pierre took advantage of the lull to do some writing in the study.

Anthony arrived just after lunch to see the twins. He spent some time giving them a medical.

"Dolly, they are robust and strong, just like Rett. He should be proud of them," Anthony remarked.

"I cannot get over how much Eleanor resembles him. I think Sanja looks more like Gita."

"Babies change constantly. They are very lucky to have such a large family."

After they were put into their cribs Anthony became very serious.

"Dolly... can I be frank?"

"Of course, Tony, we are good friends."

"I think Mathew is leaving me soon."

"You can't mean it, Tony, why do you think that?"

"Well, his grandmother is seriously ill. I'm afraid after she is gone, he will go to Montreal. I saw a letter with a Canadian postmark."

"Have you spoken to him about it?"

"Not for some months, I thought he had changed his mind."

"You must clear the air, Tony. Perhaps he intends for you both to go? God knows there is need of doctors everywhere. Joan told me about the desperate state Africa is in and how desperate they are for medical staff."

"Canada is not the same, Dolly. Montreal is a thriving city and at the forefront of medical research, according to Mathew."

"Please get this sorted out, Tony, you need to know where you stand. We will support you in any decision you make, you know we will."

Anthony embraced her and they went downstairs, where he had tea and cake with Violet. Anthony played with Grace for a while and seemed at ease with her. He took his leave of them, still troubled. He walked to the churchyard, sat on a bench, and pondered his dilemma. His thoughts were jumbled; he did not know what he felt. He weighed his options. Could he leave his practice, friends and family to follow Mathew if he was asked? What if he stayed but Mathew went? His heart took a leap inside his chest. He did not want to return to his life of denial.

He was pondering his fate when someone broke through his melancholy.

"So this is what a doctor does when no one is watching?" Victoria was walking past with Robin. She was pushing Anne in a pram and they came up to Anthony.

"Going to feed the ducks, I'm afraid," said Robin, feigning disappointment.

"Oh, come along darling, you just pretend it is for Anne, we all know it is because you enjoy it." Victoria sounded happier than Anthony could remember.

"She is growing like a weed, Vicky, and beautiful too... you have a rival for all the fellows' affections my dear." Anthony was buoyed by the couple's mood.

"Have you seen Rett's twins?" Victoria enquired.

"I have just come from there. Rett should be a proud man."

"We are going to the farm after the park. Anne should sleep after the air," Robin offered.

"When will we see you as a proud daddy, Tony? You are slow getting started. We are all leaving you behind," Victoria said, totally unaware of the real Anthony.

"I'll leave that up to others for now, you are all doing a splendid job of it." Anthony felt bile rise in his throat. He was heartsick that he would never have the family he once presumed he would have.

For the next six months everyone settled into their lives on the farm. Pierre launched another successful book, while happily Dolly and Mimi became the co-carers of her brother's children. Mimi looked a lot healthier than when she arrived, although she had bouts of deep melancholy. Sanja continued his studies, paying even more attention now to world affairs. He came home to the farm for every holiday. Joan wrote regularly describing the horrific life of the lepers in Africa, and occasionally the village did some fundraising to send her much-needed items.

After the death of his grandmother Mathew decided to go to Montreal for a year. Anthony accepted this decision better than had been anticipated. He reasoned that he could do more good in Cotter's Marsh. He was now training his own intern, a young doctor from the midlands called Alan Wilson. There was even room for a nurse in the growing practice. Anthony and his father settled on a red-headed girl, whose enthusiasm far outweighed her medical knowledge.

"Can't teach the love of medicine, even if we can teach the mechanics," Dr. Preston reasoned.

Anthony's father was now semi retired, and Anthony was happy to remain where he was loved. He knew he was no adventurer; his sexuality was enough to grapple with every day.

Timir surprised everyone by stepping out with Millie Thompson, a dairy maid at the adjoining farm. Mimi thought it quite amusing. Nan had also met someone. He was introduced to her one night at the picture palace. She was very shy to disclose the information, but her mother was thrilled for her. His name was David Meadows. He was a local man, living in Grimoldsby. He was working in the rope factory that furnished nets for the fishing industry.

It was time. Everett had asked that his children go to him. Mimi thought long and hard about leaving Sanja alone in England. She eventually decided to stay in England until he had finished his studies. Albert and Violet told her that she could stay at the farm as long as she wished. She was healthy and seemed to have accepted the deaths of her husband and daughter. Timir was given the choice to return to India, or stay in England. Dolly could see the pain in his eyes. He said that he had only a brother there and would like to continue to work for Albert. Albert and Violet were elated because Timir took over all the heavier work that Albert struggled with.

"I will live here for a while longer with your permission. Then perhaps Millie and I will rent a cottage," he went shy with these words and lowered his eyes in embarrassment.

"We are indebted to you, Timir, for leaving your country to help with my grandchildren. I will be honoured to have you stay and work here," Albert was relieved.

"Dolly, will you accompany me for a walk, cherie?" Pierre asked, gently guiding her outside.

Dolly and Pierre walked arm in arm without speaking until they reached the outer barn of the property.

"Dolly, would you like us both to take the children back to their father in India?" Pierre turned to face her.

Dolly could not speak, her eyes said it all. She took his face in her hands and kissed him passionately.

"I believe this means yes?"

Dolly pulled Pierre into the barn and pushed him playfully onto the haystacks.

"Are your intentions honourable, young lady?" Pierre's eyes were on fire, as was his body.

"No," Dolly answered.